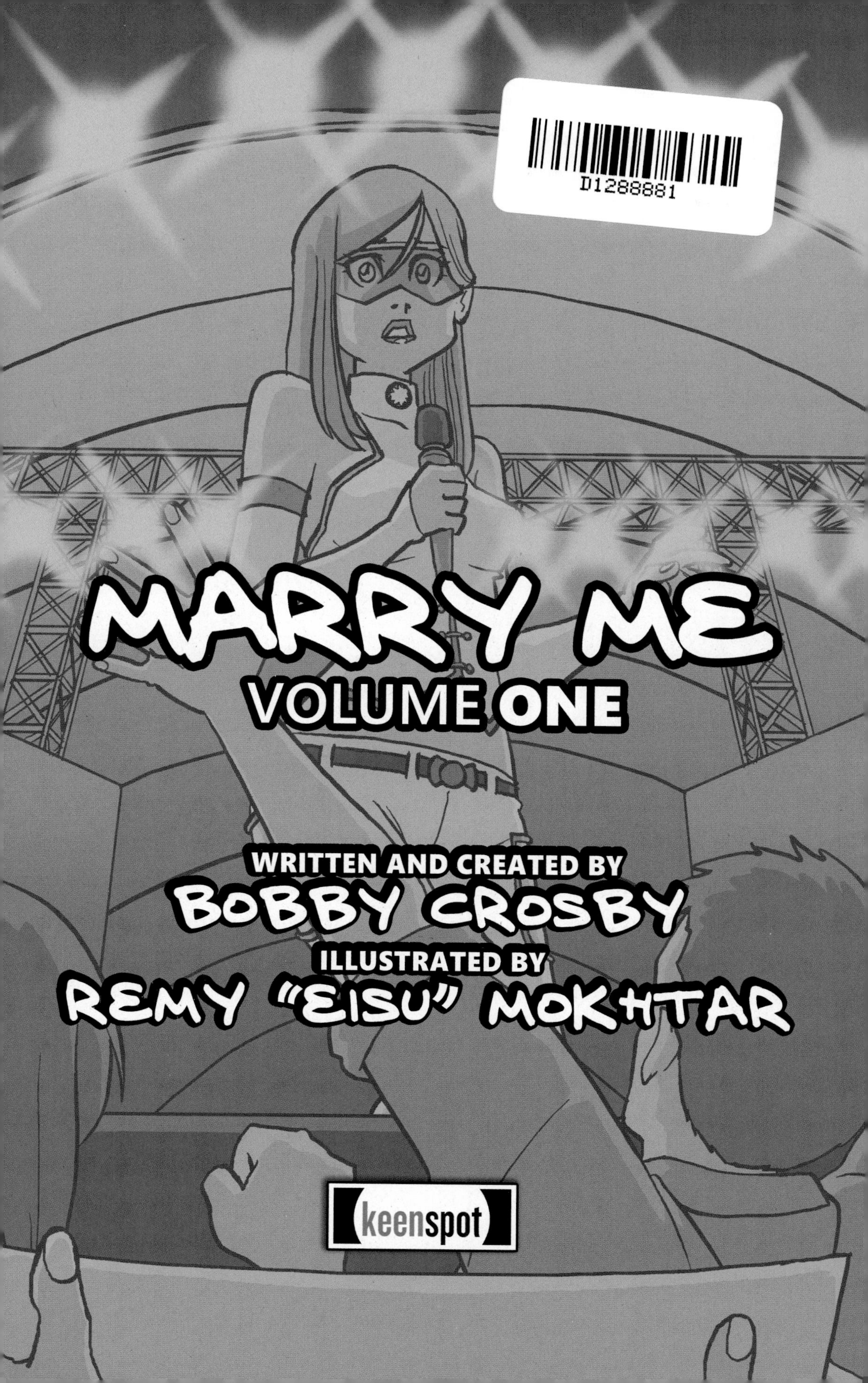
MARRY ME
VOLUME ONE
WRITTEN AND CREATED BY
BOBBY CROSBY
ILLUSTRATED BY
REMY "EISU" MOKHTAR
keenspot

MARRY ME VOL. 1

MARRY ME and all related characters are © and ™ 2007-2018 by Bobby Crosby.

This book collects material originally published online as serialized webcomics at marrymemovie.com beginning in February 2007 and in a printed graphic novel published by Blatant Comics in July 2008.

Published by
Keenspot Entertainment
P.O. Box 1463
Apple Valley, CA 92307
E-Mail: keenspot@keenspot.com
Web: www.keenspot.com

For Keenspot
CEO & EiC Chris Crosby
PRESIDENT Bobby Crosby

SOFTCOVER **ISBN** 1-932775-74-
HARDCOVER **ISBN** 1-932775-84-
First Printing, July 2018
Printed in Canada

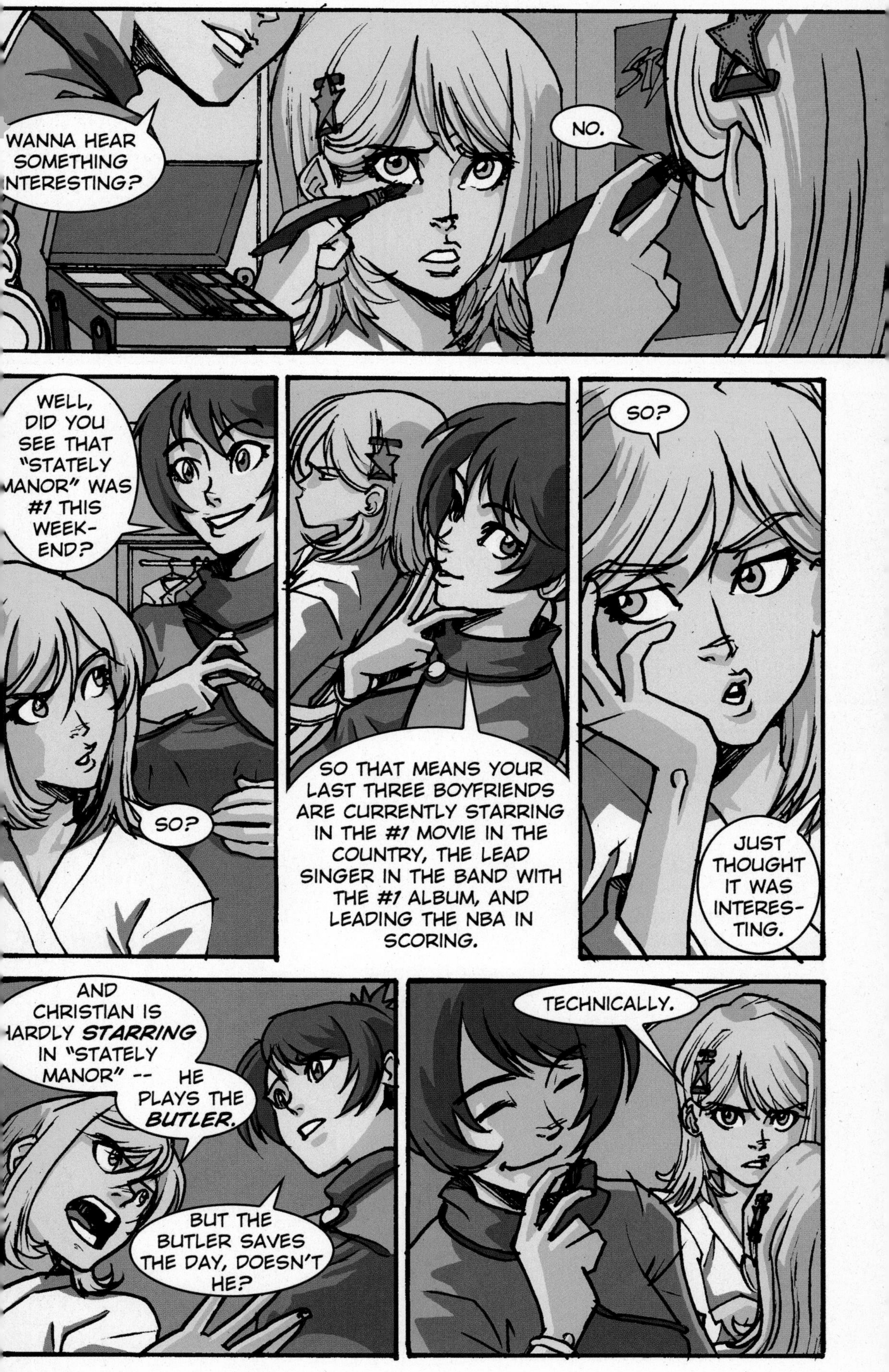
WANNA HEAR SOMETHING INTERESTING?
NO.
WELL, DID YOU SEE THAT "STATELY MANOR" WAS #1 THIS WEEK-END?
SO?
SO THAT MEANS YOUR LAST THREE BOYFRIENDS ARE CURRENTLY STARRING IN THE #1 MOVIE IN THE COUNTRY, THE LEAD SINGER IN THE BAND WITH THE #1 ALBUM, AND LEADING THE NBA IN SCORING.
SO?
JUST THOUGHT IT WAS INTERES-TING.
AND CHRISTIAN IS HARDLY *STARRING* IN "STATELY MANOR" -- HE PLAYS THE *BUTLER*.
BUT THE BUTLER SAVES THE DAY, DOESN'T HE?
TECHNICALLY.

THAT'S YOUR PRE-SHOW PEP TALK? TELLING ME HOW HUGELY SUCCESSFUL MY EX-BOYFRIENDS ARE?

I THOUGHT IT WAS FUNNY.

WHAT'S FUNNY IS WHAT ELSE THEY ALL HAVE IN COMMON.

KNOCK KNOCK!

TEN MINUTES!

COME ON, LET'S GET YOU DRESSED.

UGH.

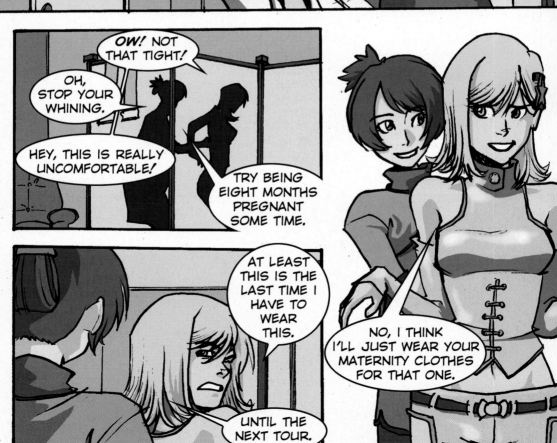

OW! NOT THAT TIGHT!

OH, STOP YOUR WHINING.

HEY, THIS IS REALLY UNCOMFORTABLE!

TRY BEING EIGHT MONTHS PREGNANT SOME TIME.

AT LEAST THIS IS THE LAST TIME I HAVE TO WEAR THIS.

UNTIL THE NEXT TOUR.

NO, I THINK I'LL JUST WEAR YOUR MATERNITY CLOTHES FOR THAT ONE.

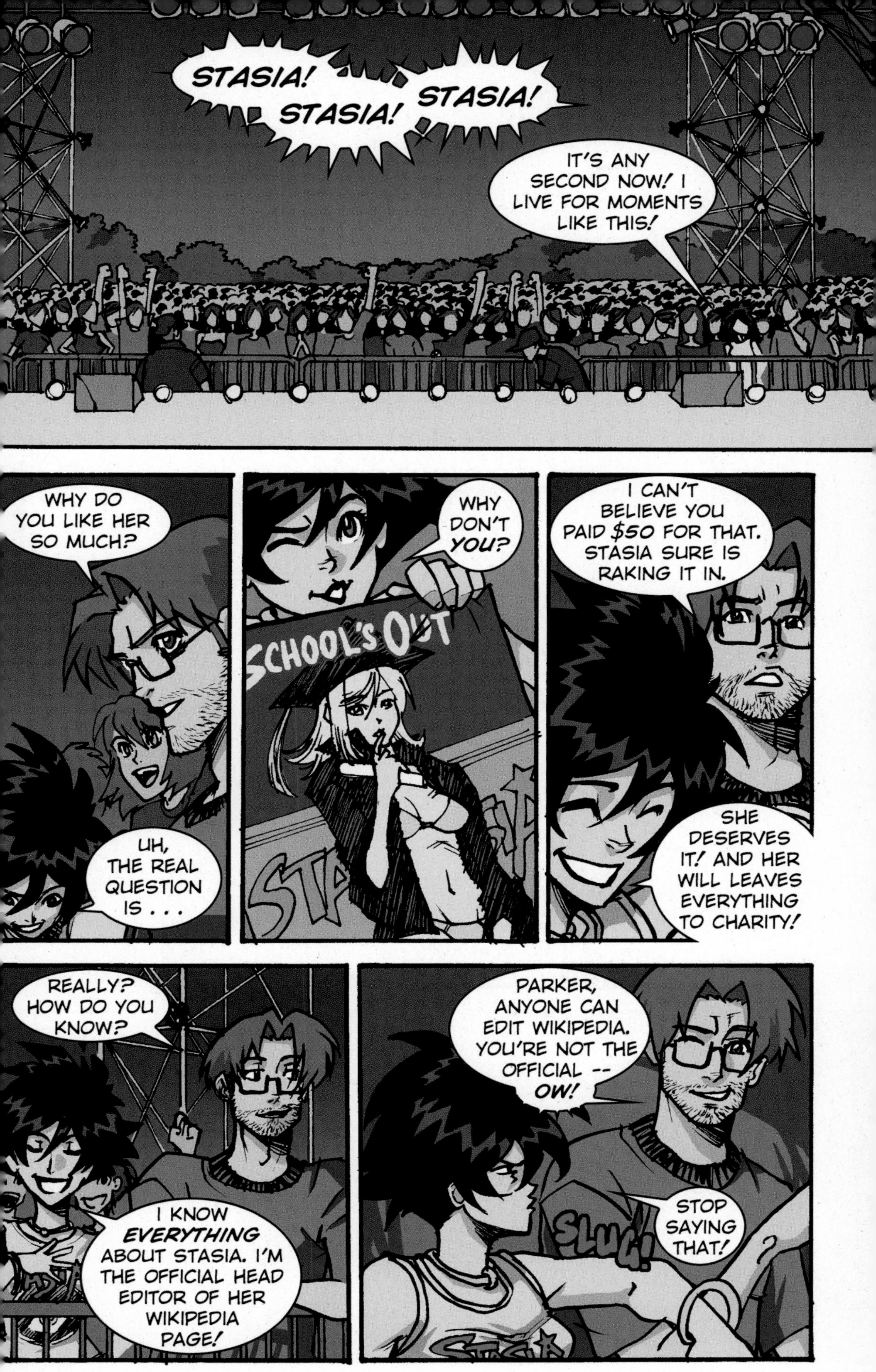
STASIA!
STASIA!
STASIA!
IT'S ANY SECOND NOW! I LIVE FOR MOMENTS LIKE THIS!
WHY DO YOU LIKE HER SO MUCH?
UH, THE REAL QUESTION IS . . .
WHY DON'T YOU?
SCHOOL'S OUT
I CAN'T BELIEVE YOU PAID $50 FOR THAT. STASIA SURE IS RAKING IT IN.
SHE DESERVES IT! AND HER WILL LEAVES EVERYTHING TO CHARITY!
REALLY? HOW DO YOU KNOW?
I KNOW EVERYTHING ABOUT STASIA. I'M THE OFFICIAL HEAD EDITOR OF HER WIKIPEDIA PAGE!
PARKER, ANYONE CAN EDIT WIKIPEDIA. YOU'RE NOT THE OFFICIAL -- OW!
SLUG!
STOP SAYING THAT!

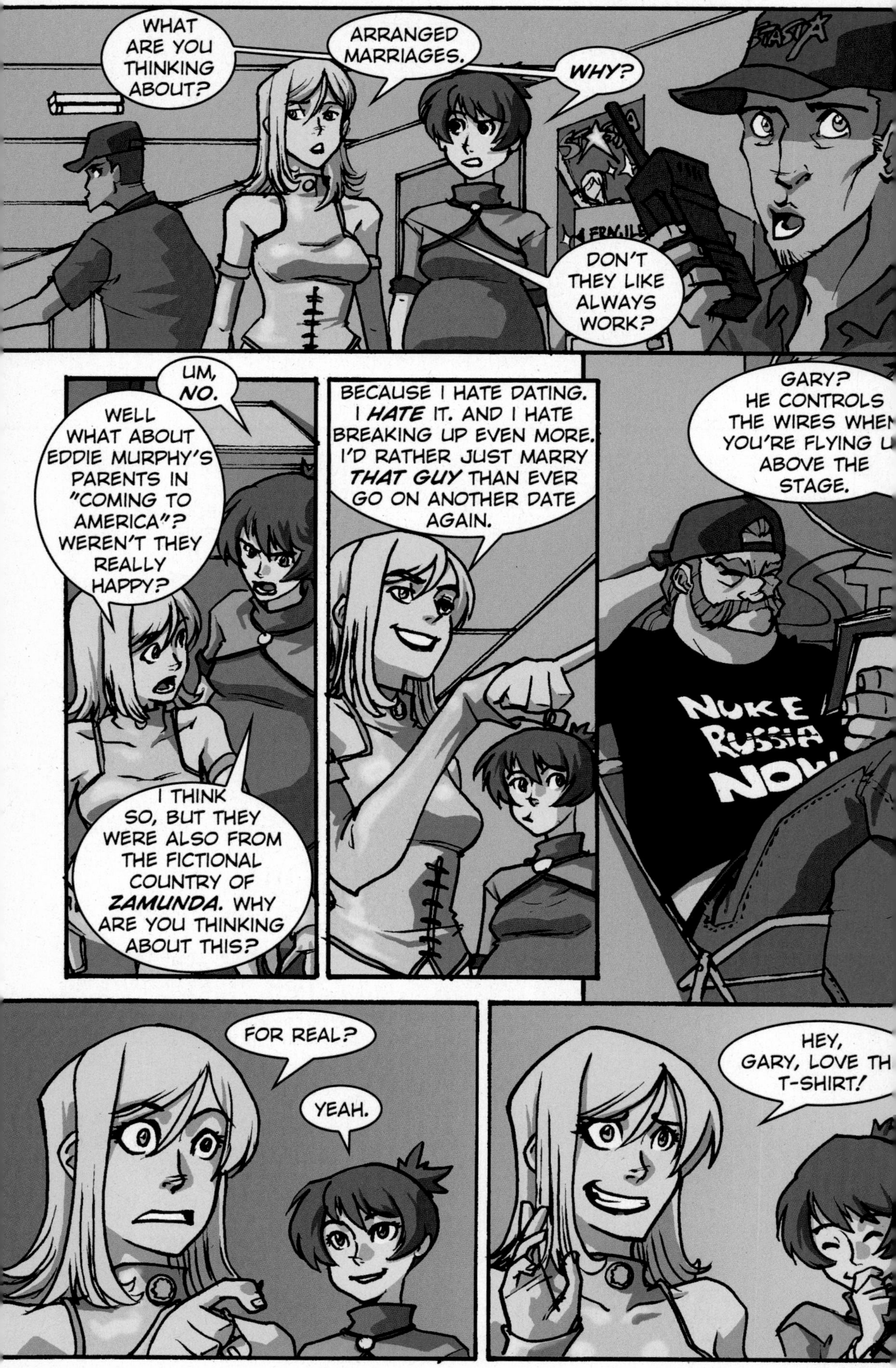

WHAT ARE YOU THINKING ABOUT?
ARRANGED MARRIAGES.
WHY?
DON'T THEY LIKE ALWAYS WORK?
STASIA
FRAGILE
UM, NO.
WELL WHAT ABOUT EDDIE MURPHY'S PARENTS IN "COMING TO AMERICA"? WEREN'T THEY REALLY HAPPY?
I THINK SO, BUT THEY WERE ALSO FROM THE FICTIONAL COUNTRY OF ZAMUNDA. WHY ARE YOU THINKING ABOUT THIS?
BECAUSE I HATE DATING. I HATE IT. AND I HATE BREAKING UP EVEN MORE. I'D RATHER JUST MARRY THAT GUY THAN EVER GO ON ANOTHER DATE AGAIN.
GARY? HE CONTROLS THE WIRES WHEN YOU'RE FLYING U ABOVE THE STAGE.
NUKE RUSSIA NOW
FOR REAL?
YEAH.
HEY, GARY, LOVE TH T-SHIRT!

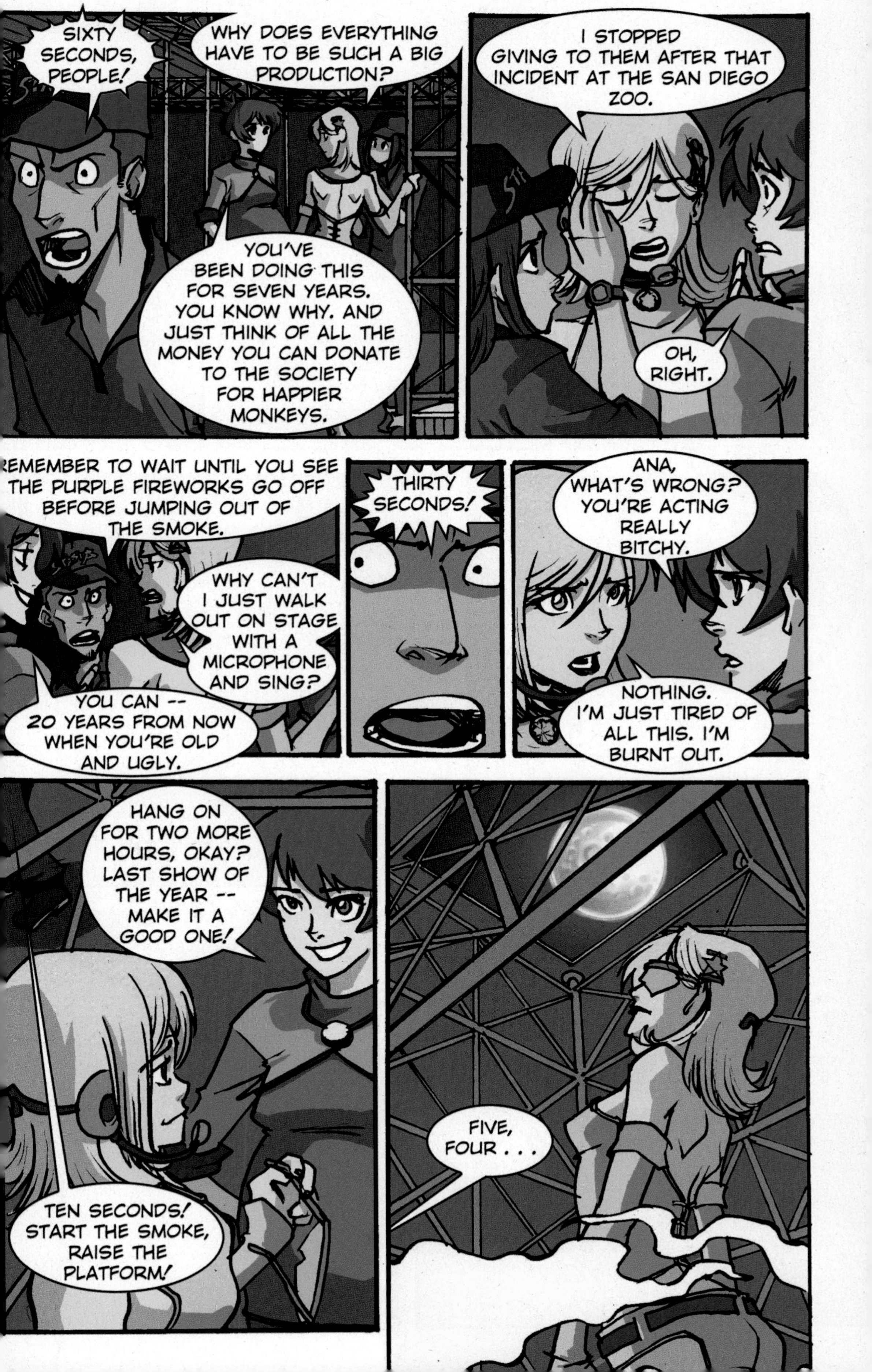
SIXTY SECONDS, PEOPLE!
WHY DOES EVERYTHING HAVE TO BE SUCH A BIG PRODUCTION?
YOU'VE BEEN DOING THIS FOR SEVEN YEARS. YOU KNOW WHY. AND JUST THINK OF ALL THE MONEY YOU CAN DONATE TO THE SOCIETY FOR HAPPIER MONKEYS.
I STOPPED GIVING TO THEM AFTER THAT INCIDENT AT THE SAN DIEGO ZOO.
OH, RIGHT.
REMEMBER TO WAIT UNTIL YOU SEE THE PURPLE FIREWORKS GO OFF BEFORE JUMPING OUT OF THE SMOKE.
WHY CAN'T I JUST WALK OUT ON STAGE WITH A MICROPHONE AND SING?
YOU CAN -- 20 YEARS FROM NOW WHEN YOU'RE OLD AND UGLY.
THIRTY SECONDS!
ANA, WHAT'S WRONG? YOU'RE ACTING REALLY BITCHY.
NOTHING. I'M JUST TIRED OF ALL THIS. I'M BURNT OUT.
HANG ON FOR TWO MORE HOURS, OKAY? LAST SHOW OF THE YEAR -- MAKE IT A GOOD ONE!
TEN SECONDS! START THE SMOKE, RAISE THE PLATFORM!
FIVE, FOUR . . .

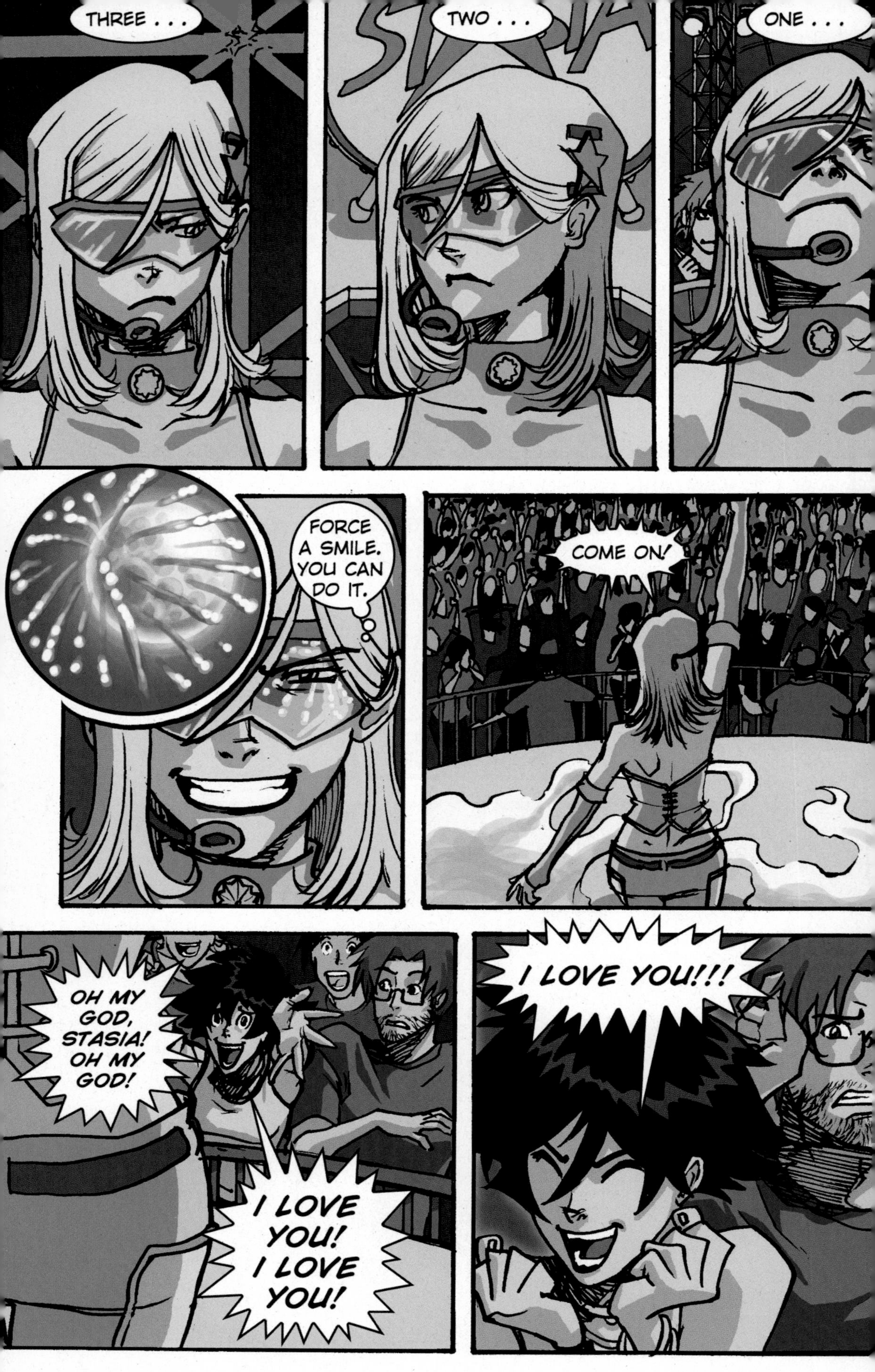
THREE . . .
TWO . . .
ONE . . .
FORCE A SMILE. YOU CAN DO IT.
COME ON!
OH MY GOD, STASIA! OH MY GOD!
I LOVE YOU! I LOVE YOU!
I LOVE YOU!!!

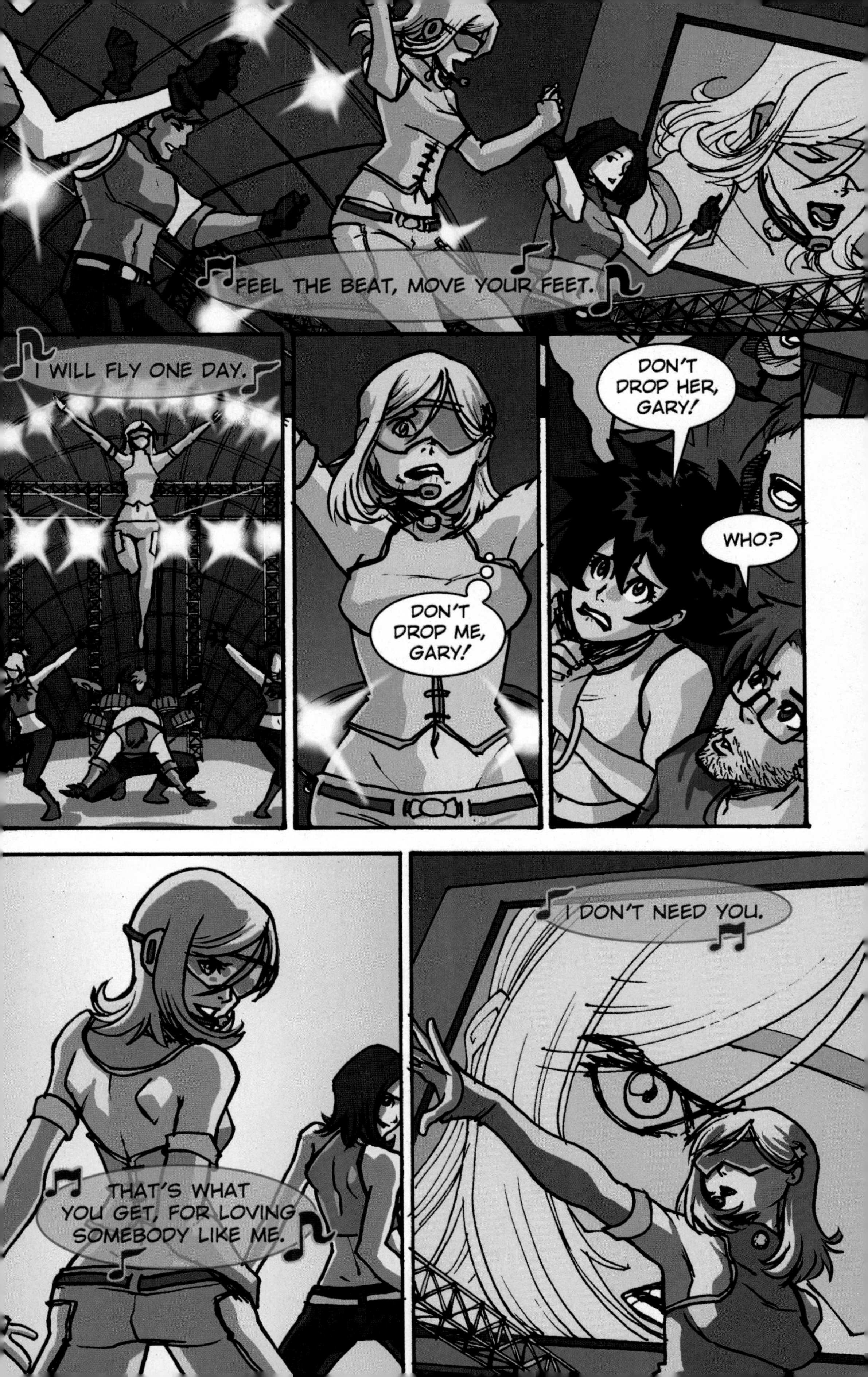
FEEL THE BEAT, MOVE YOUR FEET.
I WILL FLY ONE DAY.
DON'T DROP ME, GARY!
DON'T DROP HER, GARY!
WHO?
THAT'S WHAT YOU GET, FOR LOVING SOMEBODY LIKE ME.
I DON'T NEED YOU.

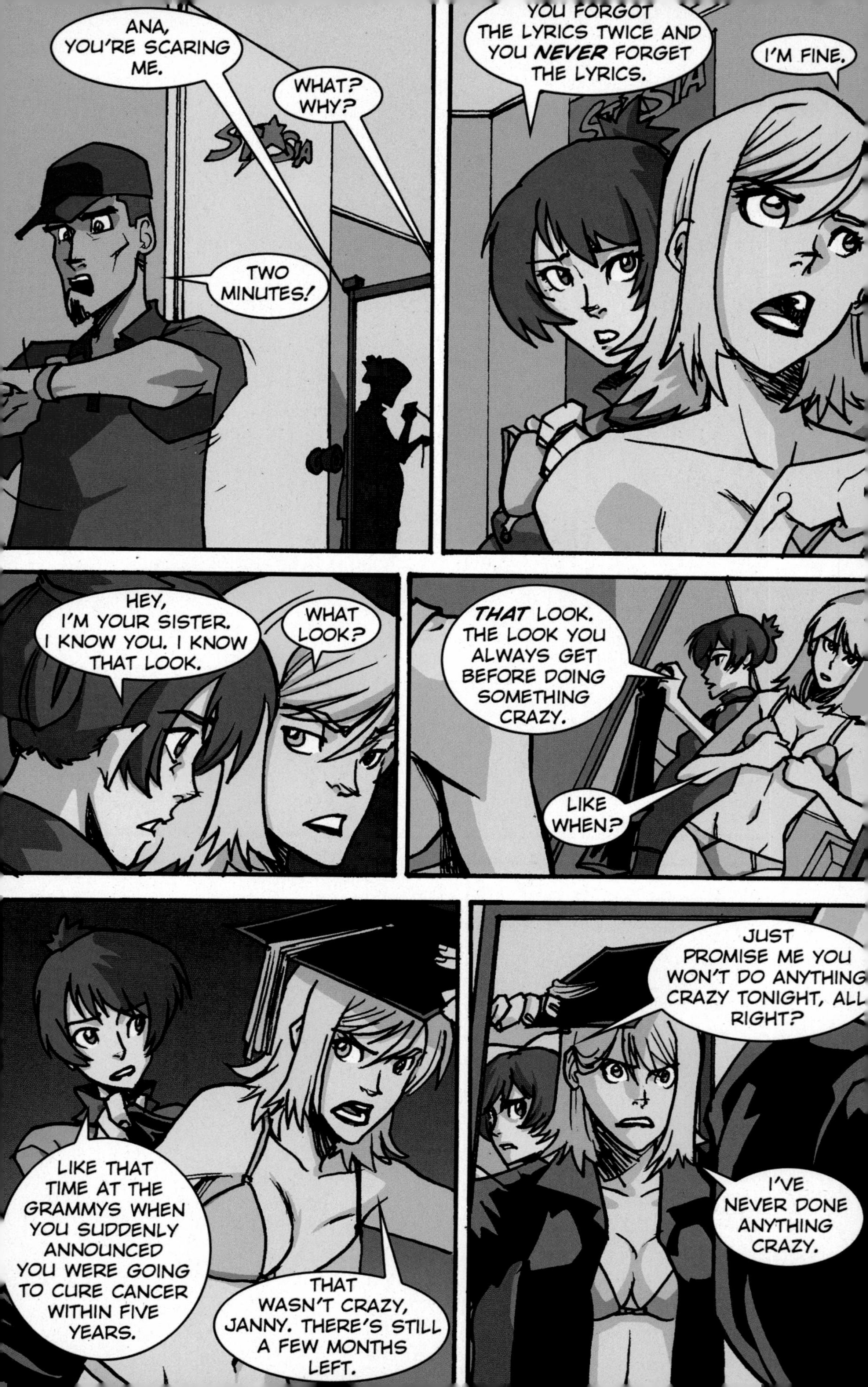
ANA, YOU'RE SCARING ME.
WHAT? WHY?
TWO MINUTES!
YOU FORGOT THE LYRICS TWICE AND YOU *NEVER* FORGET THE LYRICS.
I'M FINE.
HEY, I'M YOUR SISTER. I KNOW YOU. I KNOW THAT LOOK.
WHAT LOOK?
THAT LOOK. THE LOOK YOU ALWAYS GET BEFORE DOING SOMETHING CRAZY.
LIKE WHEN?
LIKE THAT TIME AT THE GRAMMYS WHEN YOU SUDDENLY ANNOUNCED YOU WERE GOING TO CURE CANCER WITHIN FIVE YEARS.
THAT WASN'T CRAZY, JANNY. THERE'S STILL A FEW MONTHS LEFT.
JUST PROMISE ME YOU WON'T DO ANYTHING CRAZY TONIGHT, ALL RIGHT?
I'VE NEVER DONE ANYTHING CRAZY.

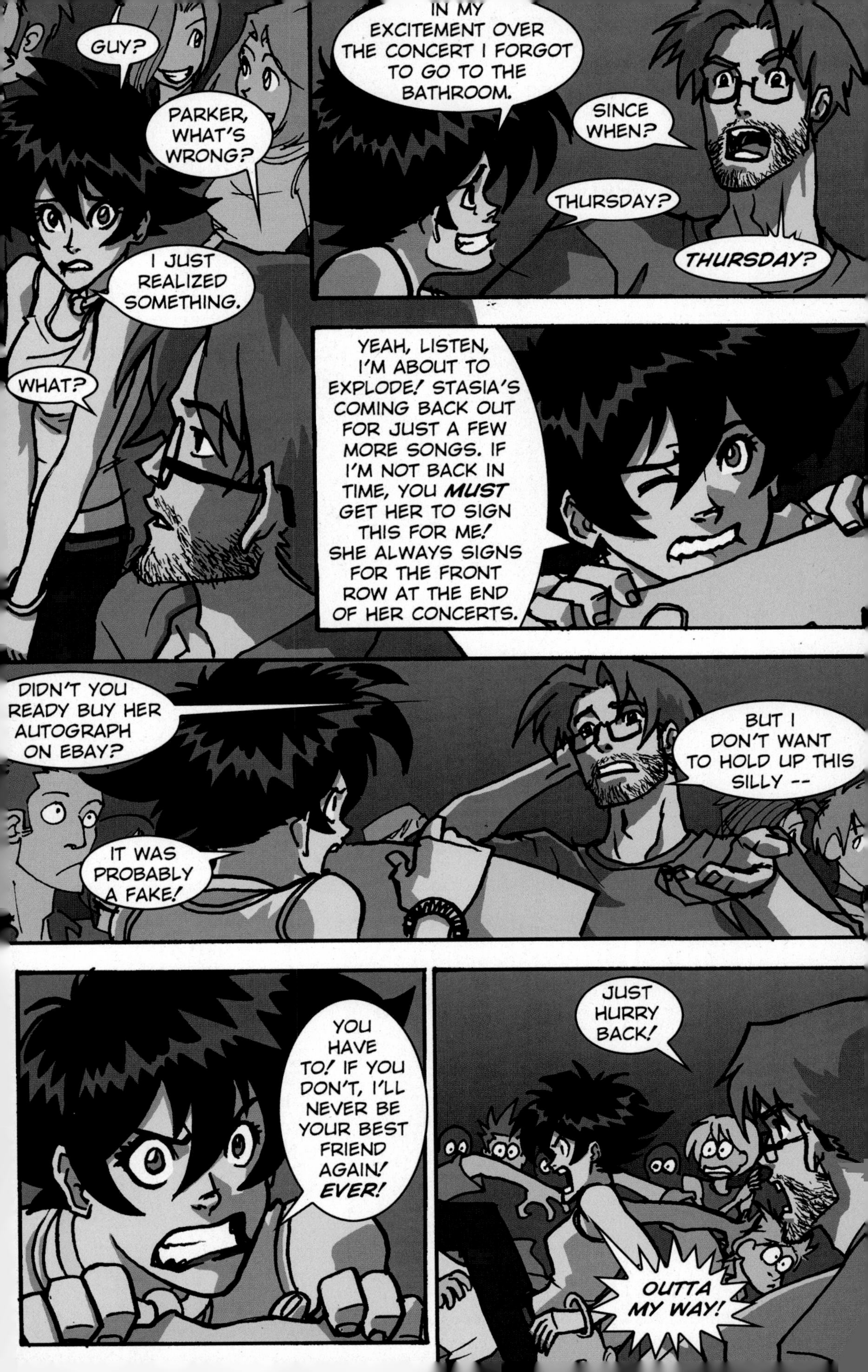
GUY?
PARKER, WHAT'S WRONG?
I JUST REALIZED SOMETHING.
WHAT?
IN MY EXCITEMENT OVER THE CONCERT I FORGOT TO GO TO THE BATHROOM.
SINCE WHEN?
THURSDAY?
THURSDAY?
YEAH, LISTEN, I'M ABOUT TO EXPLODE! STASIA'S COMING BACK OUT FOR JUST A FEW MORE SONGS. IF I'M NOT BACK IN TIME, YOU MUST GET HER TO SIGN THIS FOR ME! SHE ALWAYS SIGNS FOR THE FRONT ROW AT THE END OF HER CONCERTS.
DIDN'T YOU READY BUY HER AUTOGRAPH ON EBAY?
IT WAS PROBABLY A FAKE!
BUT I DON'T WANT TO HOLD UP THIS SILLY --
YOU HAVE TO! IF YOU DON'T, I'LL NEVER BE YOUR BEST FRIEND AGAIN! EVER!
JUST HURRY BACK!
OUTTA MY WAY!

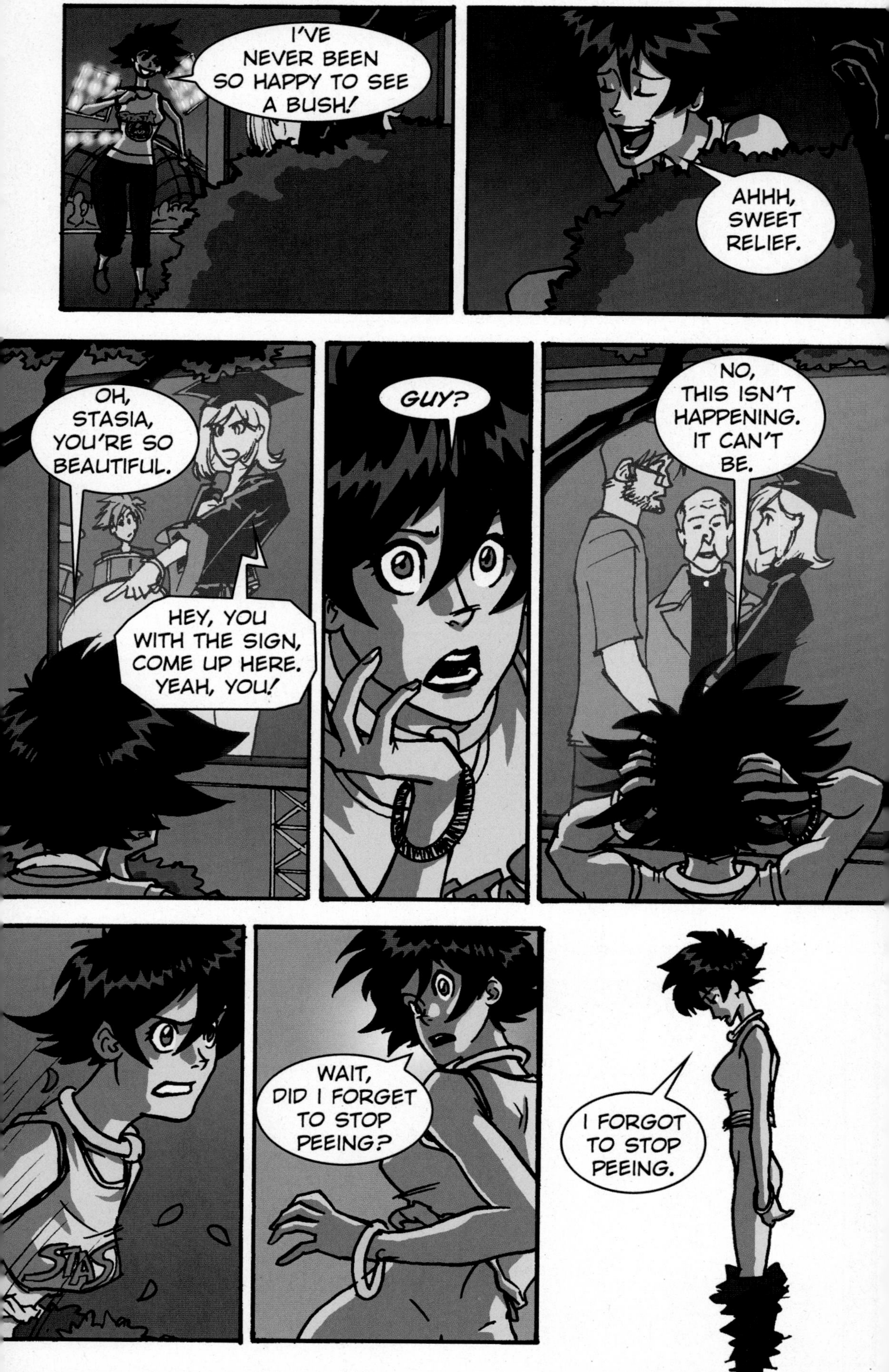
I'VE NEVER BEEN SO HAPPY TO SEE A BUSH!
AHHH, SWEET RELIEF.
OH, STASIA, YOU'RE SO BEAUTIFUL.
HEY, YOU WITH THE SIGN, COME UP HERE. YEAH, YOU!
GUY?
NO, THIS ISN'T HAPPENING. IT CAN'T BE.
WAIT, DID I FORGET TO STOP PEEING?
I FORGOT TO STOP PEEING.

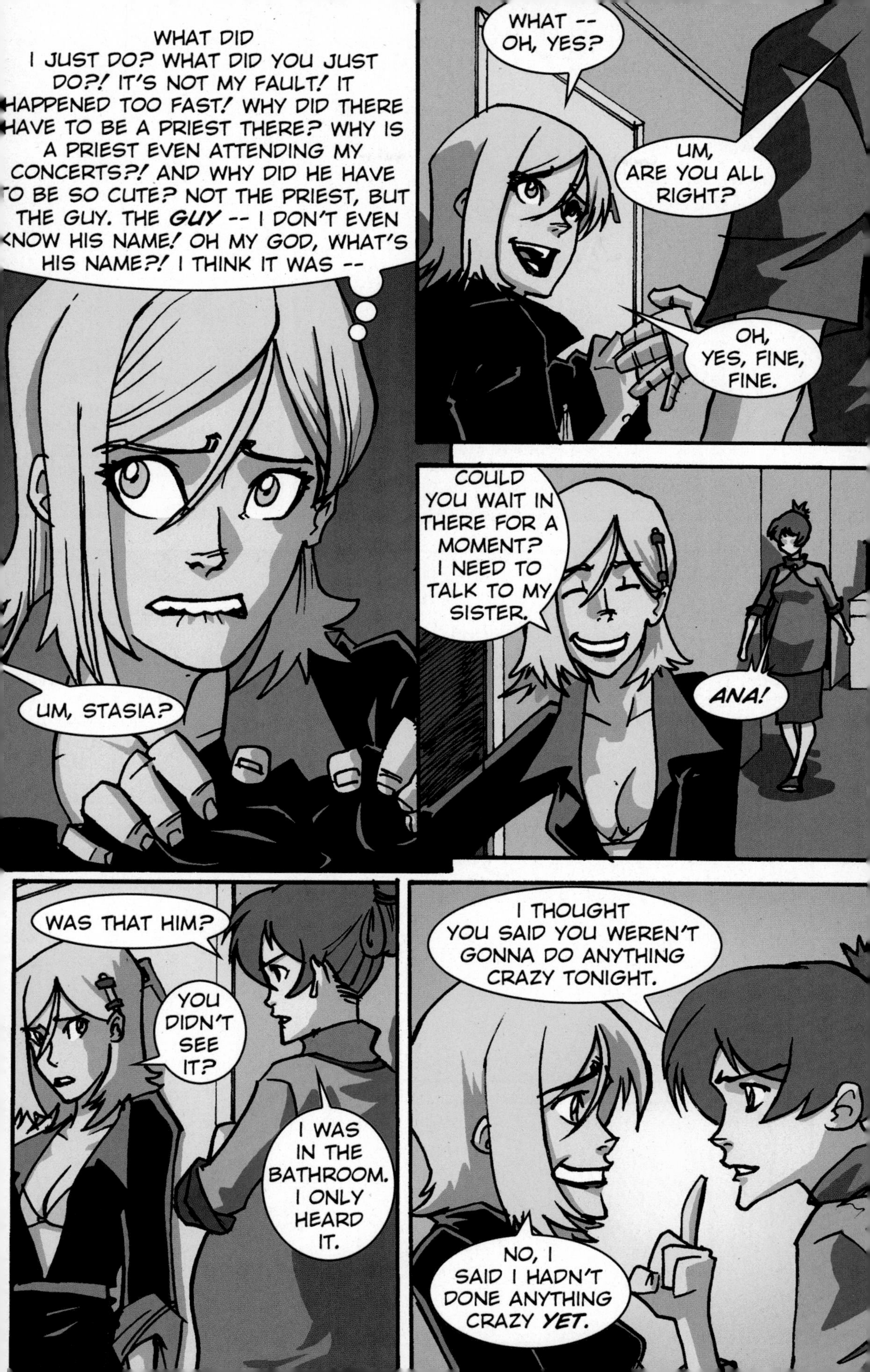
WHAT DID I JUST DO? WHAT DID YOU JUST DO?! IT'S NOT MY FAULT! IT HAPPENED TOO FAST! WHY DID THERE HAVE TO BE A PRIEST THERE? WHY IS A PRIEST EVEN ATTENDING MY CONCERTS?! AND WHY DID HE HAVE TO BE SO CUTE? NOT THE PRIEST, BUT THE GUY. THE GUY -- I DON'T EVEN KNOW HIS NAME! OH MY GOD, WHAT'S HIS NAME?! I THINK IT WAS --
UM, STASIA?
WHAT -- OH, YES?
UM, ARE YOU ALL RIGHT?
OH, YES, FINE, FINE.
COULD YOU WAIT IN THERE FOR A MOMENT? I NEED TO TALK TO MY SISTER.
ANA!
WAS THAT HIM?
YOU DIDN'T SEE IT?
I WAS IN THE BATHROOM. I ONLY HEARD IT.
I THOUGHT YOU SAID YOU WEREN'T GONNA DO ANYTHING CRAZY TONIGHT.
NO, I SAID I HADN'T DONE ANYTHING CRAZY YET.

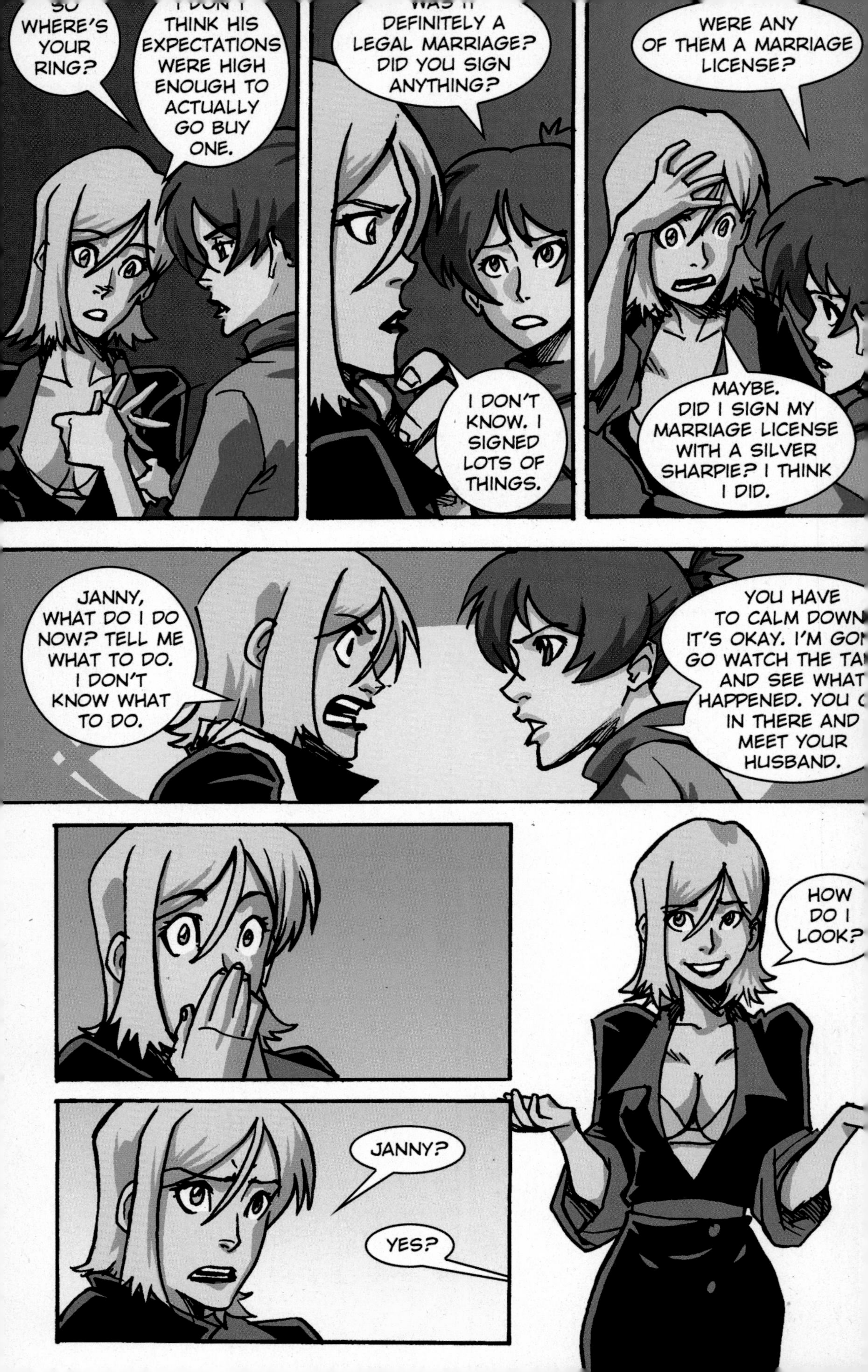

WHERE'S YOUR RING?
THINK HIS EXPECTATIONS WERE HIGH ENOUGH TO ACTUALLY GO BUY ONE.
DEFINITELY A LEGAL MARRIAGE? DID YOU SIGN ANYTHING?
I DON'T KNOW. I SIGNED LOTS OF THINGS.
WERE ANY OF THEM A MARRIAGE LICENSE?
MAYBE. DID I SIGN MY MARRIAGE LICENSE WITH A SILVER SHARPIE? I THINK I DID.
JANNY, WHAT DO I DO NOW? TELL ME WHAT TO DO. I DON'T KNOW WHAT TO DO.
YOU HAVE TO CALM DOWN IT'S OKAY. I'M GO GO WATCH THE TA AND SEE WHAT HAPPENED. YOU IN THERE AND MEET YOUR HUSBAND.
HOW DO I LOOK?
JANNY?
YES?

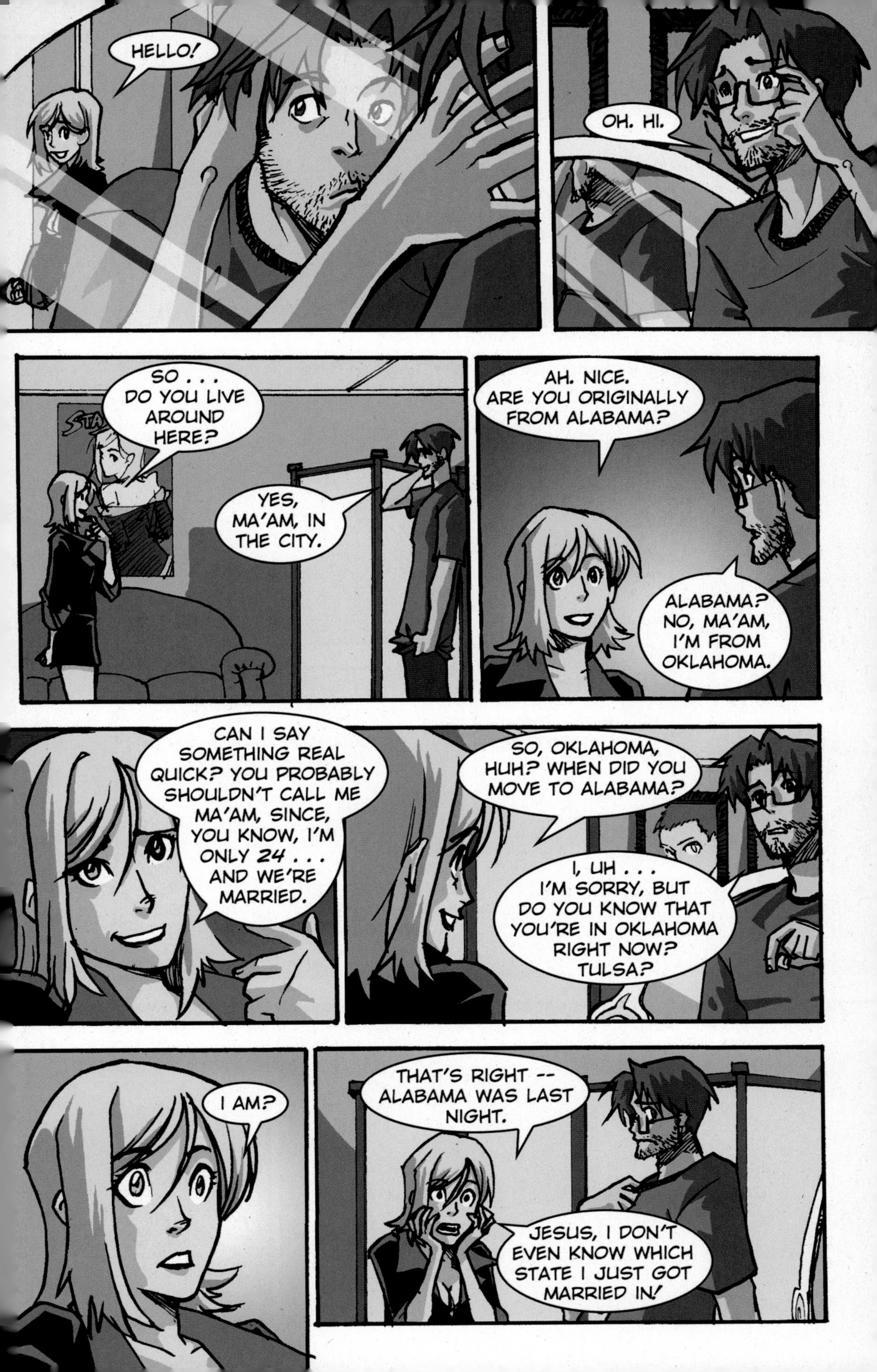
HELLO!
OH. HI.
SO . . . DO YOU LIVE AROUND HERE?
YES, MA'AM, IN THE CITY.
AH. NICE. ARE YOU ORIGINALLY FROM ALABAMA?
ALABAMA? NO, MA'AM, I'M FROM OKLAHOMA.
CAN I SAY SOMETHING REAL QUICK? YOU PROBABLY SHOULDN'T CALL ME MA'AM, SINCE, YOU KNOW, I'M ONLY 24 . . . AND WE'RE MARRIED.
SO, OKLAHOMA, HUH? WHEN DID YOU MOVE TO ALABAMA?
I, UH . . . I'M SORRY, BUT DO YOU KNOW THAT YOU'RE IN OKLAHOMA RIGHT NOW? TULSA?
I AM?
THAT'S RIGHT -- ALABAMA WAS LAST NIGHT.
JESUS, I DON'T EVEN KNOW WHICH STATE I JUST GOT MARRIED IN!

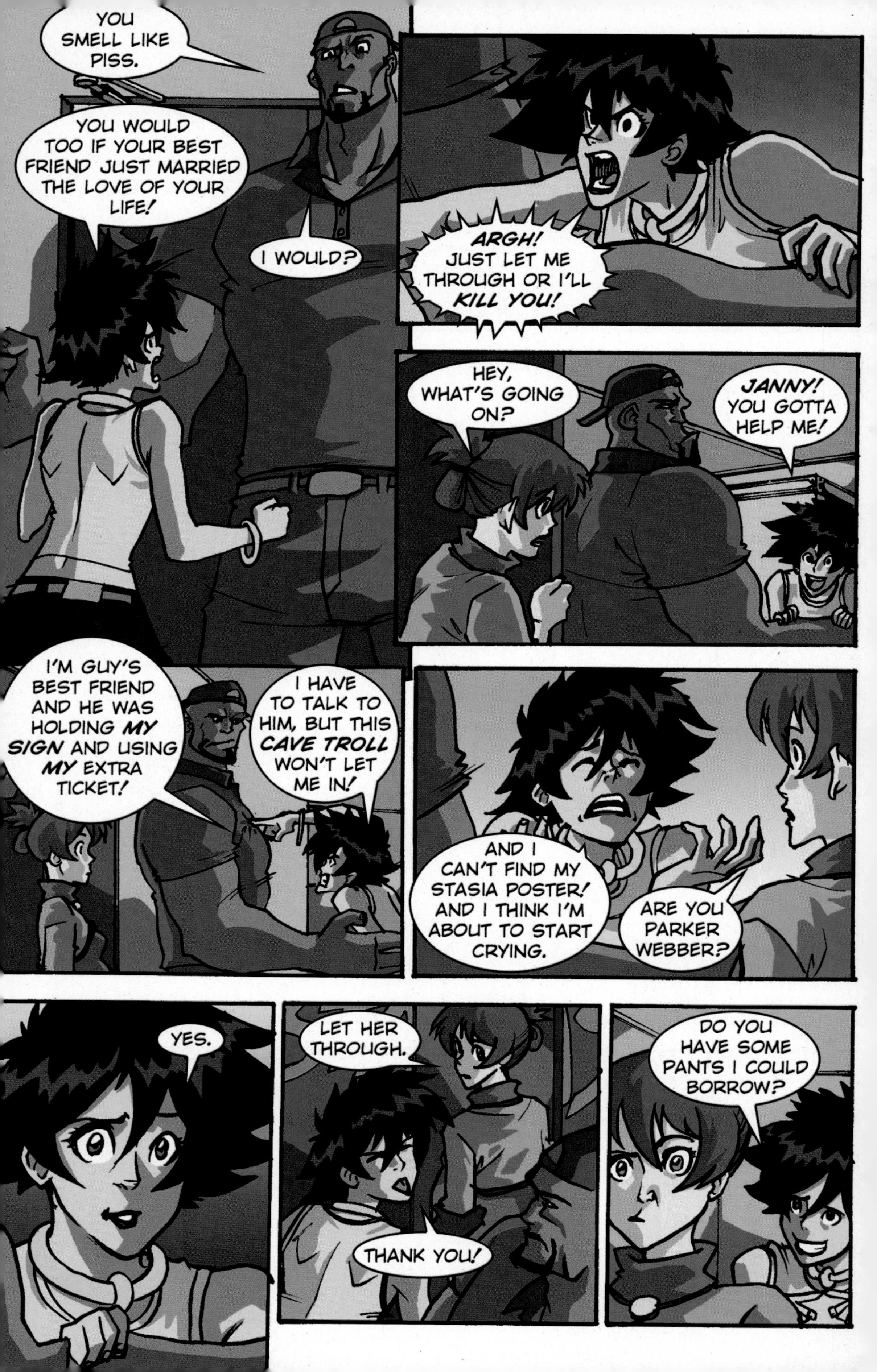
YOU SMELL LIKE PISS.
YOU WOULD TOO IF YOUR BEST FRIEND JUST MARRIED THE LOVE OF YOUR LIFE!
I WOULD?
ARGH! JUST LET ME THROUGH OR I'LL KILL YOU!
HEY, WHAT'S GOING ON?
JANNY! YOU GOTTA HELP ME!
I'M GUY'S BEST FRIEND AND HE WAS HOLDING MY SIGN AND USING MY EXTRA TICKET!
I HAVE TO TALK TO HIM, BUT THIS CAVE TROLL WON'T LET ME IN!
AND I CAN'T FIND MY STASIA POSTER! AND I THINK I'M ABOUT TO START CRYING.
ARE YOU PARKER WEBBER?
YES.
LET HER THROUGH.
THANK YOU!
DO YOU HAVE SOME PANTS I COULD BORROW?

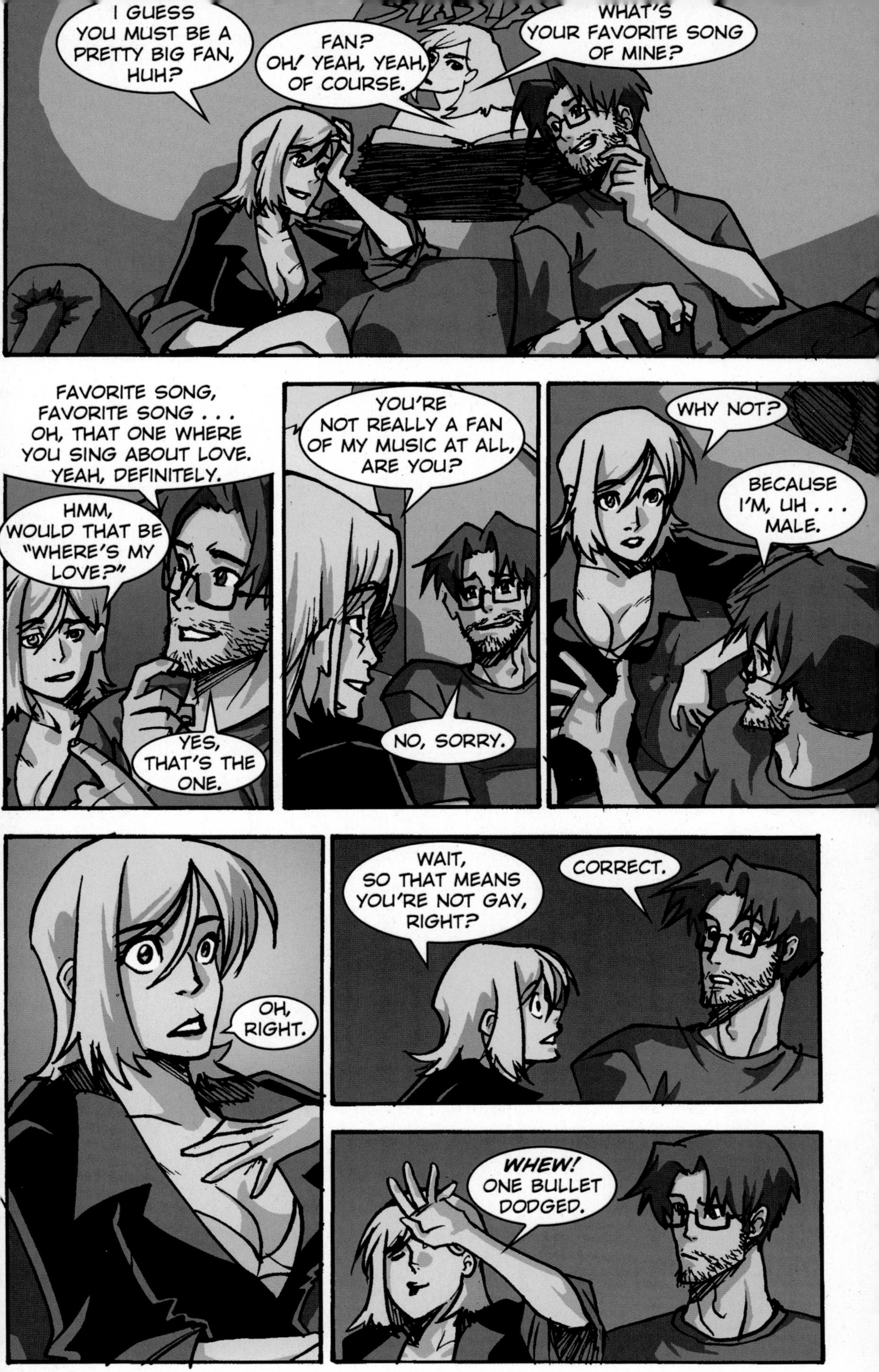
I GUESS YOU MUST BE A PRETTY BIG FAN, HUH?
FAN? OH! YEAH, YEAH, OF COURSE.
WHAT'S YOUR FAVORITE SONG OF MINE?
FAVORITE SONG, FAVORITE SONG . . . OH, THAT ONE WHERE YOU SING ABOUT LOVE. YEAH, DEFINITELY.
HMM, WOULD THAT BE "WHERE'S MY LOVE?"
YES, THAT'S THE ONE.
YOU'RE NOT REALLY A FAN OF MY MUSIC AT ALL, ARE YOU?
NO, SORRY.
WHY NOT?
BECAUSE I'M, UH . . . MALE.
OH, RIGHT.
WAIT, SO THAT MEANS YOU'RE NOT GAY, RIGHT?
CORRECT.
WHEW! ONE BULLET DODGED.

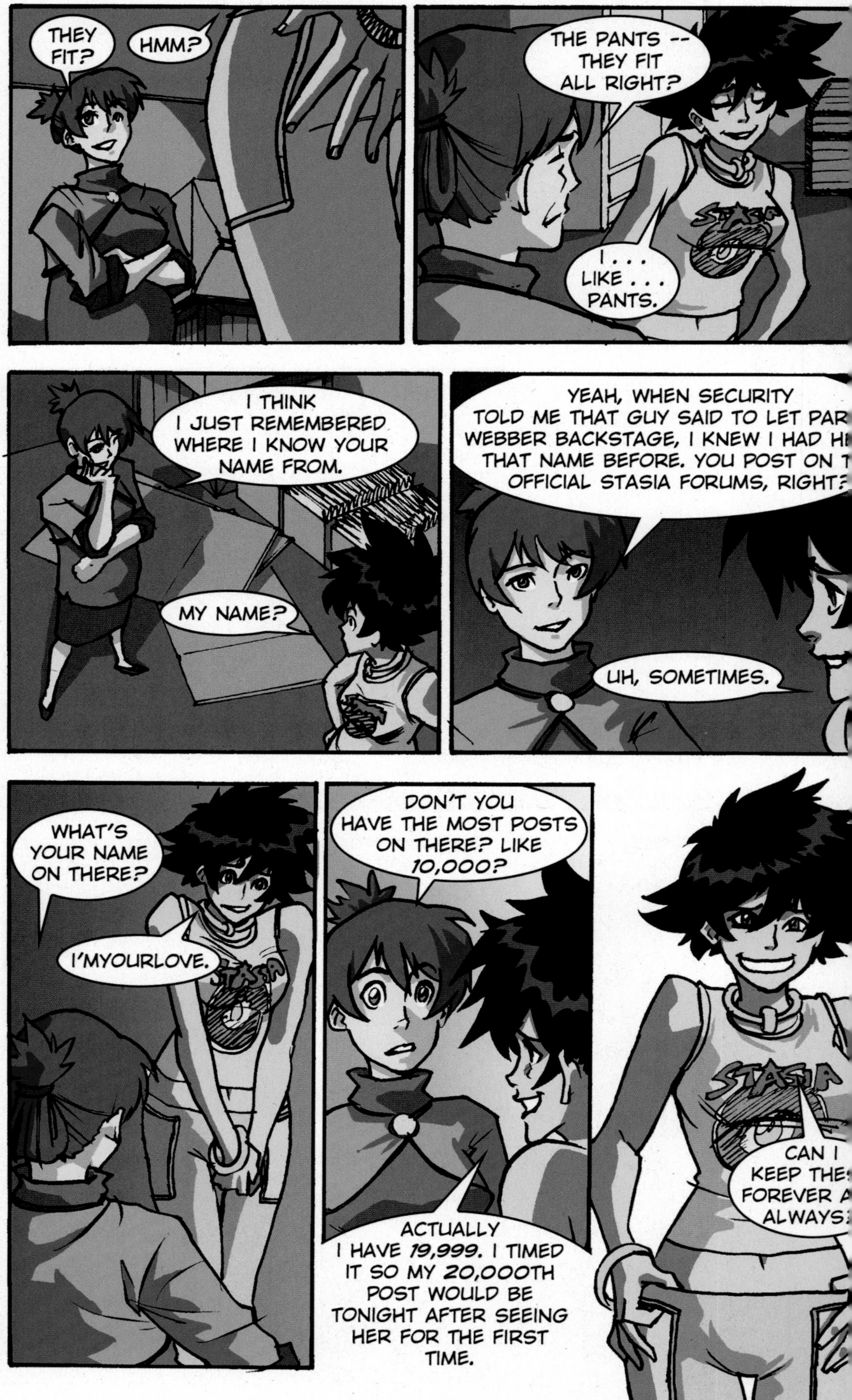
THEY FIT?
HMM?
THE PANTS -- THEY FIT ALL RIGHT?
I . . . LIKE . . . PANTS.
I THINK I JUST REMEMBERED WHERE I KNOW YOUR NAME FROM.
MY NAME?
YEAH, WHEN SECURITY TOLD ME THAT GUY SAID TO LET PAR WEBBER BACKSTAGE, I KNEW I HAD H THAT NAME BEFORE. YOU POST ON T OFFICIAL STASIA FORUMS, RIGHT?
UH, SOMETIMES.
WHAT'S YOUR NAME ON THERE?
I'MYOURLOVE.
DON'T YOU HAVE THE MOST POSTS ON THERE? LIKE 10,000?
ACTUALLY I HAVE 19,999. I TIMED IT SO MY 20,000TH POST WOULD BE TONIGHT AFTER SEEING HER FOR THE FIRST TIME.
CAN I KEEP THE FOREVER A ALWAYS?

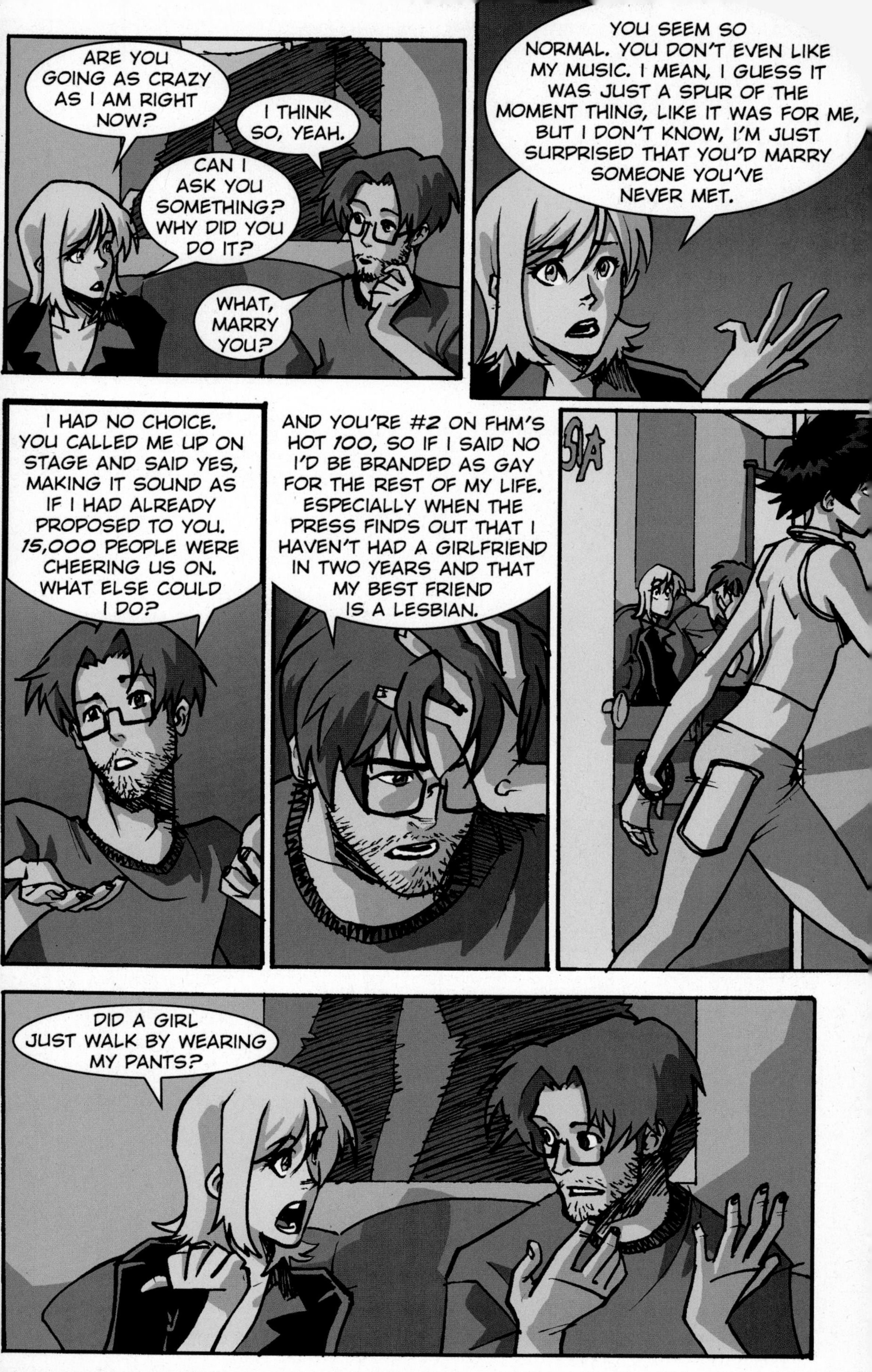
ARE YOU GOING AS CRAZY AS I AM RIGHT NOW?
I THINK SO, YEAH.
CAN I ASK YOU SOMETHING? WHY DID YOU DO IT?
WHAT, MARRY YOU?
YOU SEEM SO NORMAL. YOU DON'T EVEN LIKE MY MUSIC. I MEAN, I GUESS IT WAS JUST A SPUR OF THE MOMENT THING, LIKE IT WAS FOR ME, BUT I DON'T KNOW, I'M JUST SURPRISED THAT YOU'D MARRY SOMEONE YOU'VE NEVER MET.
I HAD NO CHOICE. YOU CALLED ME UP ON STAGE AND SAID YES, MAKING IT SOUND AS IF I HAD ALREADY PROPOSED TO YOU. 15,000 PEOPLE WERE CHEERING US ON. WHAT ELSE COULD I DO?
AND YOU'RE #2 ON FHM'S HOT 100, SO IF I SAID NO I'D BE BRANDED AS GAY FOR THE REST OF MY LIFE. ESPECIALLY WHEN THE PRESS FINDS OUT THAT I HAVEN'T HAD A GIRLFRIEND IN TWO YEARS AND THAT MY BEST FRIEND IS A LESBIAN.
DID A GIRL JUST WALK BY WEARING MY PANTS?

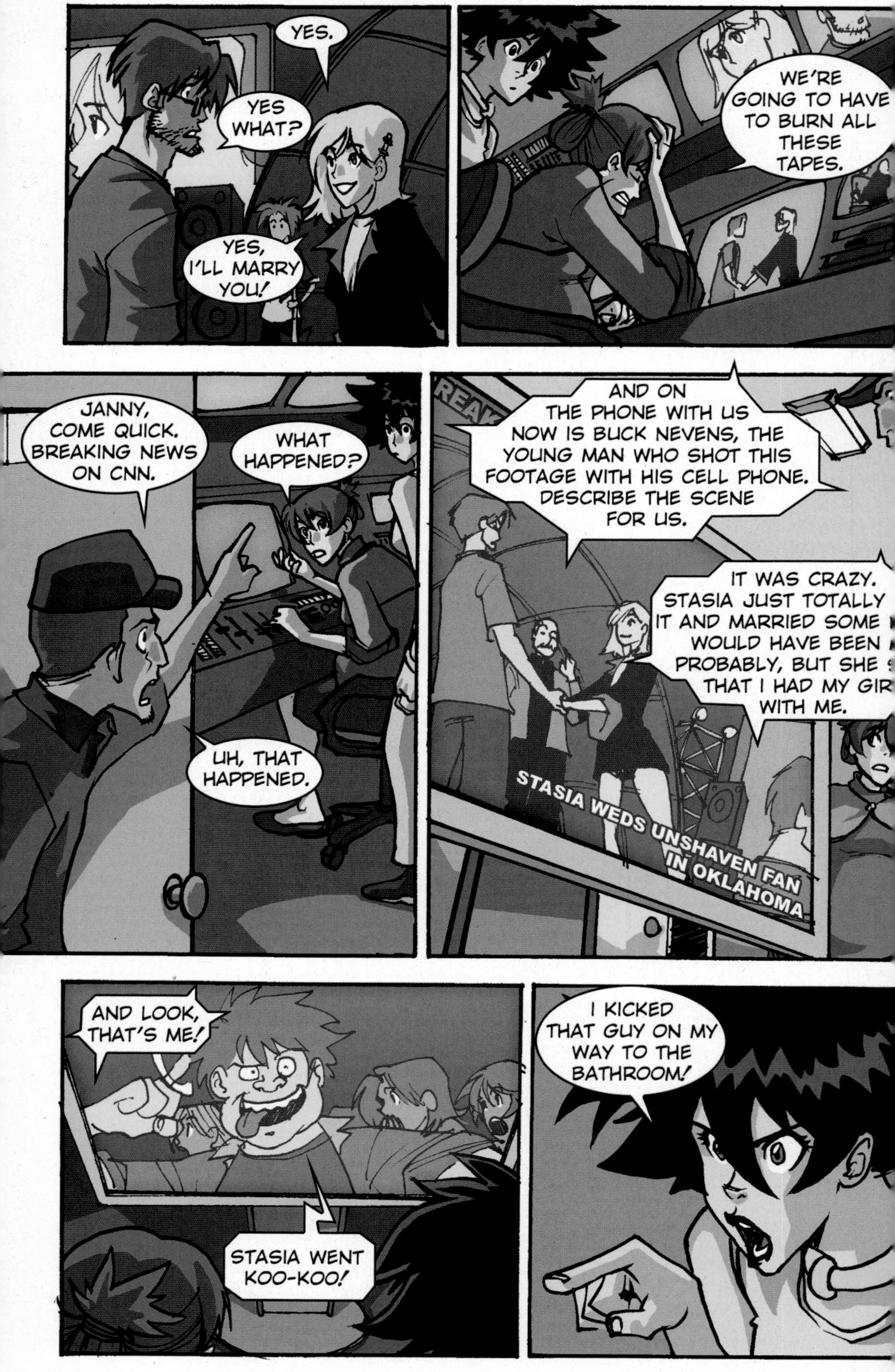
YES.
YES WHAT?
YES, I'LL MARRY YOU!
WE'RE GOING TO HAVE TO BURN ALL THESE TAPES.
JANNY, COME QUICK. BREAKING NEWS ON CNN.
WHAT HAPPENED?
UH, THAT HAPPENED.
AND ON THE PHONE WITH US NOW IS BUCK NEVENS, THE YOUNG MAN WHO SHOT THIS FOOTAGE WITH HIS CELL PHONE. DESCRIBE THE SCENE FOR US.
IT WAS CRAZY. STASIA JUST TOTALLY IT AND MARRIED SOME WOULD HAVE BEEN PROBABLY, BUT SHE THAT I HAD MY GIR WITH ME.
STASIA WEDS UNSHAVEN FAN IN OKLAHOMA
AND LOOK, THAT'S ME!
STASIA WENT KOO-KOO!
I KICKED THAT GUY ON MY WAY TO THE BATHROOM!

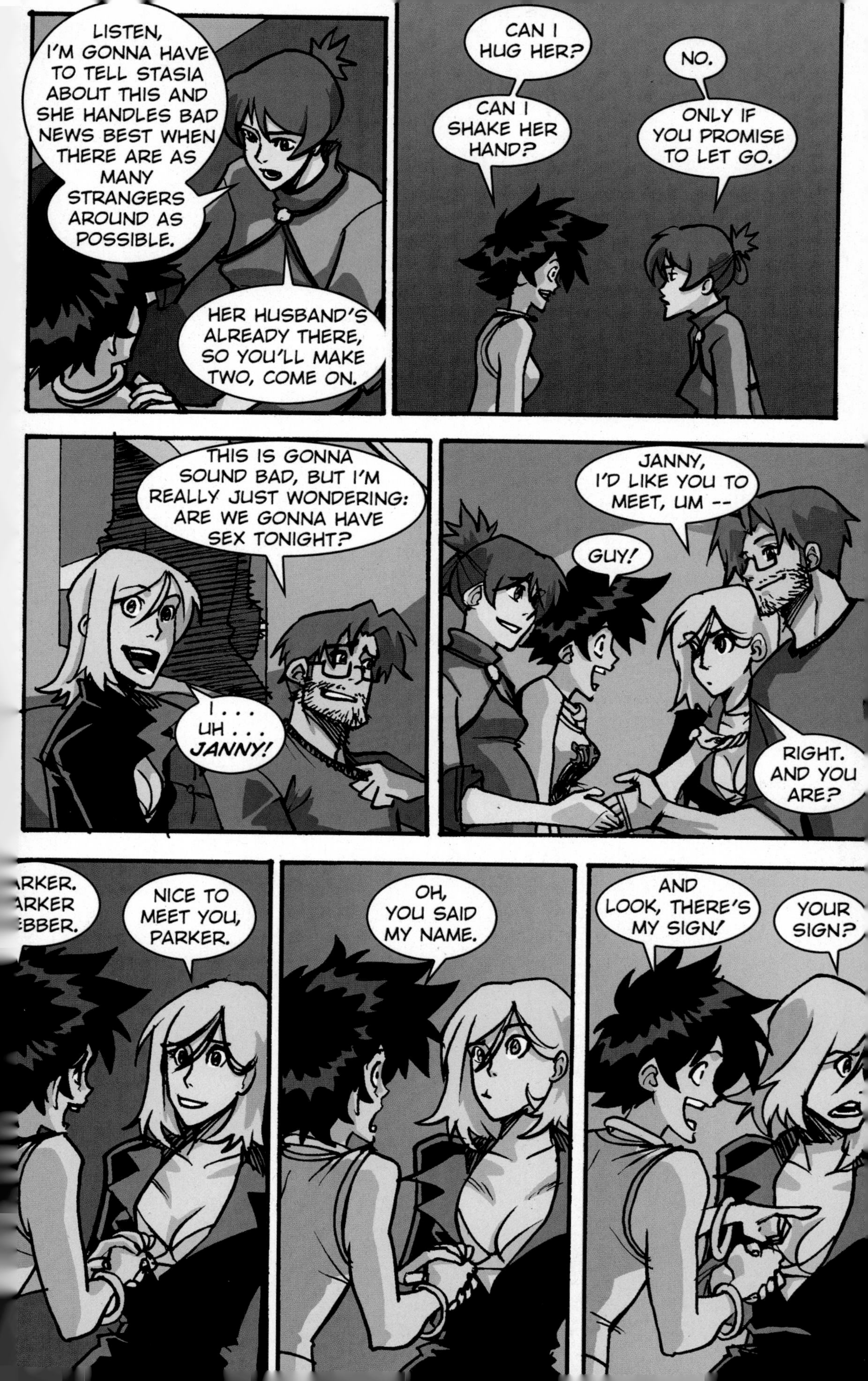

LISTEN, I'M GONNA HAVE TO TELL STASIA ABOUT THIS AND SHE HANDLES BAD NEWS BEST WHEN THERE ARE AS MANY STRANGERS AROUND AS POSSIBLE.
HER HUSBAND'S ALREADY THERE, SO YOU'LL MAKE TWO, COME ON.
CAN I HUG HER?
NO.
CAN I SHAKE HER HAND?
ONLY IF YOU PROMISE TO LET GO.
THIS IS GONNA SOUND BAD, BUT I'M REALLY JUST WONDERING: ARE WE GONNA HAVE SEX TONIGHT?
I . . . UH . . . JANNY!
JANNY, I'D LIKE YOU TO MEET, UM --
GUY!
RIGHT. AND YOU ARE?
ARKER. ARKER EBBER.
NICE TO MEET YOU, PARKER.
OH, YOU SAID MY NAME.
AND LOOK, THERE'S MY SIGN!
YOUR SIGN?

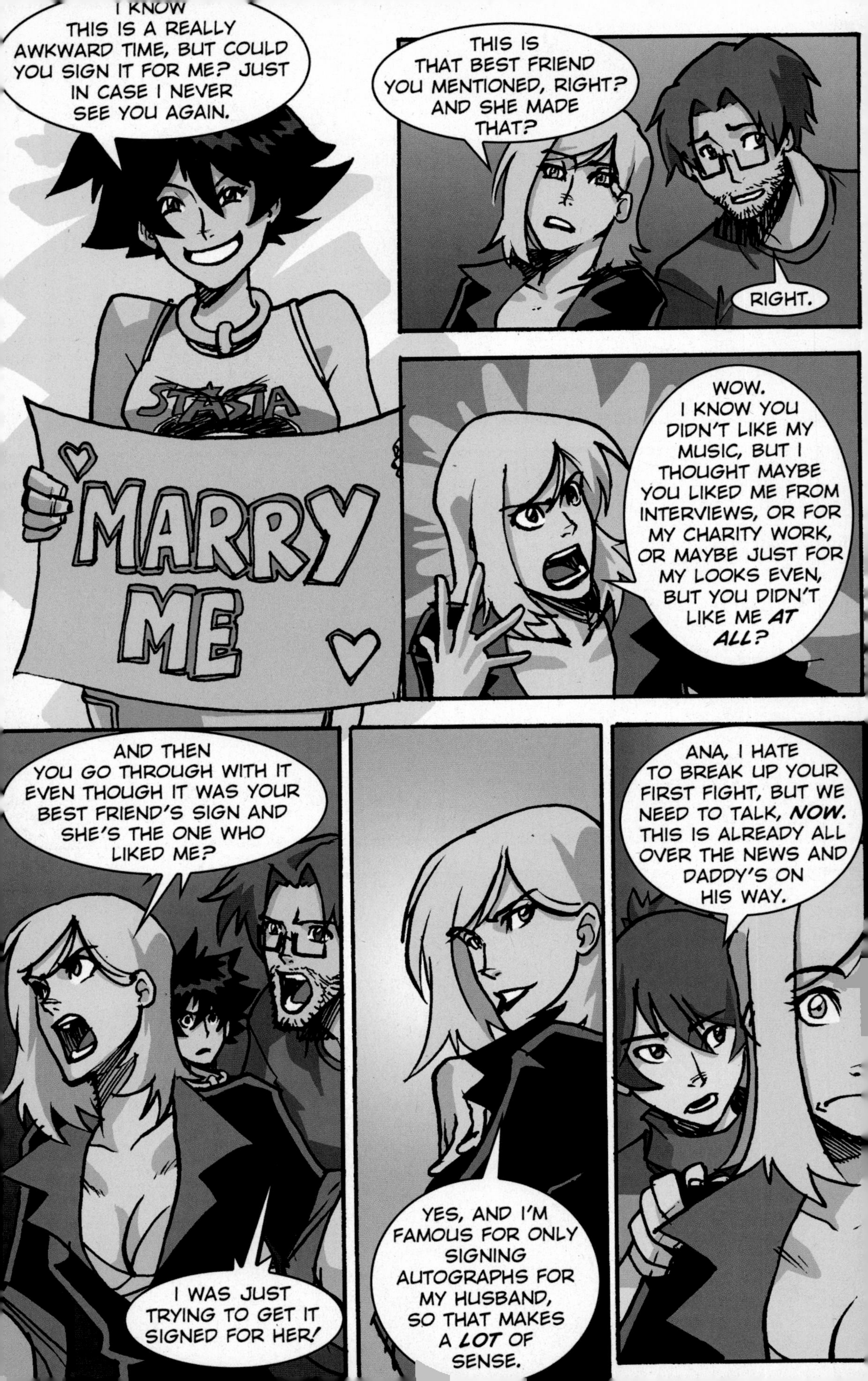
I KNOW THIS IS A REALLY AWKWARD TIME, BUT COULD YOU SIGN IT FOR ME? JUST IN CASE I NEVER SEE YOU AGAIN.
STASIA
MARRY ME
THIS IS THAT BEST FRIEND YOU MENTIONED, RIGHT? AND SHE MADE THAT?
RIGHT.
WOW. I KNOW YOU DIDN'T LIKE MY MUSIC, BUT I THOUGHT MAYBE YOU LIKED ME FROM INTERVIEWS, OR FOR MY CHARITY WORK, OR MAYBE JUST FOR MY LOOKS EVEN, BUT YOU DIDN'T LIKE ME *AT ALL*?
AND THEN YOU GO THROUGH WITH IT EVEN THOUGH IT WAS YOUR BEST FRIEND'S SIGN AND SHE'S THE ONE WHO LIKED ME?
I WAS JUST TRYING TO GET IT SIGNED FOR HER!
YES, AND I'M FAMOUS FOR ONLY SIGNING AUTOGRAPHS FOR MY HUSBAND, SO THAT MAKES A *LOT* OF SENSE.
ANA, I HATE TO BREAK UP YOUR FIRST FIGHT, BUT WE NEED TO TALK, *NOW.* THIS IS ALREADY ALL OVER THE NEWS AND DADDY'S ON HIS WAY.

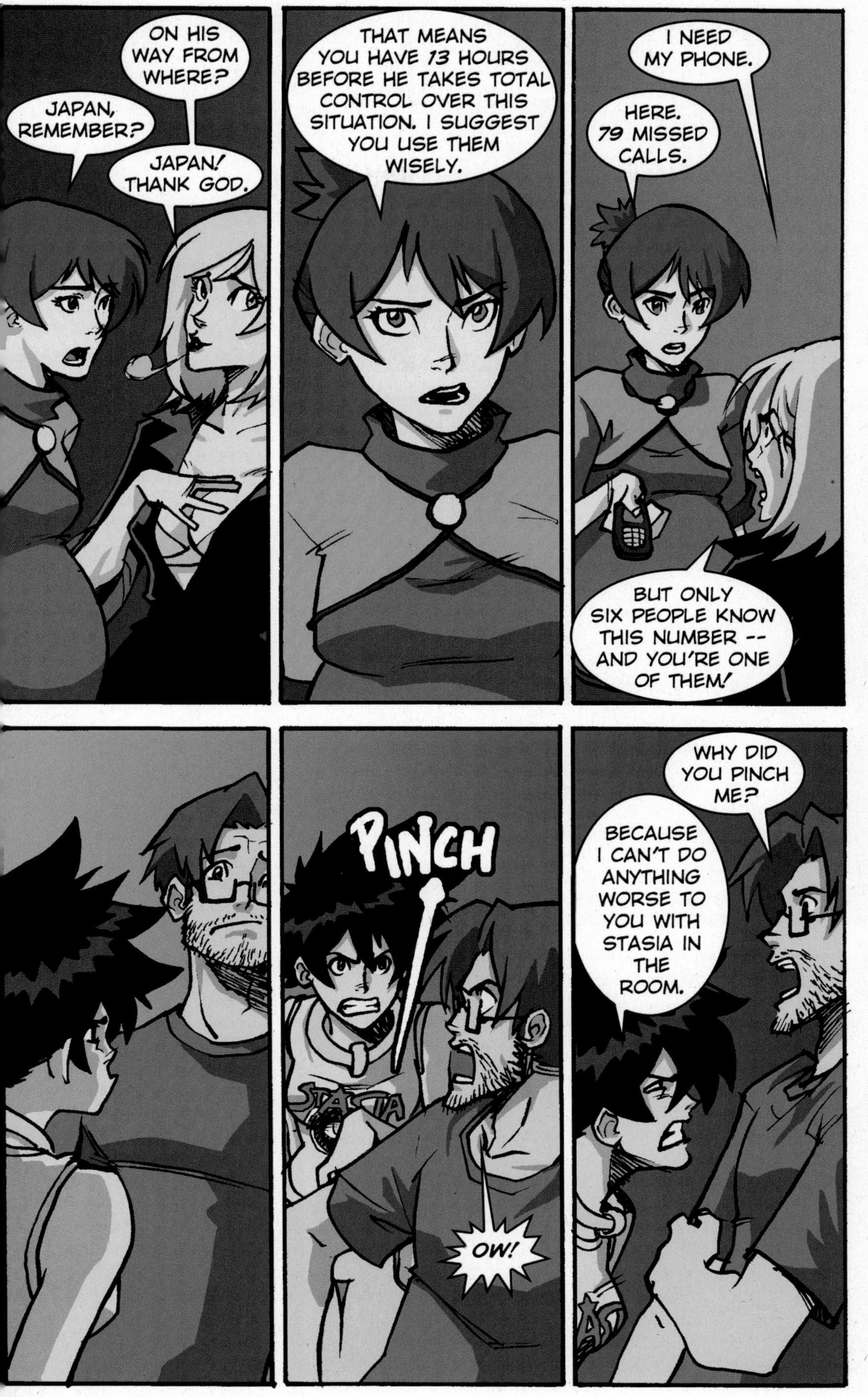
ON HIS WAY FROM WHERE?
JAPAN, REMEMBER?
JAPAN! THANK GOD.
THAT MEANS YOU HAVE 13 HOURS BEFORE HE TAKES TOTAL CONTROL OVER THIS SITUATION. I SUGGEST YOU USE THEM WISELY.
I NEED MY PHONE.
HERE. 79 MISSED CALLS.
BUT ONLY SIX PEOPLE KNOW THIS NUMBER -- AND YOU'RE ONE OF THEM!
PINCH
OW!
WHY DID YOU PINCH ME?
BECAUSE I CAN'T DO ANYTHING WORSE TO YOU WITH STASIA IN THE ROOM.

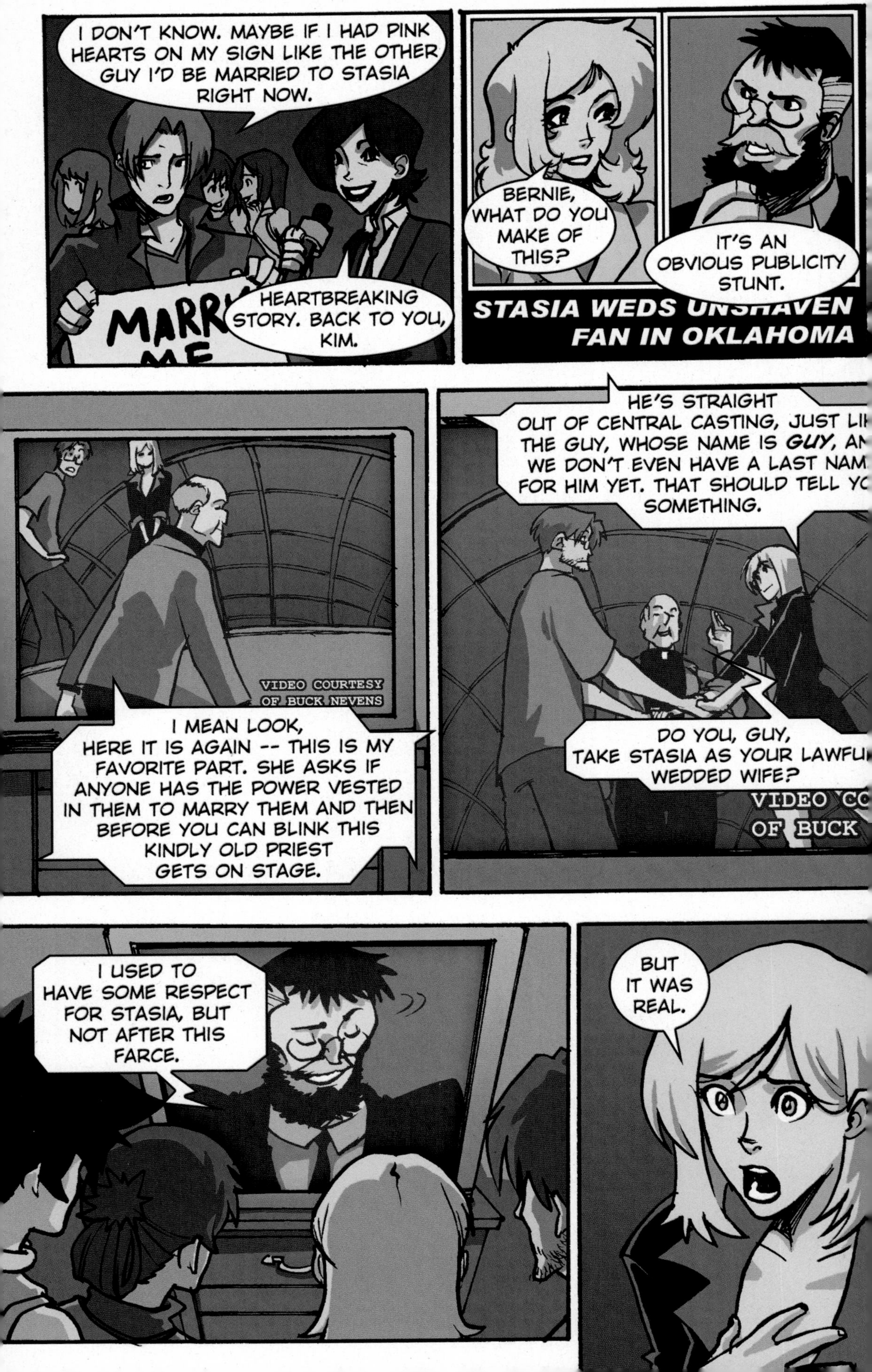
I DON'T KNOW. MAYBE IF I HAD PINK HEARTS ON MY SIGN LIKE THE OTHER GUY I'D BE MARRIED TO STASIA RIGHT NOW.
MARR
HEARTBREAKING STORY. BACK TO YOU, KIM.
BERNIE, WHAT DO YOU MAKE OF THIS?
IT'S AN OBVIOUS PUBLICITY STUNT.
STASIA WEDS UNSHAVEN FAN IN OKLAHOMA
VIDEO COURTESY OF BUCK NEVENS
I MEAN LOOK, HERE IT IS AGAIN -- THIS IS MY FAVORITE PART. SHE ASKS IF ANYONE HAS THE POWER VESTED IN THEM TO MARRY THEM AND THEN BEFORE YOU CAN BLINK THIS KINDLY OLD PRIEST GETS ON STAGE.
HE'S STRAIGHT OUT OF CENTRAL CASTING, JUST LI THE GUY, WHOSE NAME IS *GUY*, AN WE DON'T EVEN HAVE A LAST NAM FOR HIM YET. THAT SHOULD TELL YO SOMETHING.
DO YOU, GUY, TAKE STASIA AS YOUR LAWFU WEDDED WIFE?
VIDEO CO OF BUCK
I USED TO HAVE SOME RESPECT FOR STASIA, BUT NOT AFTER THIS FARCE.
BUT IT WAS REAL.

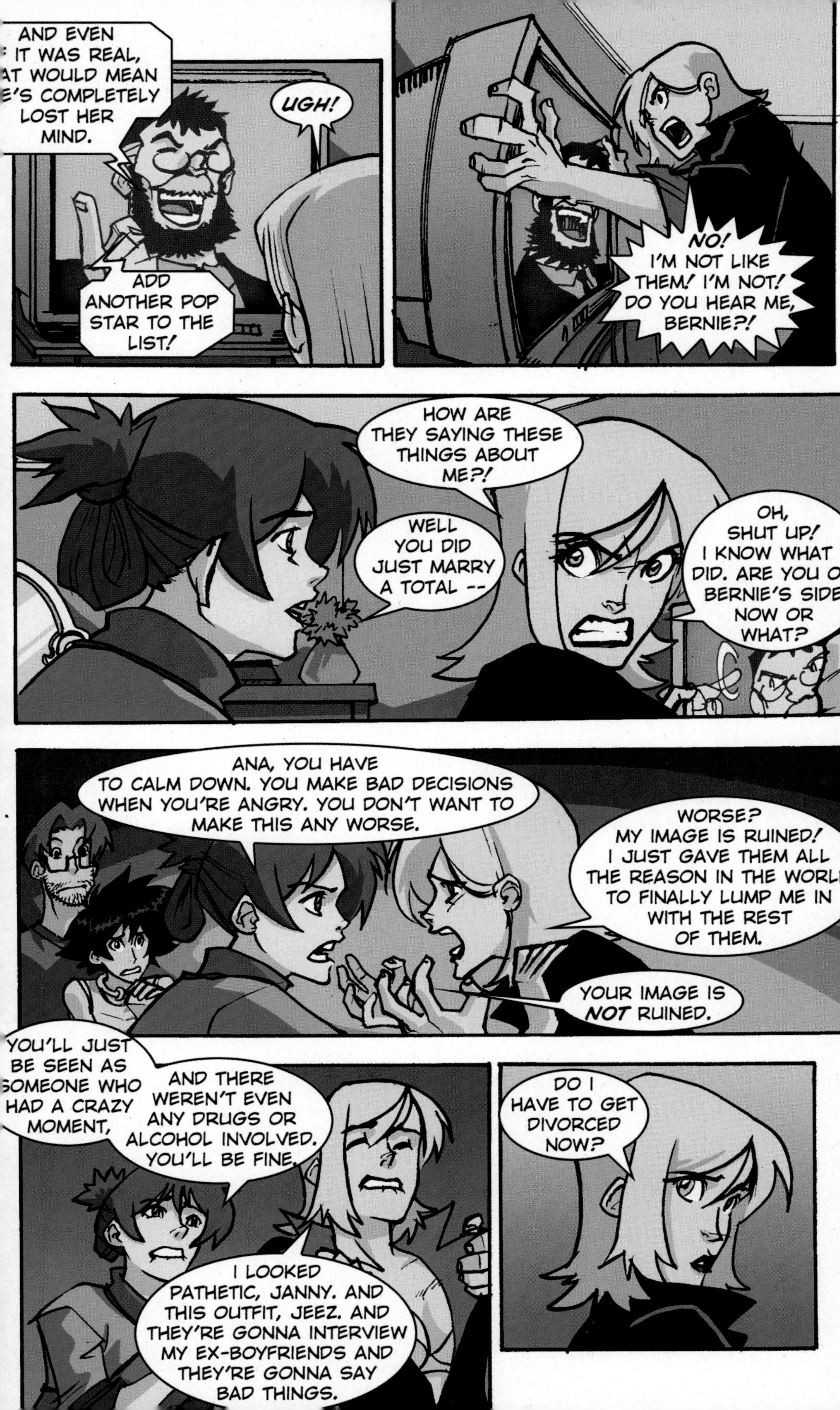
AND EVEN F IT WAS REAL, AT WOULD MEAN E'S COMPLETELY LOST HER MIND.
UGH!
ADD ANOTHER POP STAR TO THE LIST!
NO! I'M NOT LIKE THEM! I'M NOT! DO YOU HEAR ME, BERNIE?!
HOW ARE THEY SAYING THESE THINGS ABOUT ME?!
WELL YOU DID JUST MARRY A TOTAL --
OH, SHUT UP! I KNOW WHAT I DID. ARE YOU ON BERNIE'S SIDE NOW OR WHAT?
ANA, YOU HAVE TO CALM DOWN. YOU MAKE BAD DECISIONS WHEN YOU'RE ANGRY. YOU DON'T WANT TO MAKE THIS ANY WORSE.
WORSE? MY IMAGE IS RUINED! I JUST GAVE THEM ALL THE REASON IN THE WORLD TO FINALLY LUMP ME IN WITH THE REST OF THEM.
YOUR IMAGE IS NOT RUINED.
YOU'LL JUST BE SEEN AS SOMEONE WHO HAD A CRAZY MOMENT,
AND THERE WEREN'T EVEN ANY DRUGS OR ALCOHOL INVOLVED. YOU'LL BE FINE.
I LOOKED PATHETIC, JANNY. AND THIS OUTFIT, JEEZ. AND THEY'RE GONNA INTERVIEW MY EX-BOYFRIENDS AND THEY'RE GONNA SAY BAD THINGS.
DO I HAVE TO GET DIVORCED NOW?

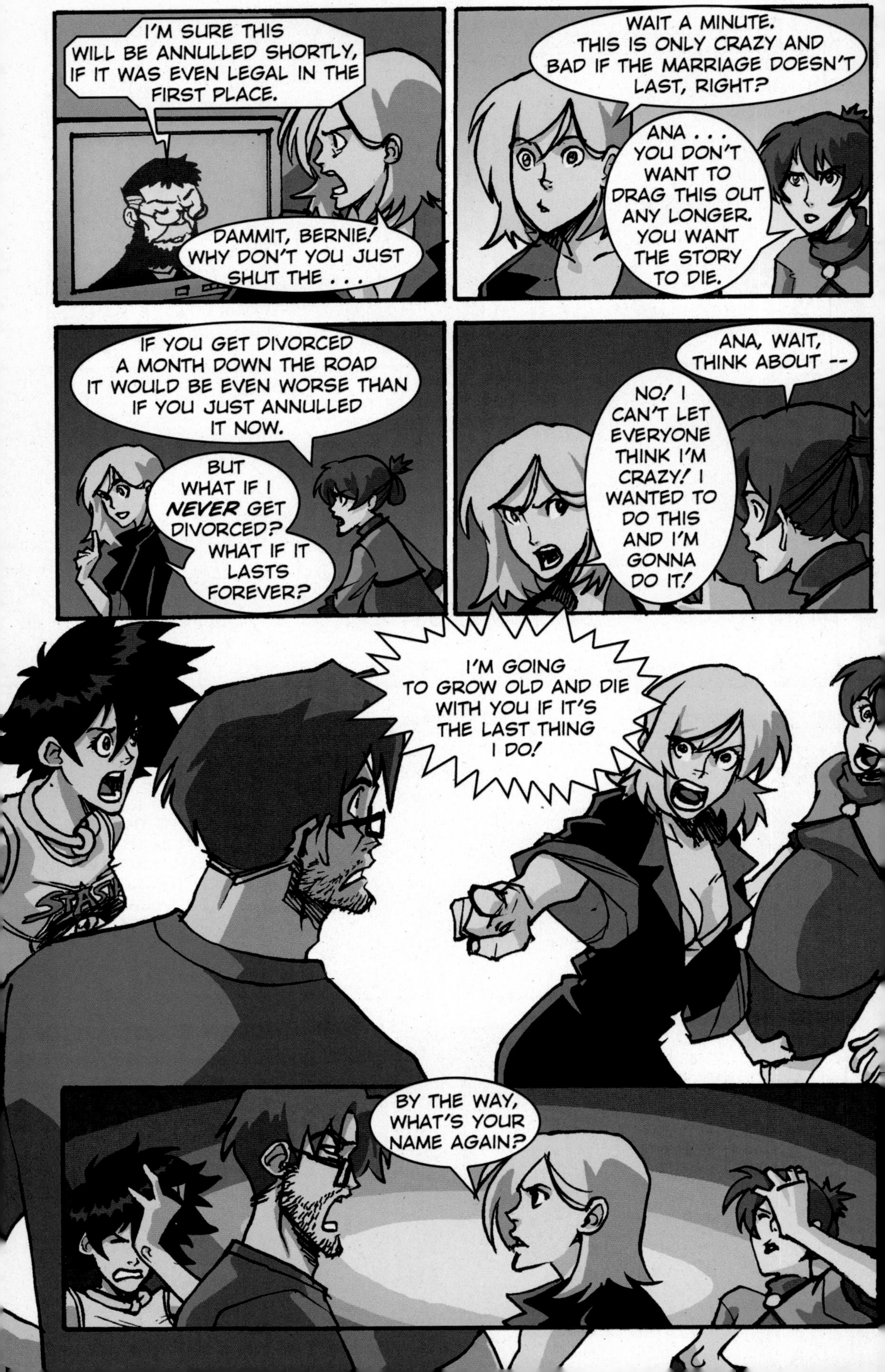
I'M SURE THIS WILL BE ANNULLED SHORTLY, IF IT WAS EVEN LEGAL IN THE FIRST PLACE.
DAMMIT, BERNIE! WHY DON'T YOU JUST SHUT THE . . .
WAIT A MINUTE. THIS IS ONLY CRAZY AND BAD IF THE MARRIAGE DOESN'T LAST, RIGHT?
ANA . . . YOU DON'T WANT TO DRAG THIS OUT ANY LONGER. YOU WANT THE STORY TO DIE.
IF YOU GET DIVORCED A MONTH DOWN THE ROAD IT WOULD BE EVEN WORSE THAN IF YOU JUST ANNULLED IT NOW.
BUT WHAT IF I NEVER GET DIVORCED? WHAT IF IT LASTS FOREVER?
ANA, WAIT, THINK ABOUT --
NO! I CAN'T LET EVERYONE THINK I'M CRAZY! I WANTED TO DO THIS AND I'M GONNA DO IT!
I'M GOING TO GROW OLD AND DIE WITH YOU IF IT'S THE LAST THING I DO!
BY THE WAY, WHAT'S YOUR NAME AGAIN?

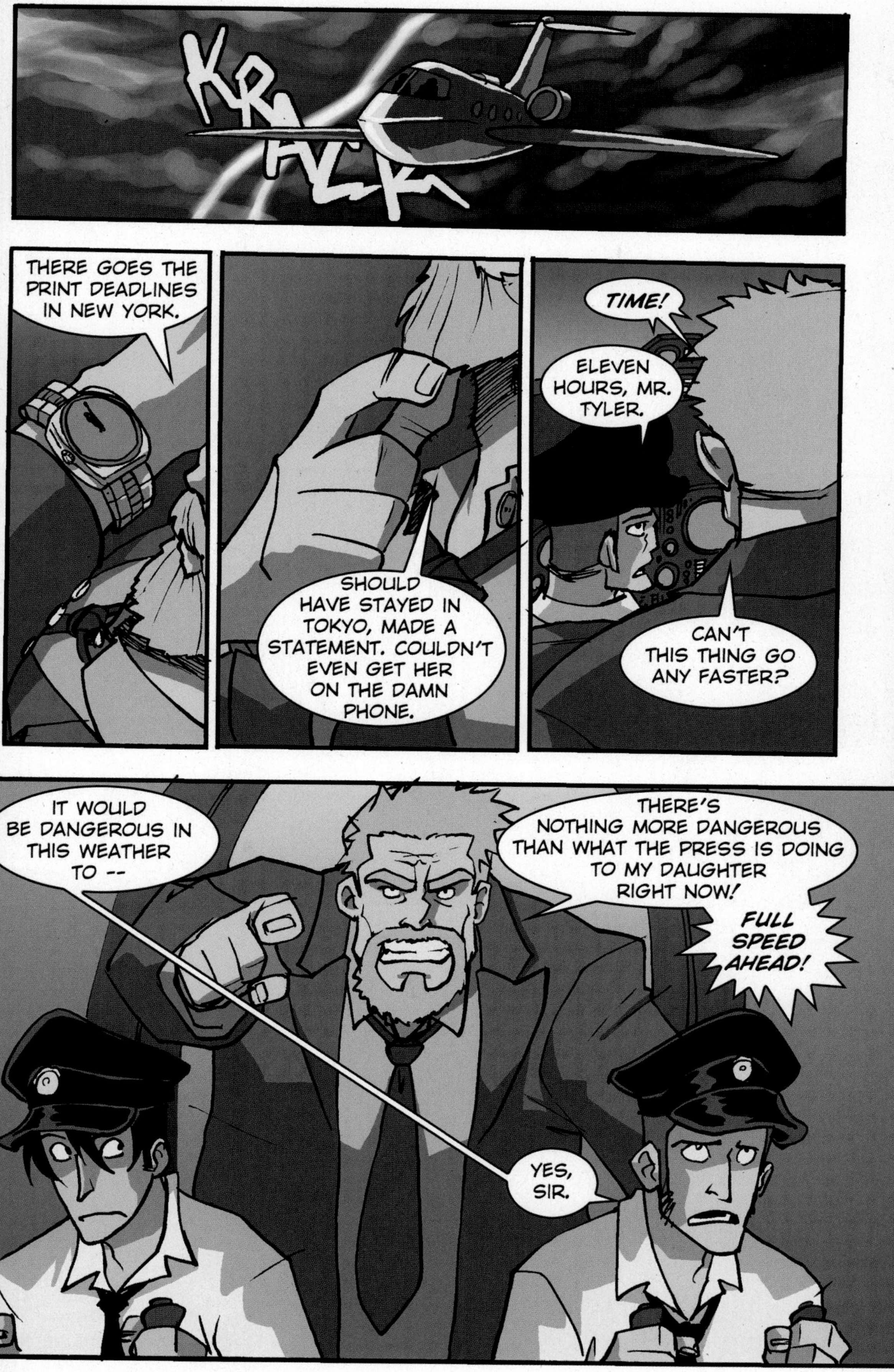
KRACK
THERE GOES THE PRINT DEADLINES IN NEW YORK.
SHOULD HAVE STAYED IN TOKYO, MADE A STATEMENT. COULDN'T EVEN GET HER ON THE DAMN PHONE.
TIME!
ELEVEN HOURS, MR. TYLER.
CAN'T THIS THING GO ANY FASTER?
IT WOULD BE DANGEROUS IN THIS WEATHER TO --
THERE'S NOTHING MORE DANGEROUS THAN WHAT THE PRESS IS DOING TO MY DAUGHTER RIGHT NOW!
FULL SPEED AHEAD!
YES, SIR.

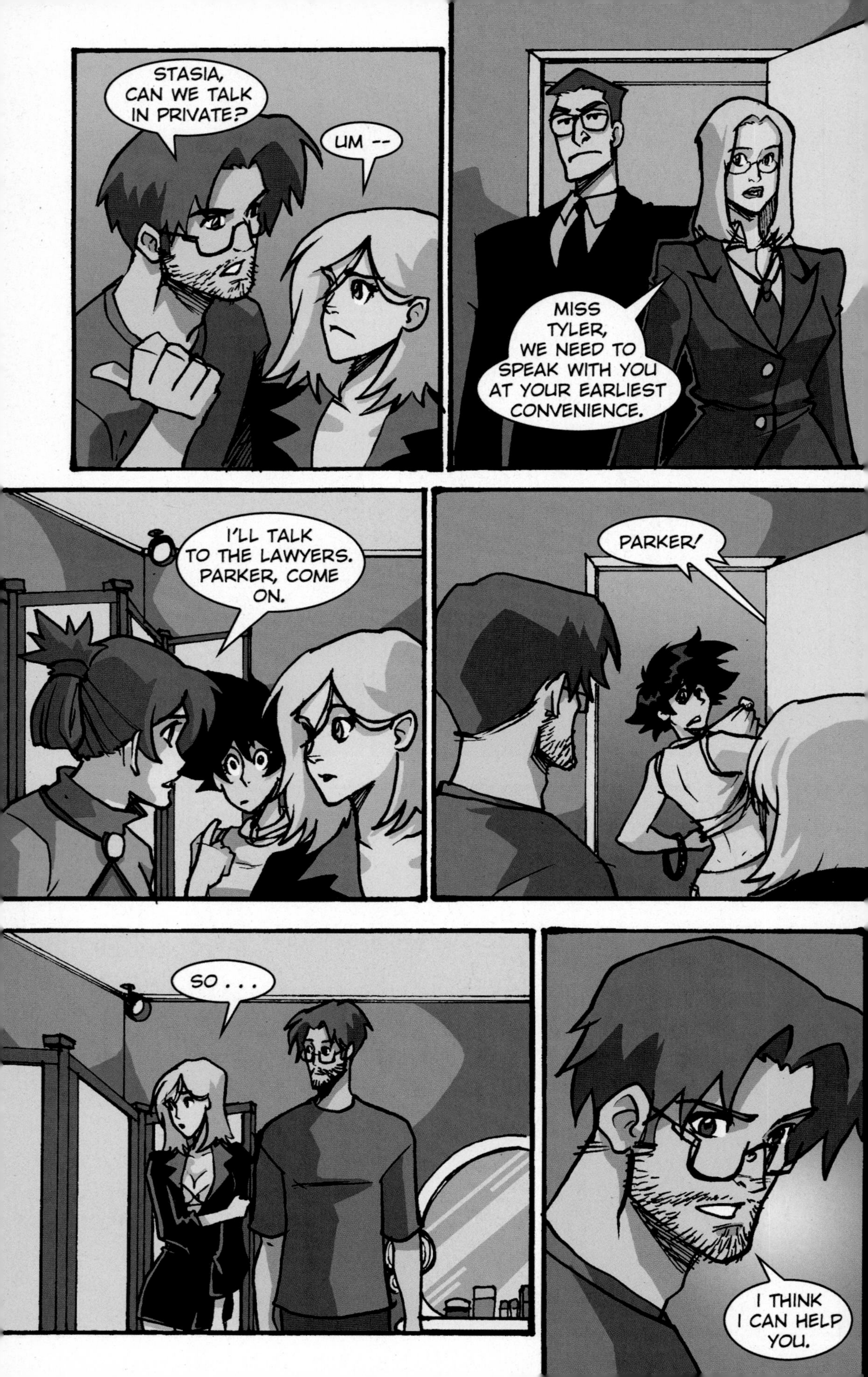
STASIA, CAN WE TALK IN PRIVATE?
UM --
MISS TYLER, WE NEED TO SPEAK WITH YOU AT YOUR EARLIEST CONVENIENCE.
I'LL TALK TO THE LAWYERS. PARKER, COME ON.
PARKER!
SO . . .
I THINK I CAN HELP YOU.

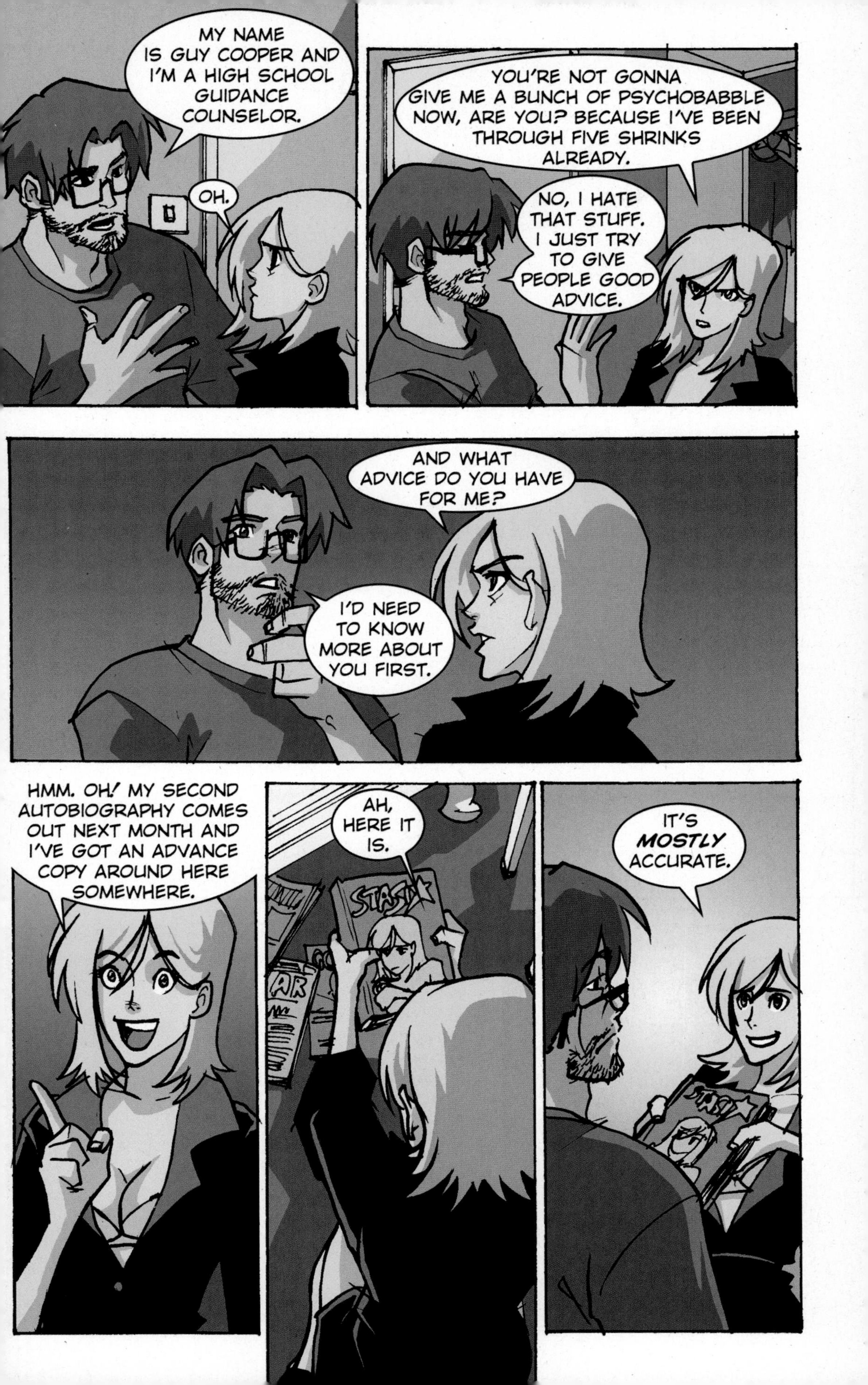
MY NAME IS GUY COOPER AND I'M A HIGH SCHOOL GUIDANCE COUNSELOR.
OH.
YOU'RE NOT GONNA GIVE ME A BUNCH OF PSYCHOBABBLE NOW, ARE YOU? BECAUSE I'VE BEEN THROUGH FIVE SHRINKS ALREADY.
NO, I HATE THAT STUFF. I JUST TRY TO GIVE PEOPLE GOOD ADVICE.
AND WHAT ADVICE DO YOU HAVE FOR ME?
I'D NEED TO KNOW MORE ABOUT YOU FIRST.
HMM. OH! MY SECOND AUTOBIOGRAPHY COMES OUT NEXT MONTH AND I'VE GOT AN ADVANCE COPY AROUND HERE SOMEWHERE.
AH, HERE IT IS.
IT'S *MOSTLY* ACCURATE.

 Stasia Forums :: View topic - 20,000th... | http://www.stasia.com/ | W Wikipedia

20,000th POST!

newtopic postreply   Stasia Forums Forum Index -> General Discussion

View previous topic :: View ne

Author	Message
I'mYourLove President of the "I <3 Stasia" Fan Club Joined: 22 May 2007 Posts: 20,000	Posted: 09 Sep 2009 09:02pm Post subject: 20,000th POST! quote edit I'm in Stasia's pants right now.

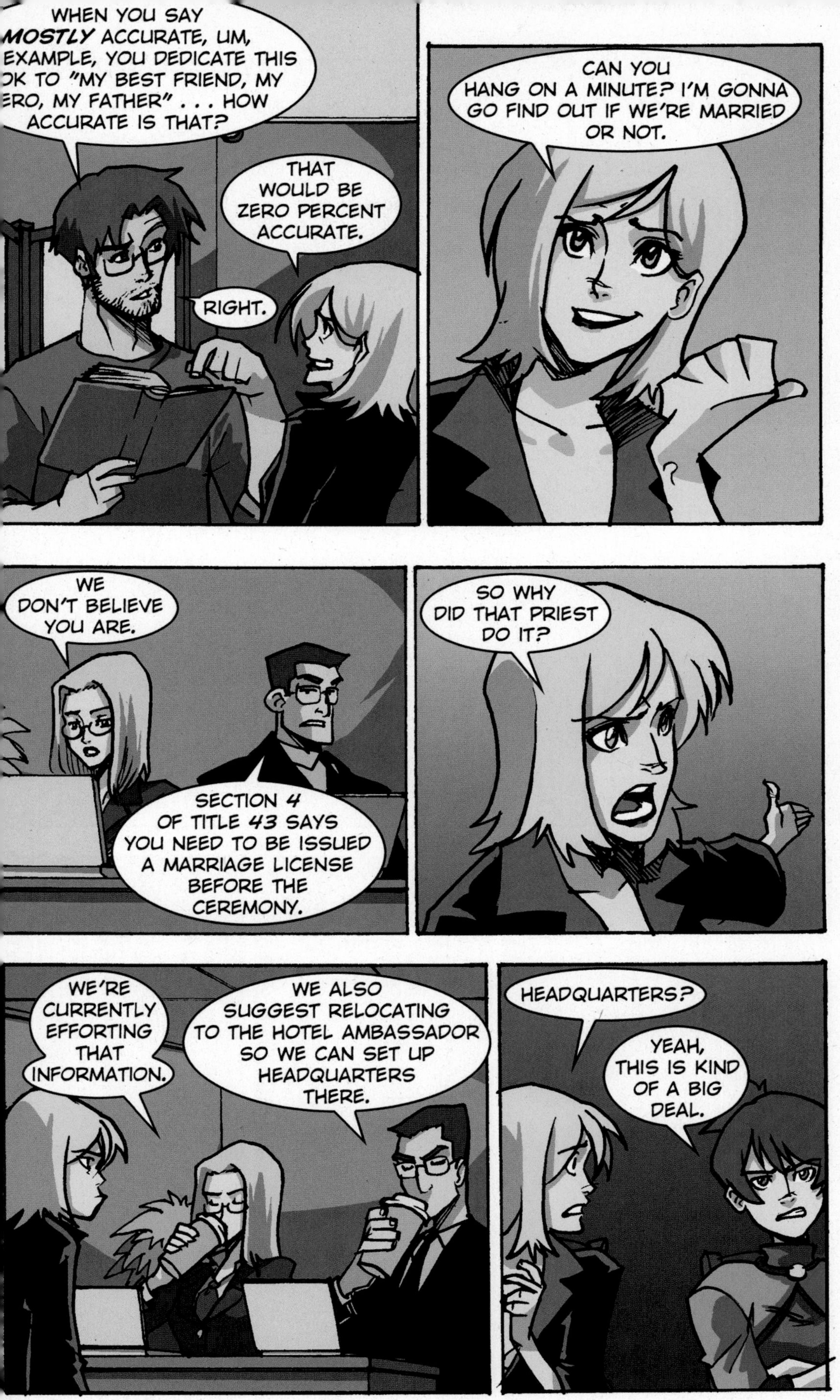
WHEN YOU SAY MOSTLY ACCURATE, UM, EXAMPLE, YOU DEDICATE THIS OK TO "MY BEST FRIEND, MY ERO, MY FATHER" . . . HOW ACCURATE IS THAT?
THAT WOULD BE ZERO PERCENT ACCURATE.
RIGHT.
CAN YOU HANG ON A MINUTE? I'M GONNA GO FIND OUT IF WE'RE MARRIED OR NOT.
WE DON'T BELIEVE YOU ARE.
SECTION 4 OF TITLE 43 SAYS YOU NEED TO BE ISSUED A MARRIAGE LICENSE BEFORE THE CEREMONY.
SO WHY DID THAT PRIEST DO IT?
WE'RE CURRENTLY EFFORTING THAT INFORMATION.
WE ALSO SUGGEST RELOCATING TO THE HOTEL AMBASSADOR SO WE CAN SET UP HEADQUARTERS THERE.
HEADQUARTERS?
YEAH, THIS IS KIND OF A BIG DEAL.

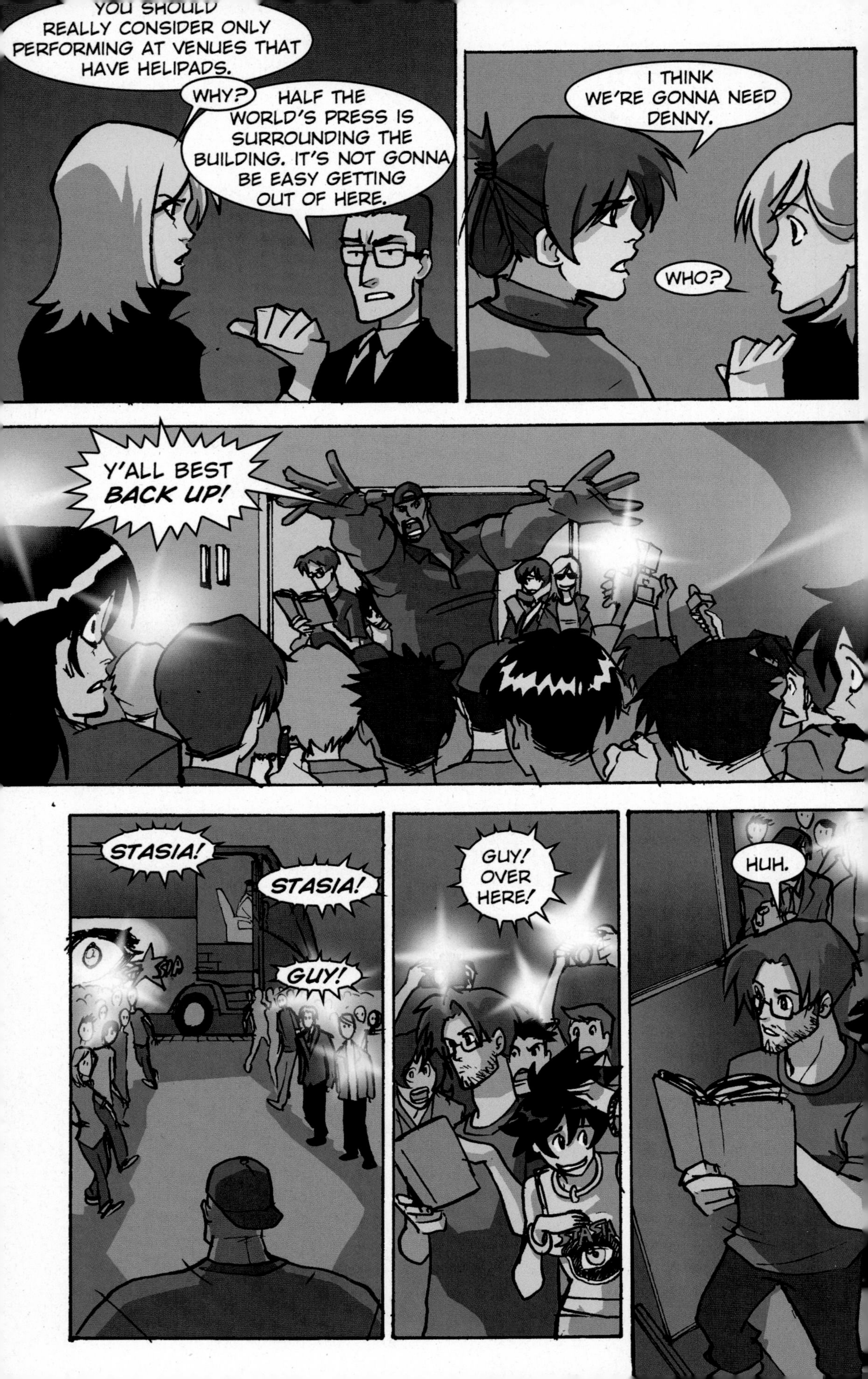
YOU SHOULD REALLY CONSIDER ONLY PERFORMING AT VENUES THAT HAVE HELIPADS.
WHY?
HALF THE WORLD'S PRESS IS SURROUNDING THE BUILDING. IT'S NOT GONNA BE EASY GETTING OUT OF HERE.
I THINK WE'RE GONNA NEED DENNY.
WHO?
Y'ALL BEST BACK UP!
STASIA!
STASIA!
GUY!
GUY! OVER HERE!
HUH.

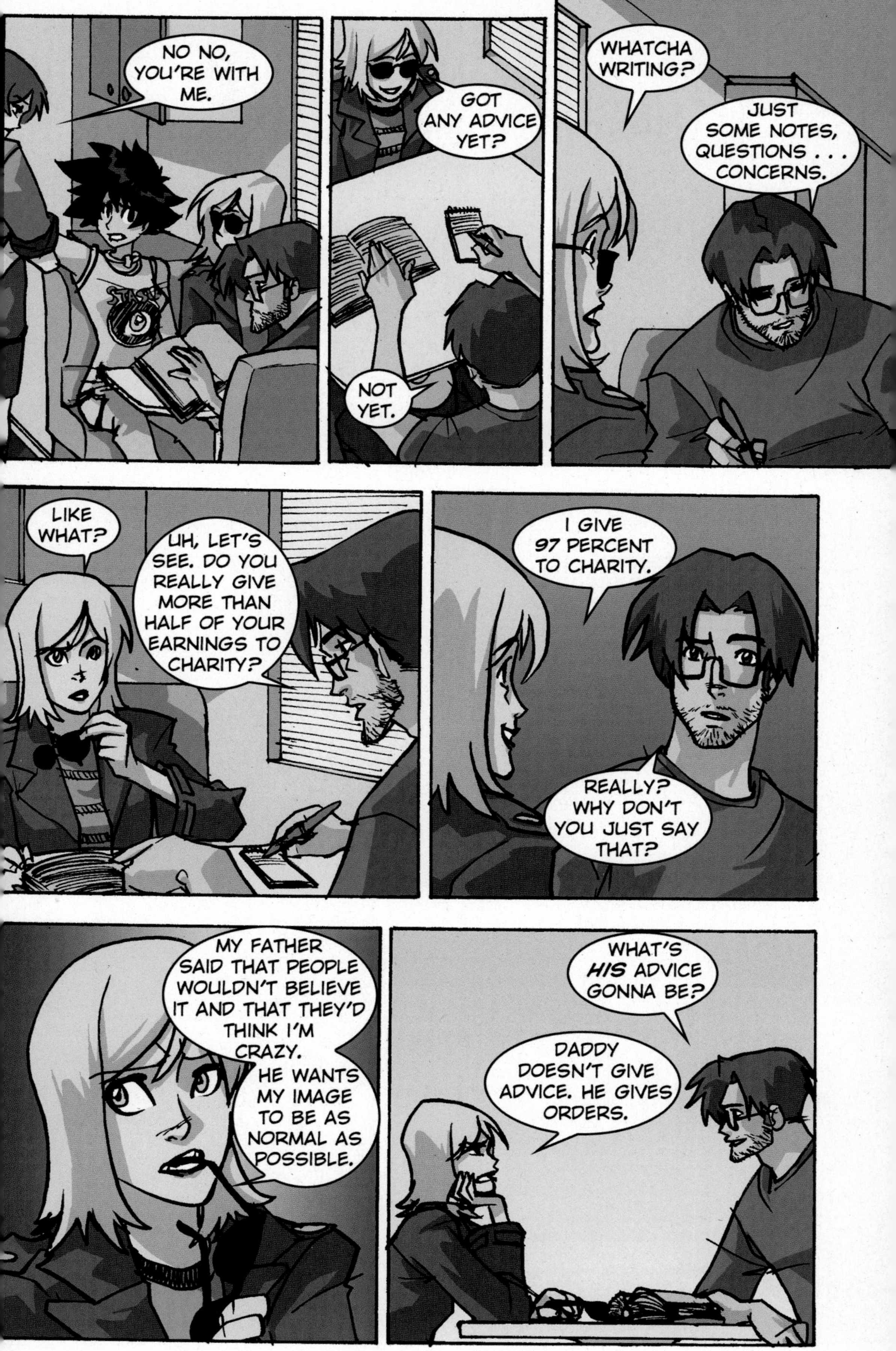
NO NO, YOU'RE WITH ME.
GOT ANY ADVICE YET?
NOT YET.
WHATCHA WRITING?
JUST SOME NOTES, QUESTIONS . . . CONCERNS.
LIKE WHAT?
UH, LET'S SEE. DO YOU REALLY GIVE MORE THAN HALF OF YOUR EARNINGS TO CHARITY?
I GIVE 97 PERCENT TO CHARITY.
REALLY? WHY DON'T YOU JUST SAY THAT?
MY FATHER SAID THAT PEOPLE WOULDN'T BELIEVE IT AND THAT THEY'D THINK I'M CRAZY.
HE WANTS MY IMAGE TO BE AS NORMAL AS POSSIBLE.
WHAT'S HIS ADVICE GONNA BE?
DADDY DOESN'T GIVE ADVICE. HE GIVES ORDERS.

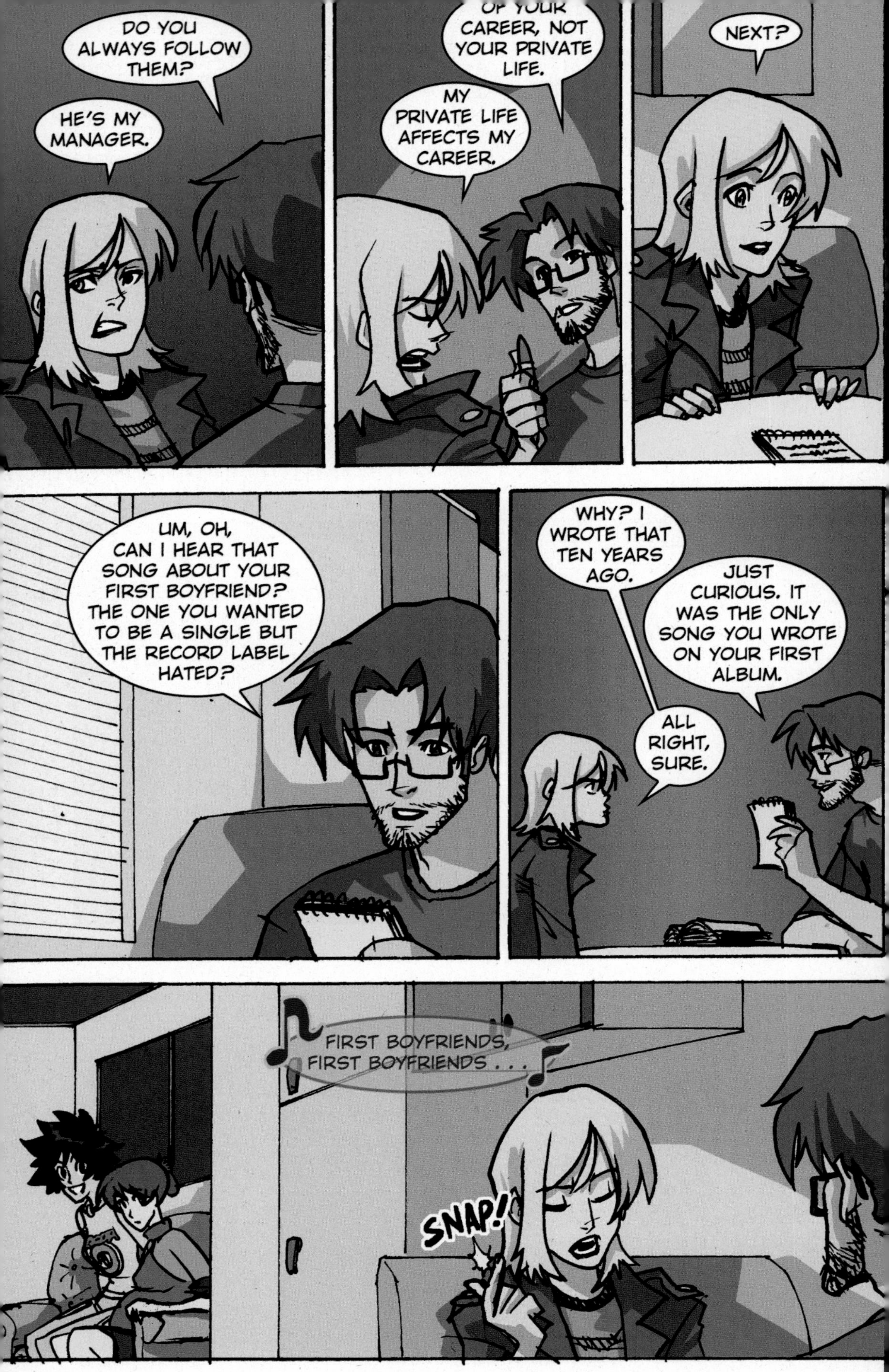
DO YOU ALWAYS FOLLOW THEM?
HE'S MY MANAGER.
OF YOUR CAREER, NOT YOUR PRIVATE LIFE.
MY PRIVATE LIFE AFFECTS MY CAREER.
NEXT?
UM, OH, CAN I HEAR THAT SONG ABOUT YOUR FIRST BOYFRIEND? THE ONE YOU WANTED TO BE A SINGLE BUT THE RECORD LABEL HATED?
WHY? I WROTE THAT TEN YEARS AGO.
JUST CURIOUS. IT WAS THE ONLY SONG YOU WROTE ON YOUR FIRST ALBUM.
ALL RIGHT, SURE.
FIRST BOYFRIENDS, FIRST BOYFRIENDS . . .
SNAP!

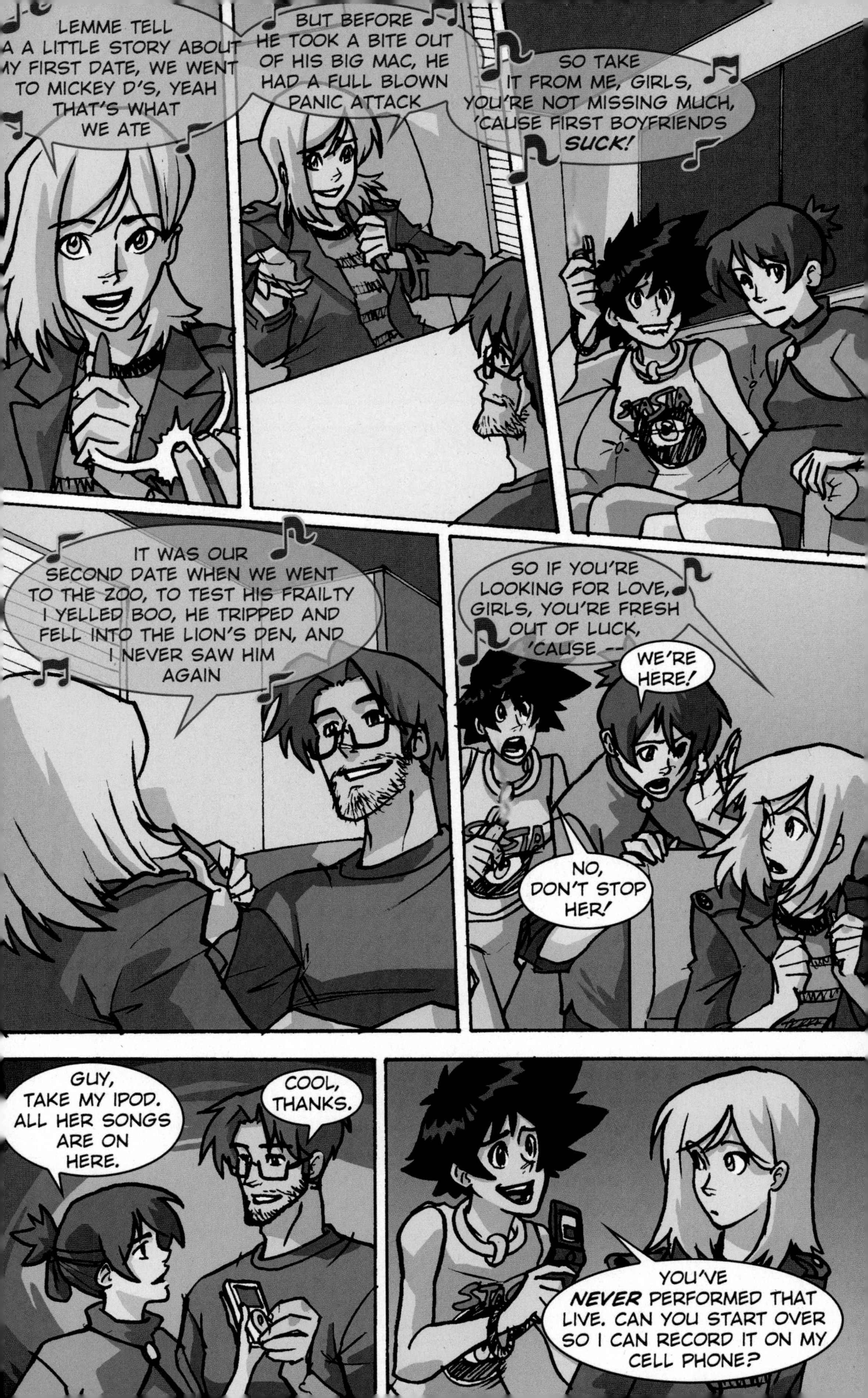
LEMME TELL A A LITTLE STORY ABOUT MY FIRST DATE, WE WENT TO MICKEY D'S, YEAH THAT'S WHAT WE ATE
BUT BEFORE HE TOOK A BITE OUT OF HIS BIG MAC, HE HAD A FULL BLOWN PANIC ATTACK
SO TAKE IT FROM ME, GIRLS, YOU'RE NOT MISSING MUCH, 'CAUSE FIRST BOYFRIENDS SUCK!
IT WAS OUR SECOND DATE WHEN WE WENT TO THE ZOO, TO TEST HIS FRAILTY I YELLED BOO, HE TRIPPED AND FELL INTO THE LION'S DEN, AND I NEVER SAW HIM AGAIN
SO IF YOU'RE LOOKING FOR LOVE, GIRLS, YOU'RE FRESH OUT OF LUCK, 'CAUSE --
WE'RE HERE!
NO, DON'T STOP HER!
GUY, TAKE MY IPOD. ALL HER SONGS ARE ON HERE.
COOL, THANKS.
YOU'VE NEVER PERFORMED THAT LIVE. CAN YOU START OVER SO I CAN RECORD IT ON MY CELL PHONE?

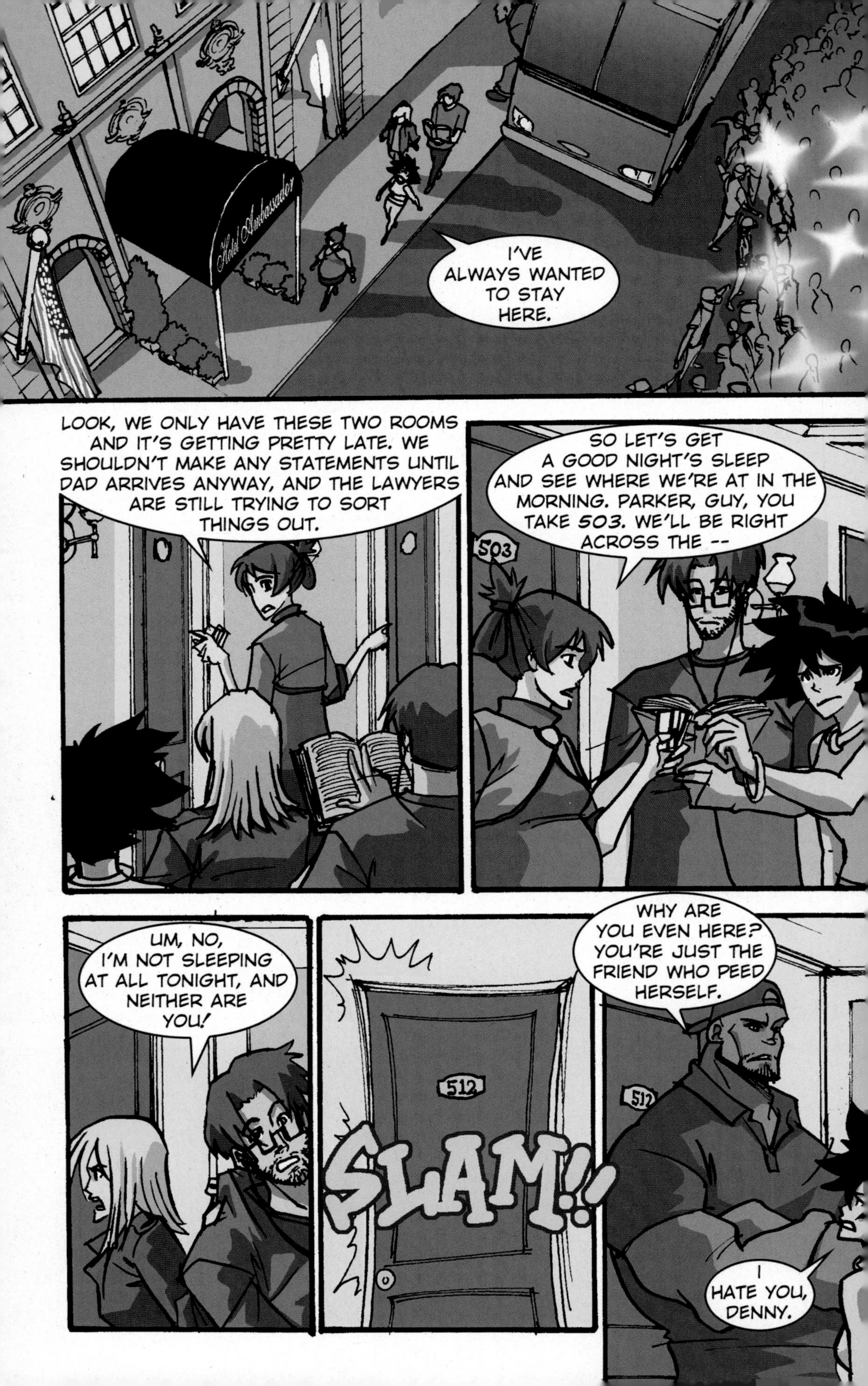
Hotel Ambassador
I'VE ALWAYS WANTED TO STAY HERE.
LOOK, WE ONLY HAVE THESE TWO ROOMS AND IT'S GETTING PRETTY LATE. WE SHOULDN'T MAKE ANY STATEMENTS UNTIL DAD ARRIVES ANYWAY, AND THE LAWYERS ARE STILL TRYING TO SORT THINGS OUT.
SO LET'S GET A GOOD NIGHT'S SLEEP AND SEE WHERE WE'RE AT IN THE MORNING. PARKER, GUY, YOU TAKE 503. WE'LL BE RIGHT ACROSS THE --
503
UM, NO, I'M NOT SLEEPING AT ALL TONIGHT, AND NEITHER ARE YOU!
512
SLAM!!
WHY ARE YOU EVEN HERE? YOU'RE JUST THE FRIEND WHO PEED HERSELF.
512
I HATE YOU, DENNY.

YOU SURE ARE ENGROSSED IN THAT BOOK. GOOD READ?

PRETTY INTERESTING, YEAH.

WANNA SIT DOWN?

SURE.

ANY ADVICE YET?

NOT YET.

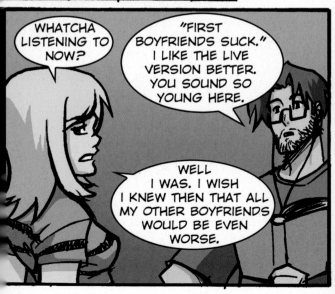

WHATCHA LISTENING TO NOW?

"FIRST BOYFRIENDS SUCK." I LIKE THE LIVE VERSION BETTER. YOU SOUND SO YOUNG HERE.

WELL I WAS. I WISH I KNEW THEN THAT ALL MY OTHER BOYFRIENDS WOULD BE EVEN WORSE.

KNOCK KNOCK!

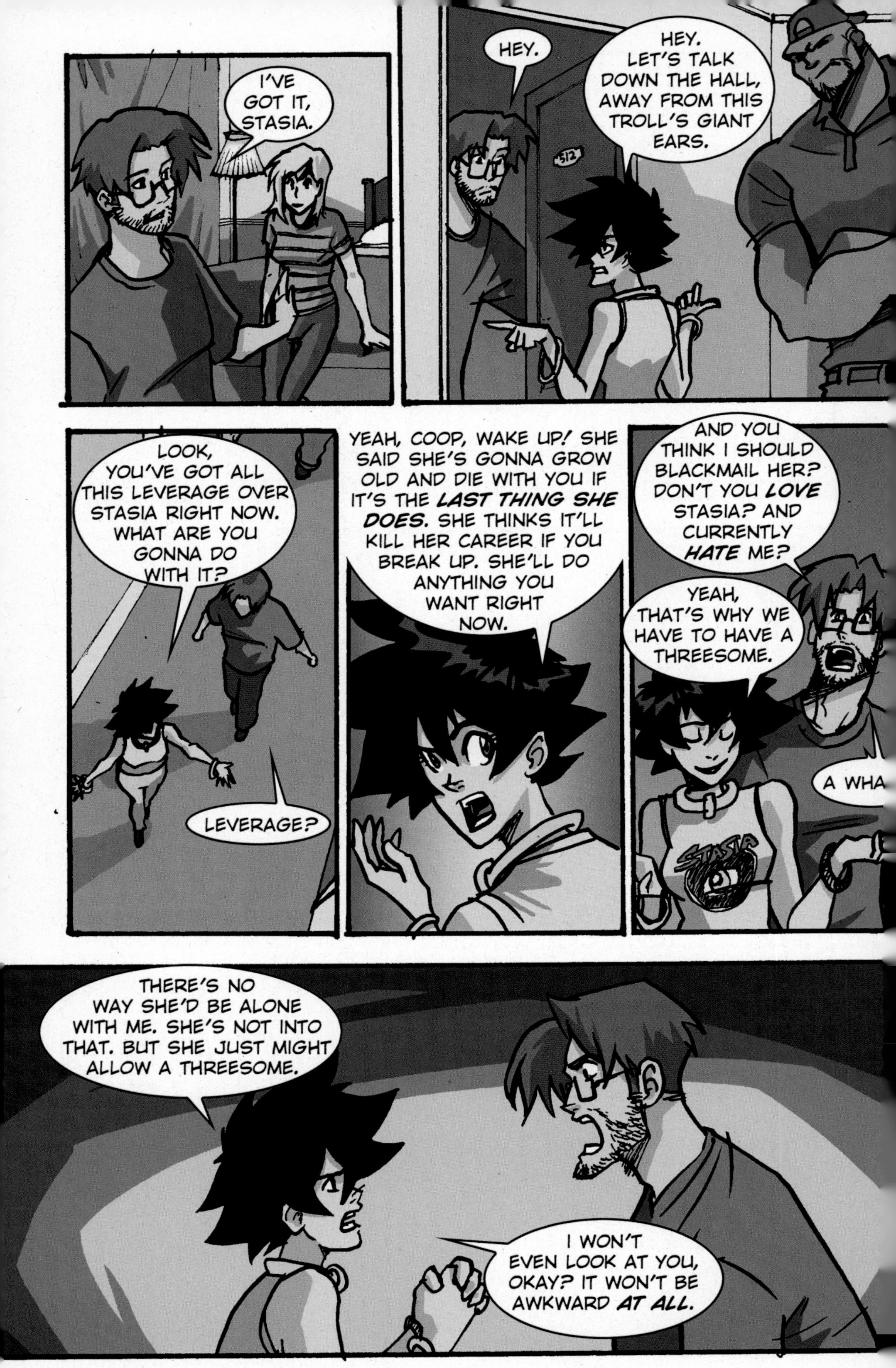
I'VE GOT IT, STASIA.
HEY.
HEY. LET'S TALK DOWN THE HALL, AWAY FROM THIS TROLL'S GIANT EARS.
512
LOOK, YOU'VE GOT ALL THIS LEVERAGE OVER STASIA RIGHT NOW. WHAT ARE YOU GONNA DO WITH IT?
LEVERAGE?
YEAH, COOP, WAKE UP! SHE SAID SHE'S GONNA GROW OLD AND DIE WITH YOU IF IT'S THE LAST THING SHE DOES. SHE THINKS IT'LL KILL HER CAREER IF YOU BREAK UP. SHE'LL DO ANYTHING YOU WANT RIGHT NOW.
AND YOU THINK I SHOULD BLACKMAIL HER? DON'T YOU LOVE STASIA? AND CURRENTLY HATE ME?
YEAH, THAT'S WHY WE HAVE TO HAVE A THREESOME.
A WHA
STASIA
THERE'S NO WAY SHE'D BE ALONE WITH ME. SHE'S NOT INTO THAT. BUT SHE JUST MIGHT ALLOW A THREESOME.
I WON'T EVEN LOOK AT YOU, OKAY? IT WON'T BE AWKWARD AT ALL.

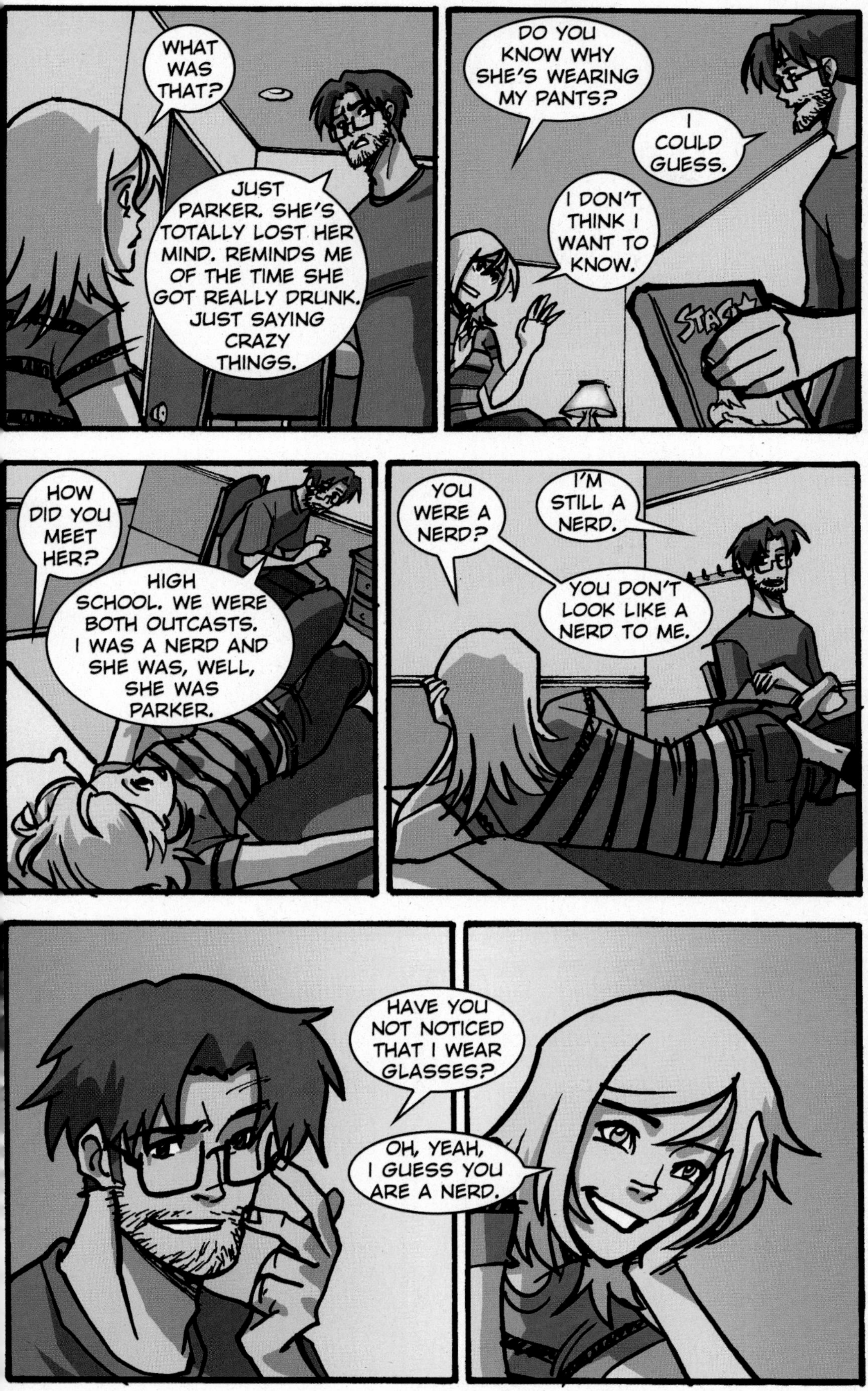
WHAT WAS THAT?
JUST PARKER. SHE'S TOTALLY LOST HER MIND. REMINDS ME OF THE TIME SHE GOT REALLY DRUNK. JUST SAYING CRAZY THINGS.
DO YOU KNOW WHY SHE'S WEARING MY PANTS?
I COULD GUESS.
I DON'T THINK I WANT TO KNOW.
HOW DID YOU MEET HER?
HIGH SCHOOL. WE WERE BOTH OUTCASTS. I WAS A NERD AND SHE WAS, WELL, SHE WAS PARKER.
YOU WERE A NERD?
I'M STILL A NERD.
YOU DON'T LOOK LIKE A NERD TO ME.
HAVE YOU NOT NOTICED THAT I WEAR GLASSES?
OH, YEAH, I GUESS YOU ARE A NERD.

COME ON.

WHAT?

LAY DOWN.

WHY?

JUST DO IT.

NO READING IN BED.

KDONK!

YOU KNOW ENOUGH ABOUT ME. IT'S TIME TO LEARN ABOUT YOU. COME ON. GUY COOPER HIS LIFE AND TIMES -- GO.

THAT WOULD JUST BORE YOU.

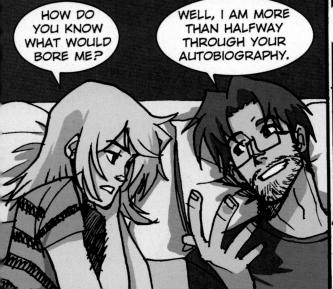

HOW DO YOU KNOW WHAT WOULD BORE ME?

WELL, I AM MORE THAN HALFWAY THROUGH YOUR AUTOBIOGRAPHY.

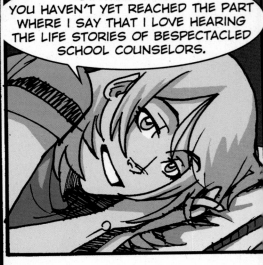

SO THAT MEANS YOU HAVEN'T YET REACHED THE PART WHERE I SAY THAT I LOVE HEARING THE LIFE STORIES OF BESPECTACLED SCHOOL COUNSELORS.

I'VE STILL GOT LIKE EIGHTY QUESTIONS TO ASK YOU.

YOU CAN PICK *ONE*. AND THEN WE'RE TALKING ABOUT YOU.

ONE QUESTION, ALL RIGHT. HMM. OKAY, THIS ONE. WHO'S YOUR HERO?

YEAH. YOU SAID THAT YOUR DAD WASN'T YOUR HERO, SO I WAS WONDERING WHO IS.

MY HERO?

I DON'T HAVE A HERO.

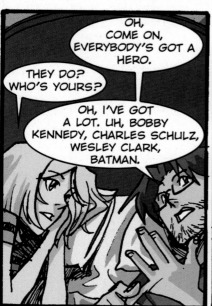

OH, COME ON, EVERYBODY'S GOT A HERO.

THEY DO? WHO'S YOURS?

OH, I'VE GOT A LOT. UH, BOBBY KENNEDY, CHARLES SCHULZ, WESLEY CLARK, BATMAN.

OOH, BATMAN -- I'LL TAKE HIM. HE'S MY HERO.

HEY, YOU CAN'T GO AROUND STEALING OTHER PEOPLE'S HEROES.

I CAN DO WHATEVER I WANT. I'M A ROCK STAR.

I THOUGHT YOU WERE A POP STAR.

THEY'RE INTERCHANGEABLE, REALLY.

ARE THEY? I DOUBT OZZY OSBOURNE WOULD LIKE BEING CALLED A POP STAR.

WELL, THEY'RE NOT INTERCHANGEABLE *THAT* WAY. ONLY THE OTHER WAY.

AH, RIGHT.

ANYWAY, YOU'VE HAD YOUR QUESTION, AND NOW YOU'RE GOING TO TELL ME ALL ABOUT YOURSELF.

I'M NOT GONNA SAY A WORD FOR THE NEXT FIVE MINUTES. I'M JUST GONNA LAY BACK AND LISTEN. GO.

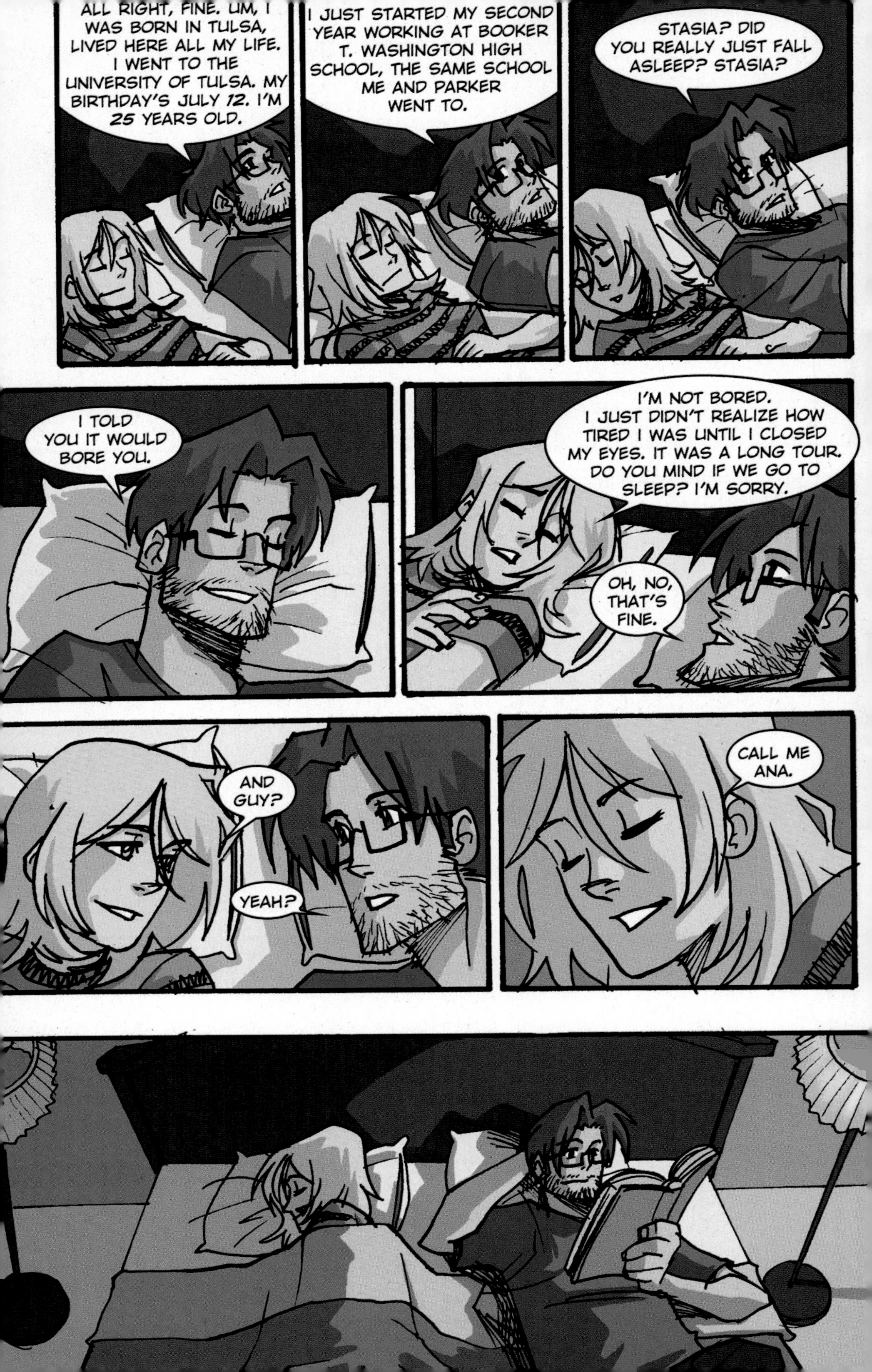
ALL RIGHT, FINE. UM, I WAS BORN IN TULSA, LIVED HERE ALL MY LIFE. I WENT TO THE UNIVERSITY OF TULSA. MY BIRTHDAY'S JULY 12. I'M 25 YEARS OLD.
I JUST STARTED MY SECOND YEAR WORKING AT BOOKER T. WASHINGTON HIGH SCHOOL, THE SAME SCHOOL ME AND PARKER WENT TO.
STASIA? DID YOU REALLY JUST FALL ASLEEP? STASIA?
I TOLD YOU IT WOULD BORE YOU.
I'M NOT BORED. I JUST DIDN'T REALIZE HOW TIRED I WAS UNTIL I CLOSED MY EYES. IT WAS A LONG TOUR. DO YOU MIND IF WE GO TO SLEEP? I'M SORRY.
OH, NO, THAT'S FINE.
AND GUY?
YEAH?
CALL ME ANA.

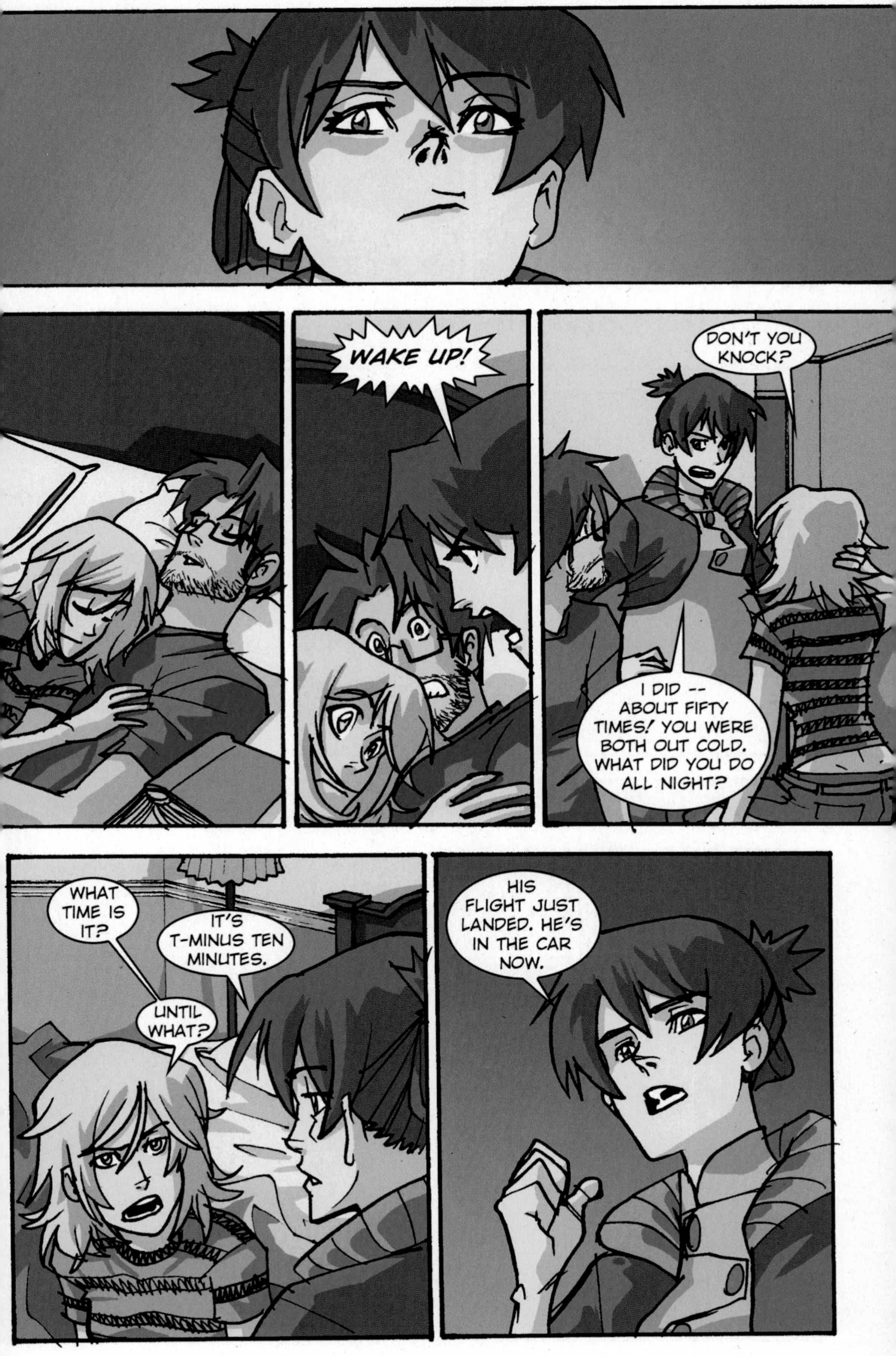
WAKE UP!
DON'T YOU KNOCK?
I DID -- ABOUT FIFTY TIMES! YOU WERE BOTH OUT COLD. WHAT DID YOU DO ALL NIGHT?
WHAT TIME IS IT?
IT'S T-MINUS TEN MINUTES.
UNTIL WHAT?
HIS FLIGHT JUST LANDED. HE'S IN THE CAR NOW.

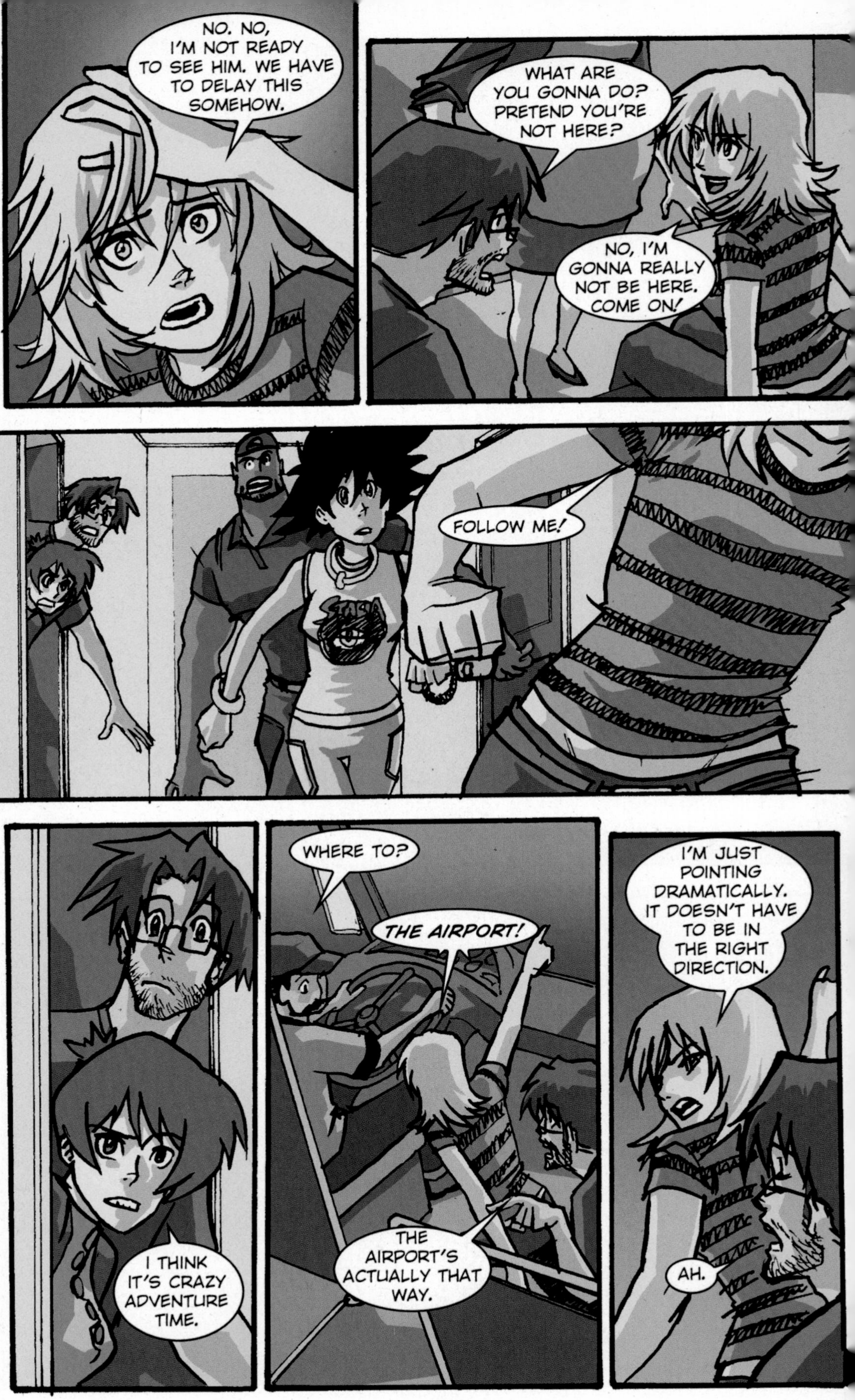
NO. NO, I'M NOT READY TO SEE HIM. WE HAVE TO DELAY THIS SOMEHOW.
WHAT ARE YOU GONNA DO? PRETEND YOU'RE NOT HERE?
NO, I'M GONNA REALLY NOT BE HERE. COME ON!
FOLLOW ME!
I THINK IT'S CRAZY ADVENTURE TIME.
WHERE TO?
THE AIRPORT!
THE AIRPORT'S ACTUALLY THAT WAY.
I'M JUST POINTING DRAMATICALLY. IT DOESN'T HAVE TO BE IN THE RIGHT DIRECTION.
AH.

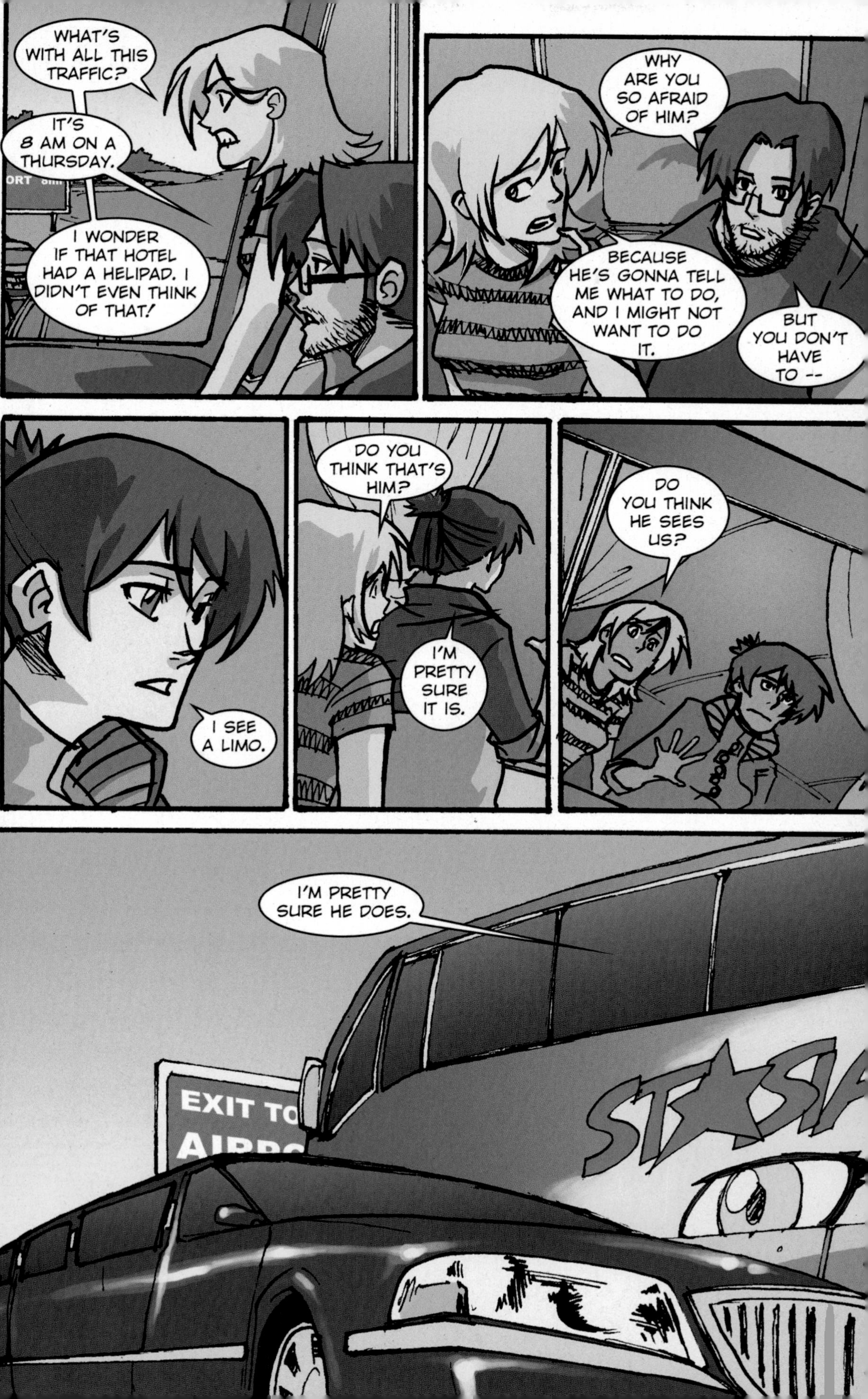
WHAT'S WITH ALL THIS TRAFFIC?
IT'S 8 AM ON A THURSDAY.
I WONDER IF THAT HOTEL HAD A HELIPAD. I DIDN'T EVEN THINK OF THAT!
WHY ARE YOU SO AFRAID OF HIM?
BECAUSE HE'S GONNA TELL ME WHAT TO DO, AND I MIGHT NOT WANT TO DO IT.
BUT YOU DON'T HAVE TO --
I SEE A LIMO.
DO YOU THINK THAT'S HIM?
I'M PRETTY SURE IT IS.
DO YOU THINK HE SEES US?
I'M PRETTY SURE HE DOES.
EXIT TO
AIRPO
ST

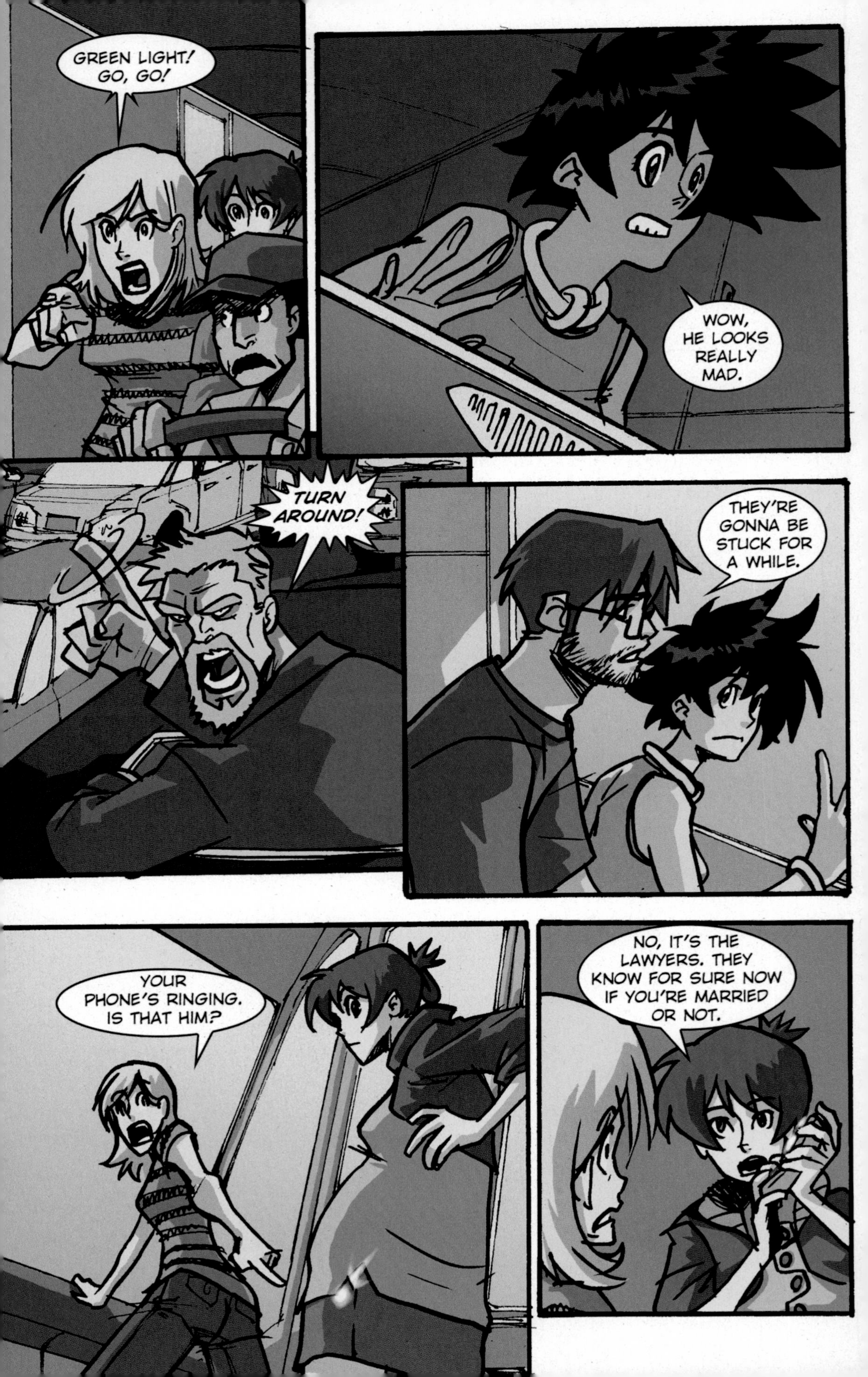
GREEN LIGHT! GO, GO!
WOW, HE LOOKS REALLY MAD.
TURN AROUND!
THEY'RE GONNA BE STUCK FOR A WHILE.
YOUR PHONE'S RINGING. IS THAT HIM?
NO, IT'S THE LAWYERS. THEY KNOW FOR SURE NOW IF YOU'RE MARRIED OR NOT.

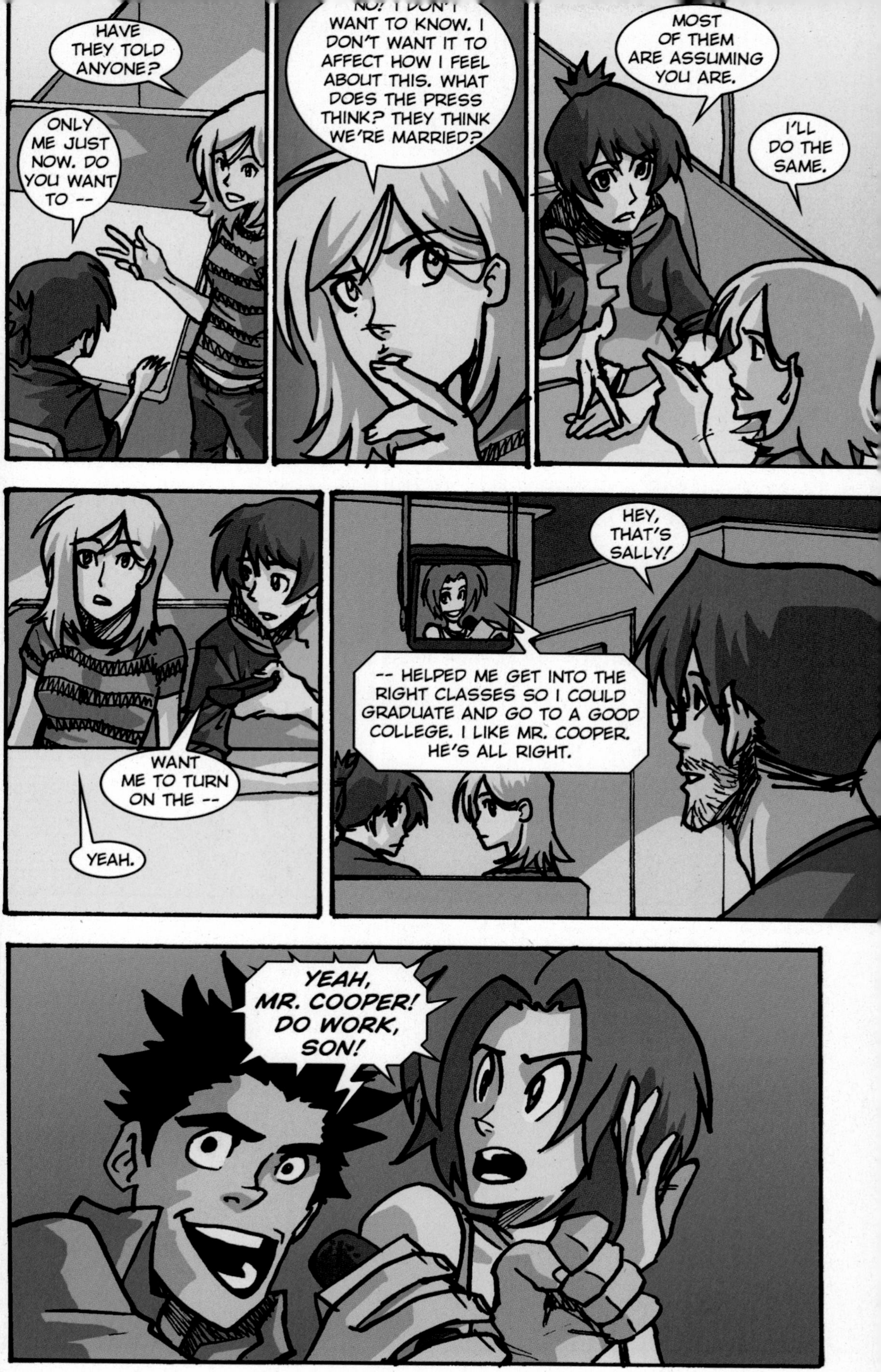
HAVE THEY TOLD ANYONE?
ONLY ME JUST NOW. DO YOU WANT TO --
NO! I DON'T WANT TO KNOW. I DON'T WANT IT TO AFFECT HOW I FEEL ABOUT THIS. WHAT DOES THE PRESS THINK? THEY THINK WE'RE MARRIED?
MOST OF THEM ARE ASSUMING YOU ARE.
I'LL DO THE SAME.
WANT ME TO TURN ON THE --
YEAH.
HEY, THAT'S SALLY!
-- HELPED ME GET INTO THE RIGHT CLASSES SO I COULD GRADUATE AND GO TO A GOOD COLLEGE. I LIKE MR. COOPER. HE'S ALL RIGHT.
YEAH, MR. COOPER! DO WORK, SON!

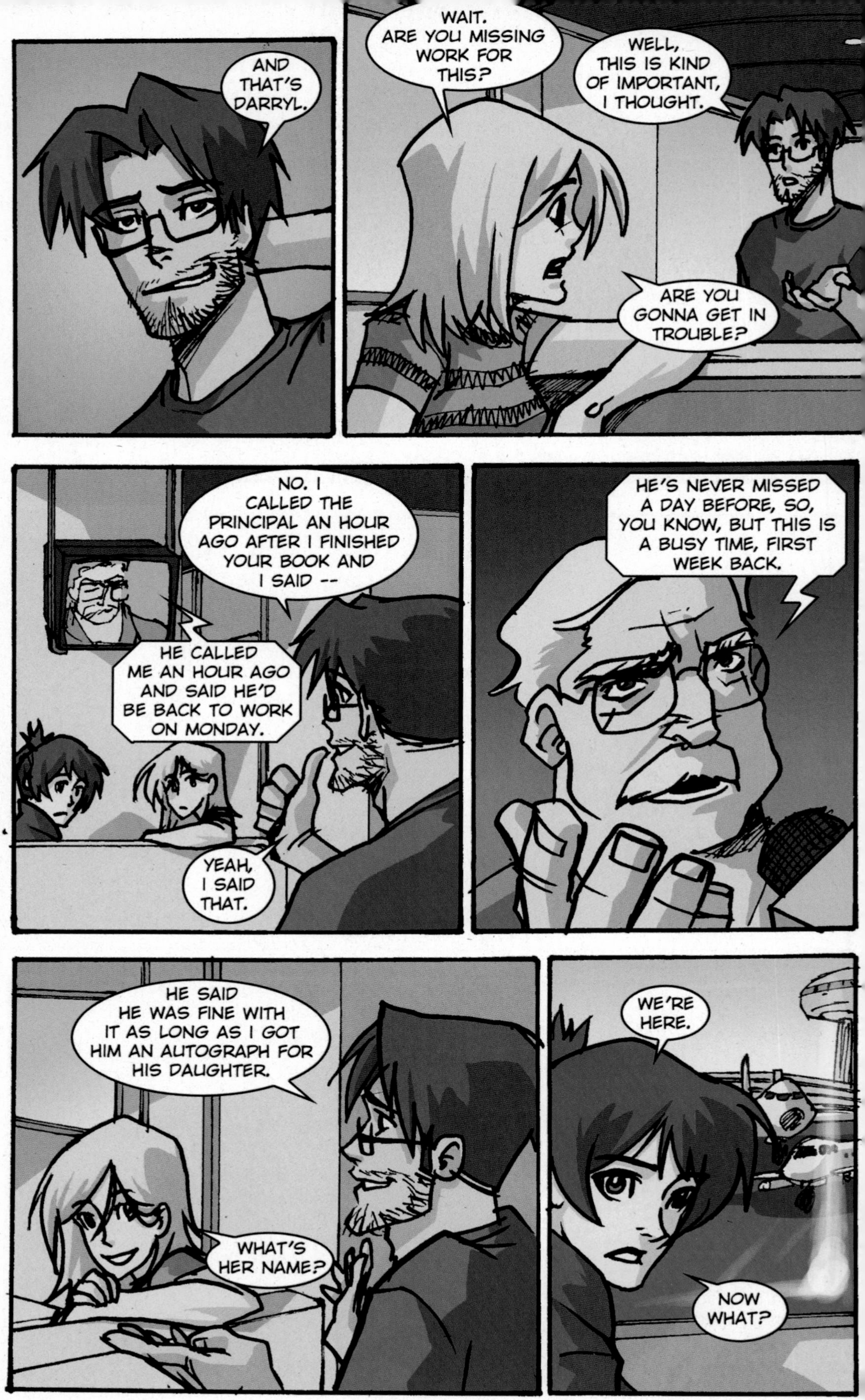
AND THAT'S DARRYL.
WAIT. ARE YOU MISSING WORK FOR THIS?
WELL, THIS IS KIND OF IMPORTANT, I THOUGHT.
ARE YOU GONNA GET IN TROUBLE?
NO. I CALLED THE PRINCIPAL AN HOUR AGO AFTER I FINISHED YOUR BOOK AND I SAID --
HE CALLED ME AN HOUR AGO AND SAID HE'D BE BACK TO WORK ON MONDAY.
YEAH, I SAID THAT.
HE'S NEVER MISSED A DAY BEFORE, SO, YOU KNOW, BUT THIS IS A BUSY TIME, FIRST WEEK BACK.
HE SAID HE WAS FINE WITH IT AS LONG AS I GOT HIM AN AUTOGRAPH FOR HIS DAUGHTER.
WHAT'S HER NAME?
WE'RE HERE.
NOW WHAT?

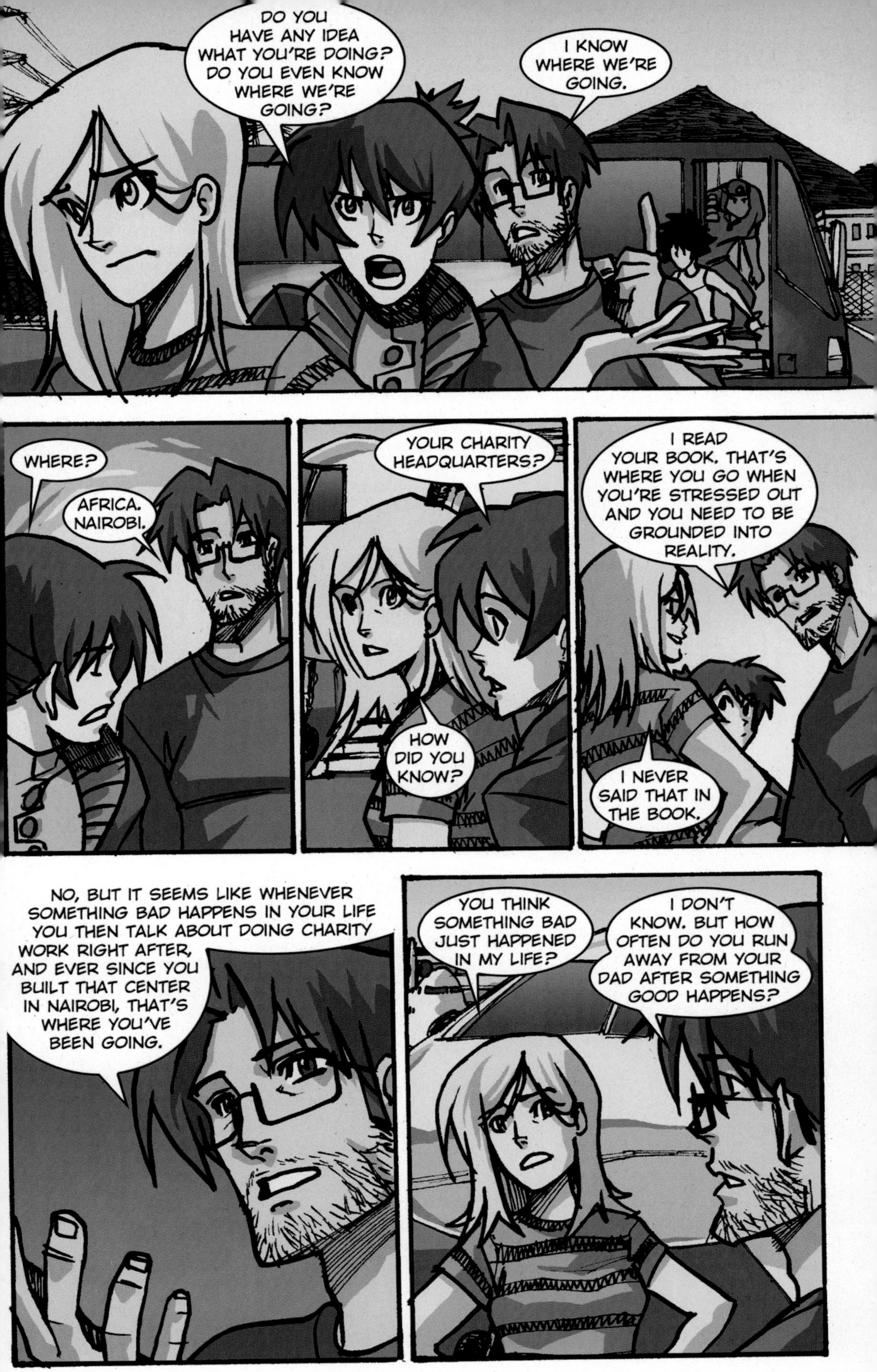
DO YOU HAVE ANY IDEA WHAT YOU'RE DOING? DO YOU EVEN KNOW WHERE WE'RE GOING?
I KNOW WHERE WE'RE GOING.
WHERE?
AFRICA. NAIROBI.
YOUR CHARITY HEADQUARTERS?
HOW DID YOU KNOW?
I READ YOUR BOOK. THAT'S WHERE YOU GO WHEN YOU'RE STRESSED OUT AND YOU NEED TO BE GROUNDED INTO REALITY.
I NEVER SAID THAT IN THE BOOK.
NO, BUT IT SEEMS LIKE WHENEVER SOMETHING BAD HAPPENS IN YOUR LIFE YOU THEN TALK ABOUT DOING CHARITY WORK RIGHT AFTER, AND EVER SINCE YOU BUILT THAT CENTER IN NAIROBI, THAT'S WHERE YOU'VE BEEN GOING.
YOU THINK SOMETHING BAD JUST HAPPENED IN MY LIFE?
I DON'T KNOW. BUT HOW OFTEN DO YOU RUN AWAY FROM YOUR DAD AFTER SOMETHING GOOD HAPPENS?

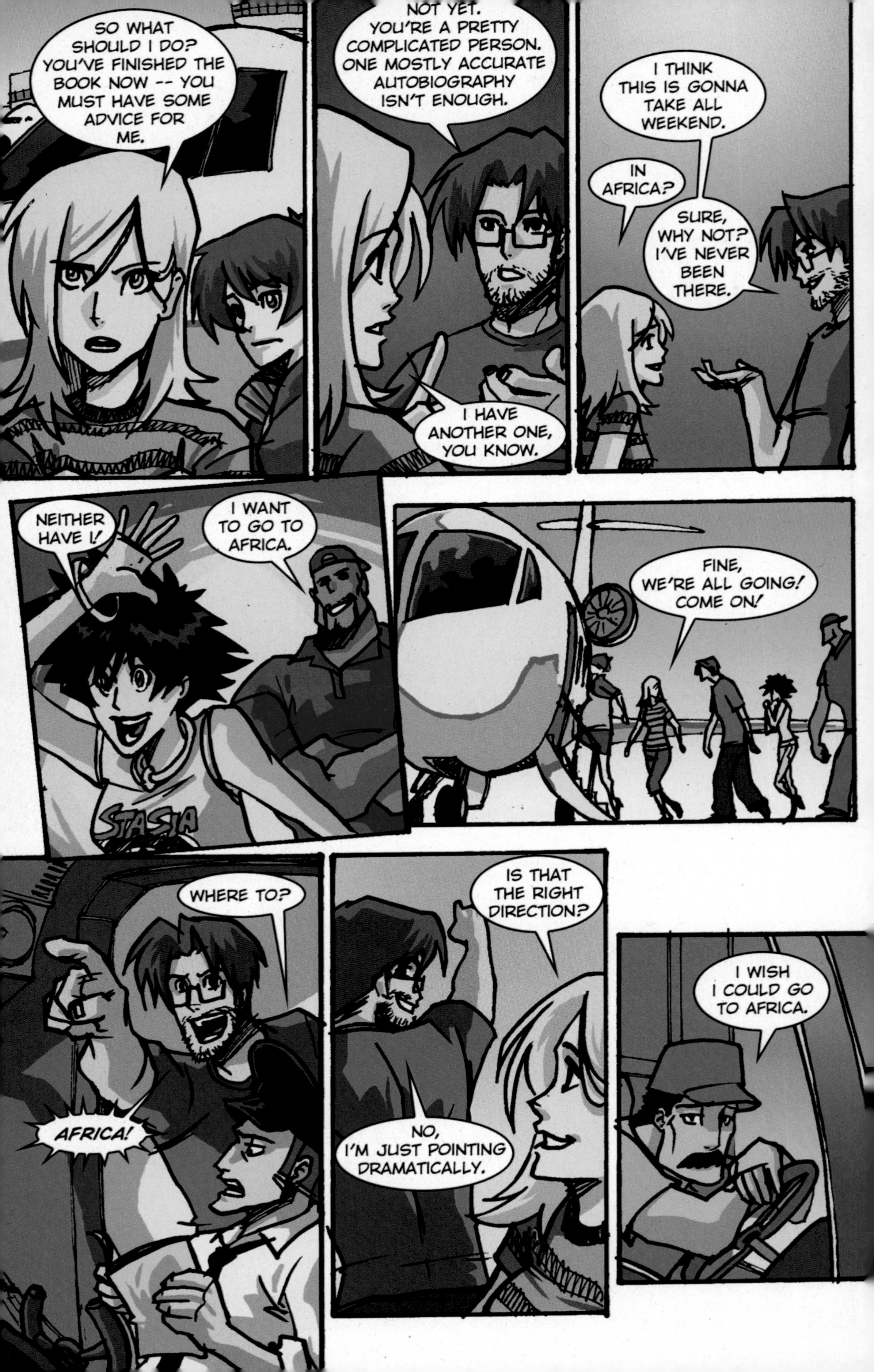
SO WHAT SHOULD I DO? YOU'VE FINISHED THE BOOK NOW -- YOU MUST HAVE SOME ADVICE FOR ME.
NOT YET. YOU'RE A PRETTY COMPLICATED PERSON. ONE MOSTLY ACCURATE AUTOBIOGRAPHY ISN'T ENOUGH.
I HAVE ANOTHER ONE, YOU KNOW.
I THINK THIS IS GONNA TAKE ALL WEEKEND.
IN AFRICA?
SURE, WHY NOT? I'VE NEVER BEEN THERE.
NEITHER HAVE I!
I WANT TO GO TO AFRICA.
STASIA
FINE, WE'RE ALL GOING! COME ON!
WHERE TO?
AFRICA!
IS THAT THE RIGHT DIRECTION?
NO, I'M JUST POINTING DRAMATICALLY.
I WISH I COULD GO TO AFRICA.

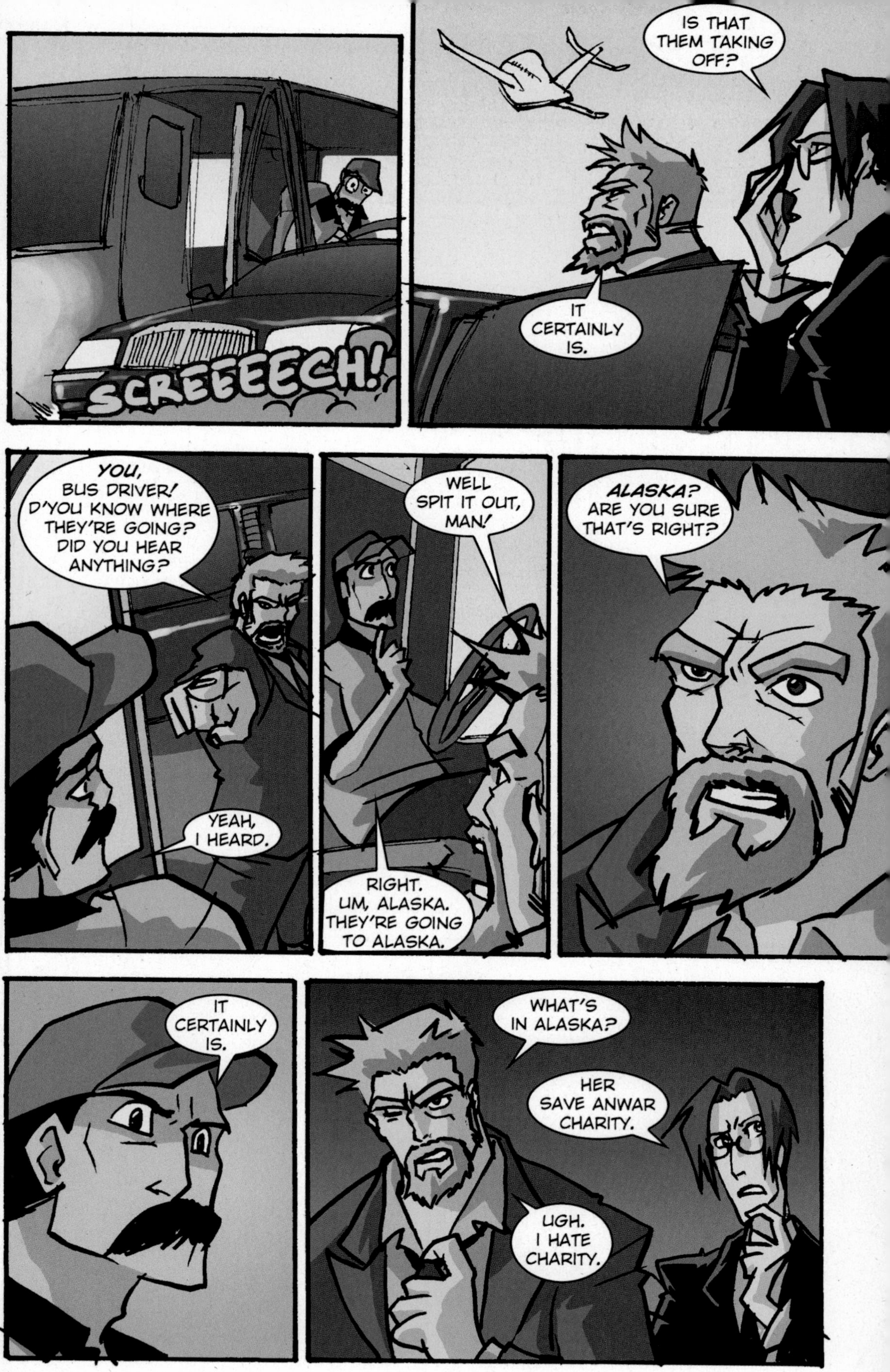

SCREEEEECH!
IS THAT THEM TAKING OFF?
IT CERTAINLY IS.
YOU, BUS DRIVER! D'YOU KNOW WHERE THEY'RE GOING? DID YOU HEAR ANYTHING?
YEAH, I HEARD.
WELL SPIT IT OUT, MAN!
RIGHT. UM, ALASKA. THEY'RE GOING TO ALASKA.
ALASKA? ARE YOU SURE THAT'S RIGHT?
IT CERTAINLY IS.
WHAT'S IN ALASKA?
HER SAVE ANWAR CHARITY.
UGH. I HATE CHARITY.

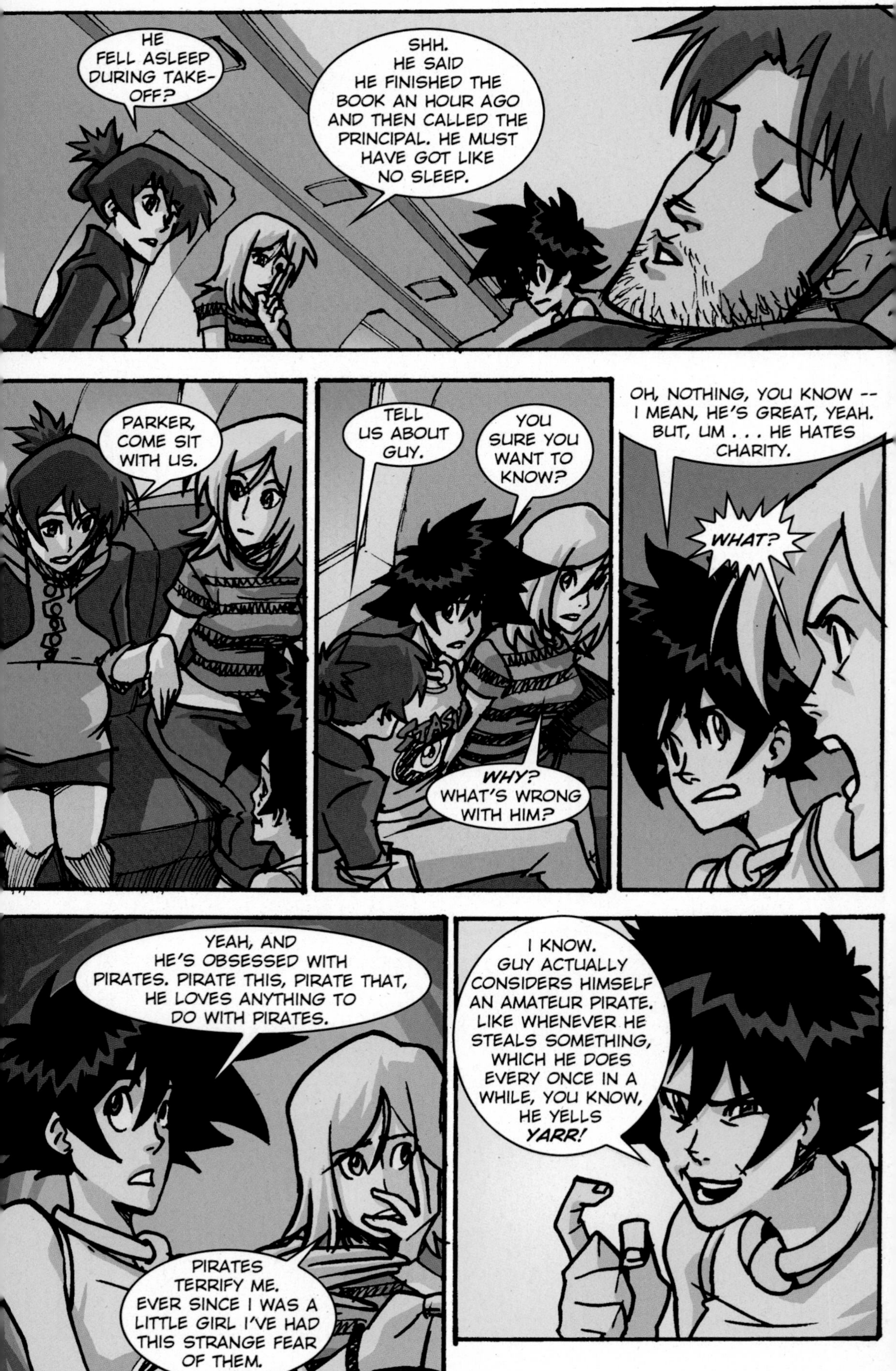
HE FELL ASLEEP DURING TAKE-OFF?
SHH. HE SAID HE FINISHED THE BOOK AN HOUR AGO AND THEN CALLED THE PRINCIPAL. HE MUST HAVE GOT LIKE NO SLEEP.
PARKER, COME SIT WITH US.
TELL US ABOUT GUY.
YOU SURE YOU WANT TO KNOW?
WHY? WHAT'S WRONG WITH HIM?
OH, NOTHING, YOU KNOW -- I MEAN, HE'S GREAT, YEAH. BUT, UM . . . HE HATES CHARITY.
WHAT?
YEAH, AND HE'S OBSESSED WITH PIRATES. PIRATE THIS, PIRATE THAT, HE LOVES ANYTHING TO DO WITH PIRATES.
PIRATES TERRIFY ME. EVER SINCE I WAS A LITTLE GIRL I'VE HAD THIS STRANGE FEAR OF THEM.
I KNOW. GUY ACTUALLY CONSIDERS HIMSELF AN AMATEUR PIRATE. LIKE WHENEVER HE STEALS SOMETHING, WHICH HE DOES EVERY ONCE IN A WHILE, YOU KNOW, HE YELLS YARR!

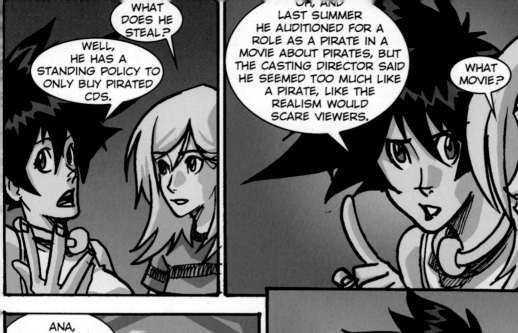

WHAT DOES HE STEAL?

WELL, HE HAS A STANDING POLICY TO ONLY BUY PIRATED CDS.

OH, AND LAST SUMMER HE AUDITIONED FOR A ROLE AS A PIRATE IN A MOVIE ABOUT PIRATES, BUT THE CASTING DIRECTOR SAID HE SEEMED TOO MUCH LIKE A PIRATE, LIKE THE REALISM WOULD SCARE VIEWERS.

WHAT MOVIE?

ANA, SHE'S MAKING IT ALL UP. YOU ARE MAKING IT ALL UP, RIGHT?

OF COURSE I'M MAKING IT ALL UP -- GUY'S PERFECT! BUT THIS IS SO UNFAIR.

I'M THE ONE WHO LOVES YOU. I'M THE ONE WHO SPENT A MONTH'S SALARY TO BUY THE TICKETS ON EBAY. I'M THE ONE WHO MADE THE SIGN. I'M THE ONE WHO DREAMS ABOUT YOU.

PARKER . . . YOU'RE FLYING ON MY PRIVATE JET, YOU'RE WEARING MY PANTS, AND I'M NOW HOLDING YOUR HAND. WILL YOU PLEASE START SEEING THIS AS A GOOD THING?

I DON'T KNOW YET HOW I FEEL ABOUT GUY. AND I DON'T KNOW HOW HE FEELS ABOUT ME. BUT I WANT TO BE YOUR FRIEND, OKAY?

OKAY.

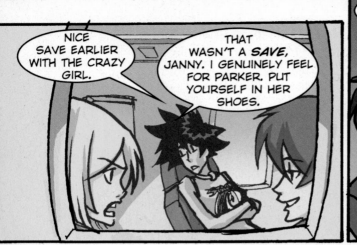

NICE SAVE EARLIER WITH THE CRAZY GIRL.

THAT WASN'T A *SAVE*, JANNY. I GENUINELY FEEL FOR PARKER. PUT YOURSELF IN HER SHOES.

ANA, YOU GENUINELY FEEL FOR *EVERYONE*.

ARE YOU COLD? SHOULD WE PUT BLANKETS ON THEM?

WHY DID YOU DO IT? WHY DID YOU GET MARRIED?

I ALMOST DID IT TWO YEARS AGO. IN DALLAS. IF HE WASN'T WEARING THAT STUPID COWBOY HAT I PROBABLY WOULD HAVE.

DALLAS . . . WASN'T THAT RIGHT AFTER LEBRON DUMPED YOU?

SORRY. BUT YOU DIDN'T ANSWER MY QUESTION. WHY? WHAT DO YOU HOPE TO ACCOMPLISH FROM THIS?

I JUST WANT TO GET LUCKY. I MEAN, I KNOW I'VE LIVED A VERY BLESSED LIFE, BUT . . . ALL OF MY RELATIONSHIPS HAVE ENDED IN DISASTER.

I WANT SOMEONE NORMAL, SOMEONE WITHOUT AN AGENDA, SOMEONE *I* CHOSE, EVEN IF IT WAS FOR STUPID REASONS. I JUST WANT TO GET LUCKY.

PARKER DID SAY HE WAS PERFECT.

NOBODY'S PERFECT.

I STILL DON'T KNOW WHY YOU DID IT LIKE THIS. WHY HIM? WHY SOME RANDOM FAN WITH A SIGN?

I WANTED SOMEONE WHO ALREADY LOVES ME, SO I DON'T HAVE TO MAKE HIM LOVE ME. I WANT . . .

WHAT?

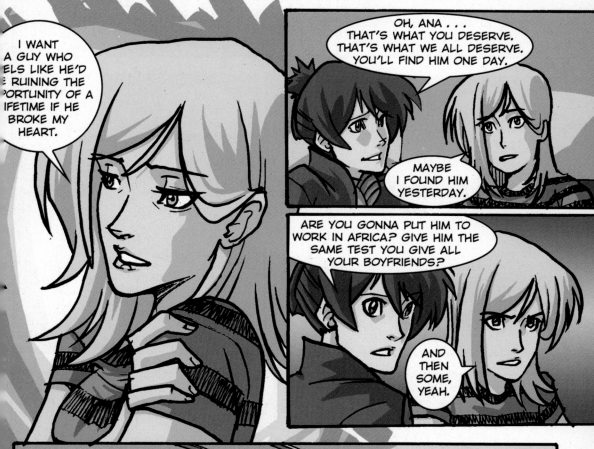

I WANT A GUY WHO FEELS LIKE HE'D BE RUINING THE OPPORTUNITY OF A LIFETIME IF HE BROKE MY HEART.

OH, ANA . . . THAT'S WHAT YOU DESERVE. THAT'S WHAT WE ALL DESERVE. YOU'LL FIND HIM ONE DAY.

MAYBE I FOUND HIM YESTERDAY.

ARE YOU GONNA PUT HIM TO WORK IN AFRICA? GIVE HIM THE SAME TEST YOU GIVE ALL YOUR BOYFRIENDS?

AND THEN SOME, YEAH.

WHAT IF HE FAILS?

THEN I'LL HOPE WE'RE NOT REALLY MARRIED.

AFRICA DOESN'T LOOK MUCH DIFFERENT THAN AMERICA TO ME.

THAT'S BECAUSE YOU'RE IN AN AIRPLANE HANGAR.

COME ON! I WANT YOU TO SEE THE CENTER!

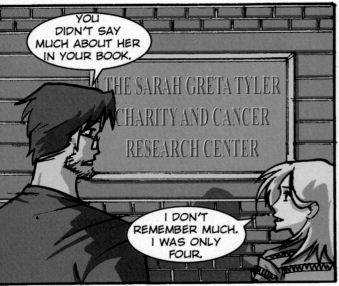

YOU DIDN'T SAY MUCH ABOUT HER IN YOUR BOOK.

THE SARAH GRETA TYLER CHARITY AND CANCER RESEARCH CENTER

I DON'T REMEMBER MUCH. I WAS ONLY FOUR.

WAS IT BREAST CANCER?

IT WAS OVARIAN. IS IT YOUR MOTHER OR --

MY GRANDMA. FOUND OUT LAST MONTH.

ON THE FOURTH FLOOR SCIENTISTS ARE WORKING ON A CURE FOR BREAST CANCER AND THEY'RE DEVELOPING DRUGS THAT WILL HELP TREAT IT. WANNA MAKE A DONATION?

HEY, ISN'T THAT THE STAR OF THAT MOVIE WE SAW SUNDAY?

UH-OH.

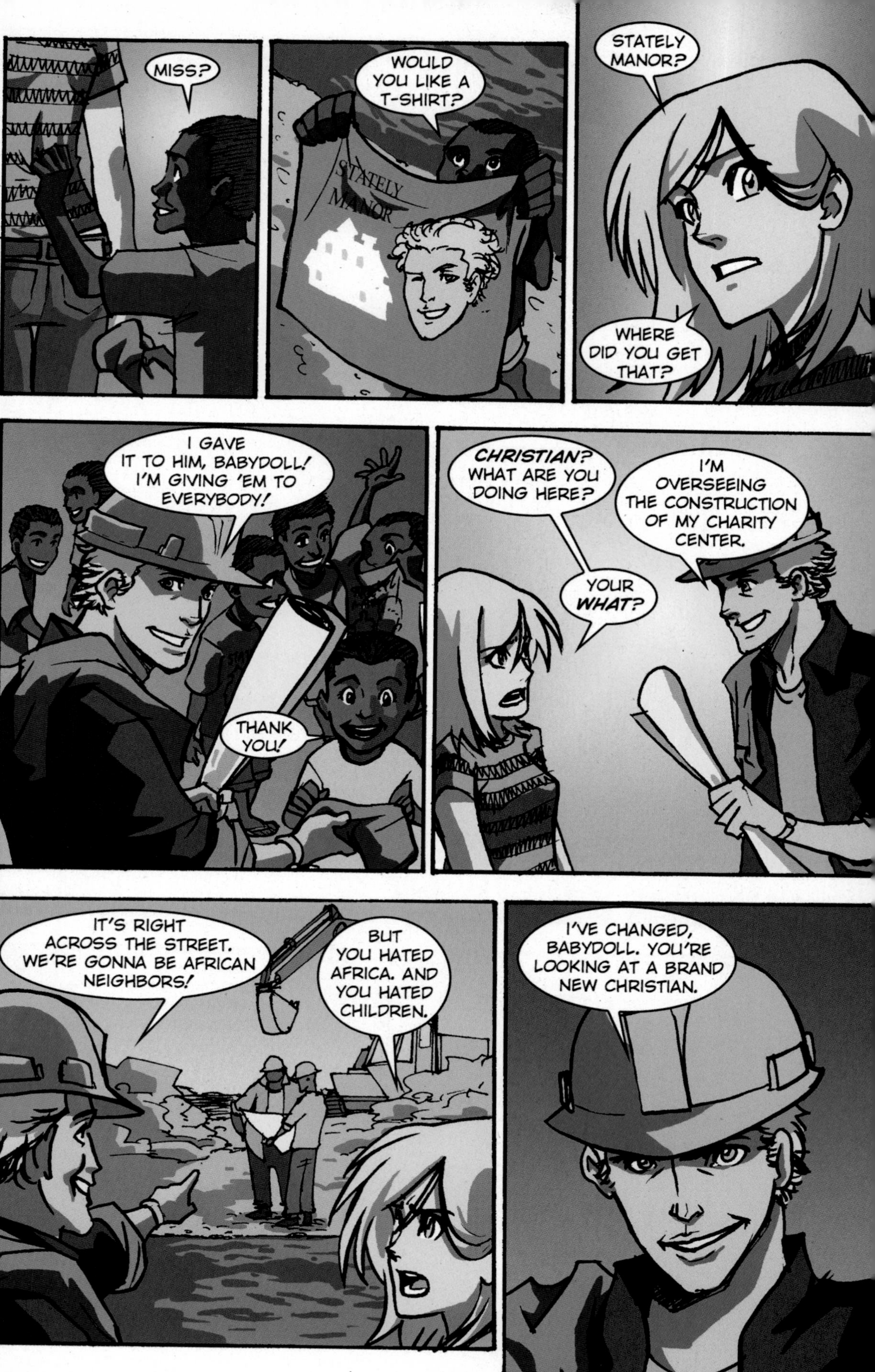
MISS?
WOULD YOU LIKE A T-SHIRT?
STATELY MANOR
STATELY MANOR?
WHERE DID YOU GET THAT?
I GAVE IT TO HIM, BABYDOLL! I'M GIVING 'EM TO EVERYBODY!
THANK YOU!
CHRISTIAN? WHAT ARE YOU DOING HERE?
I'M OVERSEEING THE CONSTRUCTION OF MY CHARITY CENTER.
YOUR WHAT?
IT'S RIGHT ACROSS THE STREET. WE'RE GONNA BE AFRICAN NEIGHBORS!
BUT YOU HATED AFRICA. AND YOU HATED CHILDREN.
I'VE CHANGED, BABYDOLL. YOU'RE LOOKING AT A BRAND NEW CHRISTIAN.

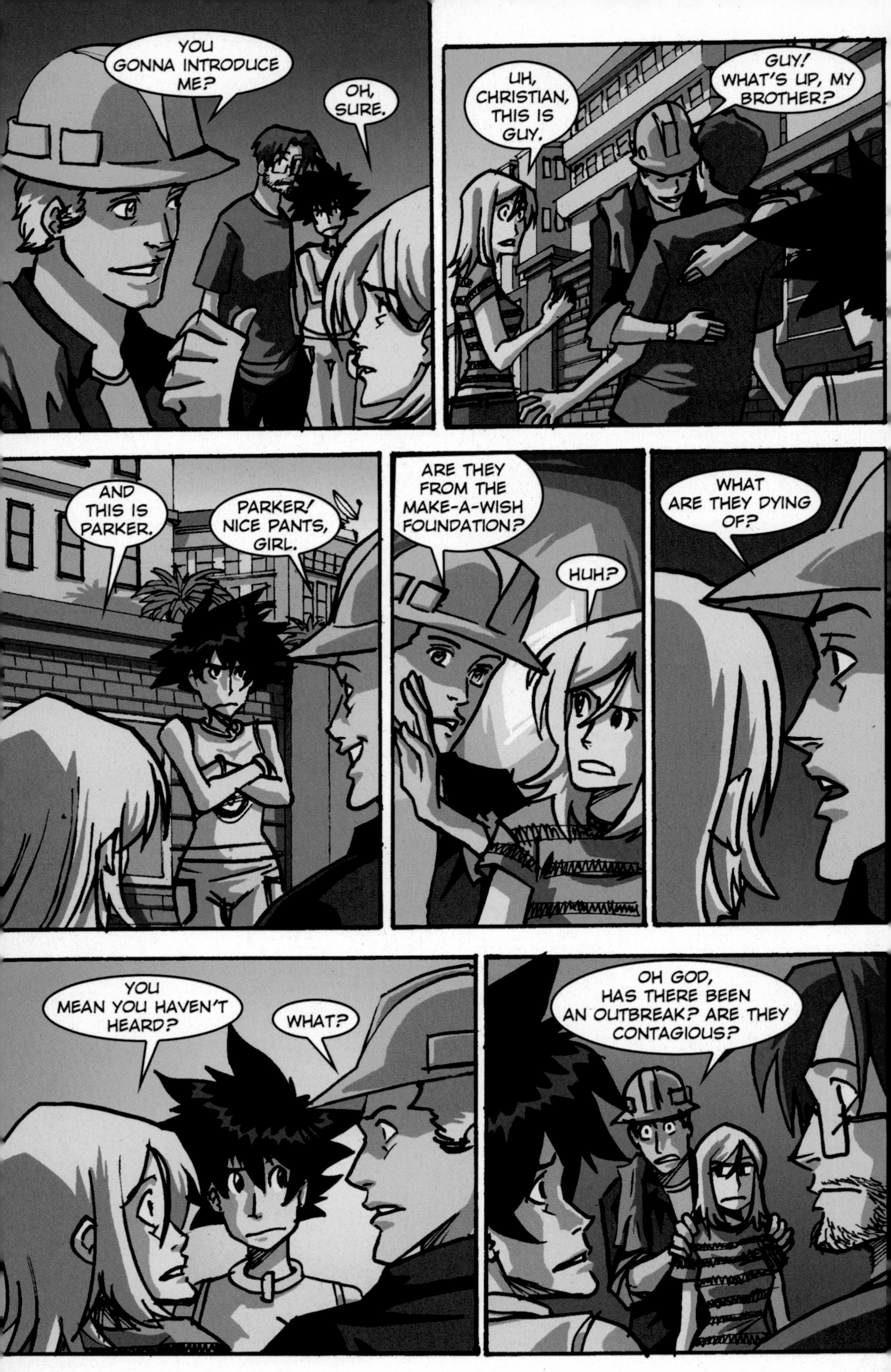
YOU GONNA INTRODUCE ME?
OH, SURE.
UH, CHRISTIAN, THIS IS GUY.
GUY! WHAT'S UP, MY BROTHER?
AND THIS IS PARKER.
PARKER! NICE PANTS, GIRL.
ARE THEY FROM THE MAKE-A-WISH FOUNDATION?
HUH?
WHAT ARE THEY DYING OF?
YOU MEAN YOU HAVEN'T HEARD?
WHAT?
OH GOD, HAS THERE BEEN AN OUTBREAK? ARE THEY CONTAGIOUS?

CHRISTIAN, CALM DOWN -- THEY'RE NOT SICK. I JUST MARRIED ONE OF THEM.

YOU . . . MARRIED . . . ONE OF THEM? THE LITTLE ONE OR THE BIG ONE?

THE BIG ONE.

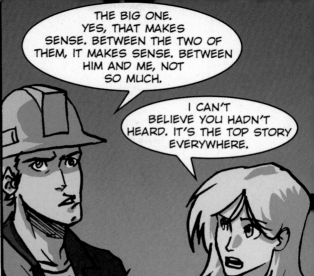

THE BIG ONE. YES, THAT MAKES SENSE. BETWEEN THE TWO OF THEM, IT MAKES SENSE. BETWEEN HIM AND ME, NOT SO MUCH.

I CAN'T BELIEVE YOU HADN'T HEARD. IT'S THE TOP STORY EVERYWHERE.

I TOTALLY CUT MYSELF OFF FROM THE WORLD WHEN I DO MY CHARITY WORK.

YOU DO?

THAT MUST BE WHY YOUR DAD'S BEEN CALLING.

MY DAD? SINCE WHEN DO YOU TALK TO HIM?

SINCE FOREVER. HE'S THE ONE WHO SET US UP. HE TOLD ME TO ASK YOU OUT. THEN HE TOLD ME TO SET UP THIS CHARITY TO WIN YOU BACK. SAID YOU'D PROBABLY COME HERE WHEN YOUR TOUR ENDED.

OF COURSE HE DID. UNBELIEVABLE.

THAT WAS SUPPOSED TO BE A SECRET, BUT I GUESS IT DOESN'T MATTER ANYMORE.

HEY, YOU'RE ALL FIRED! JOB'S OVER!

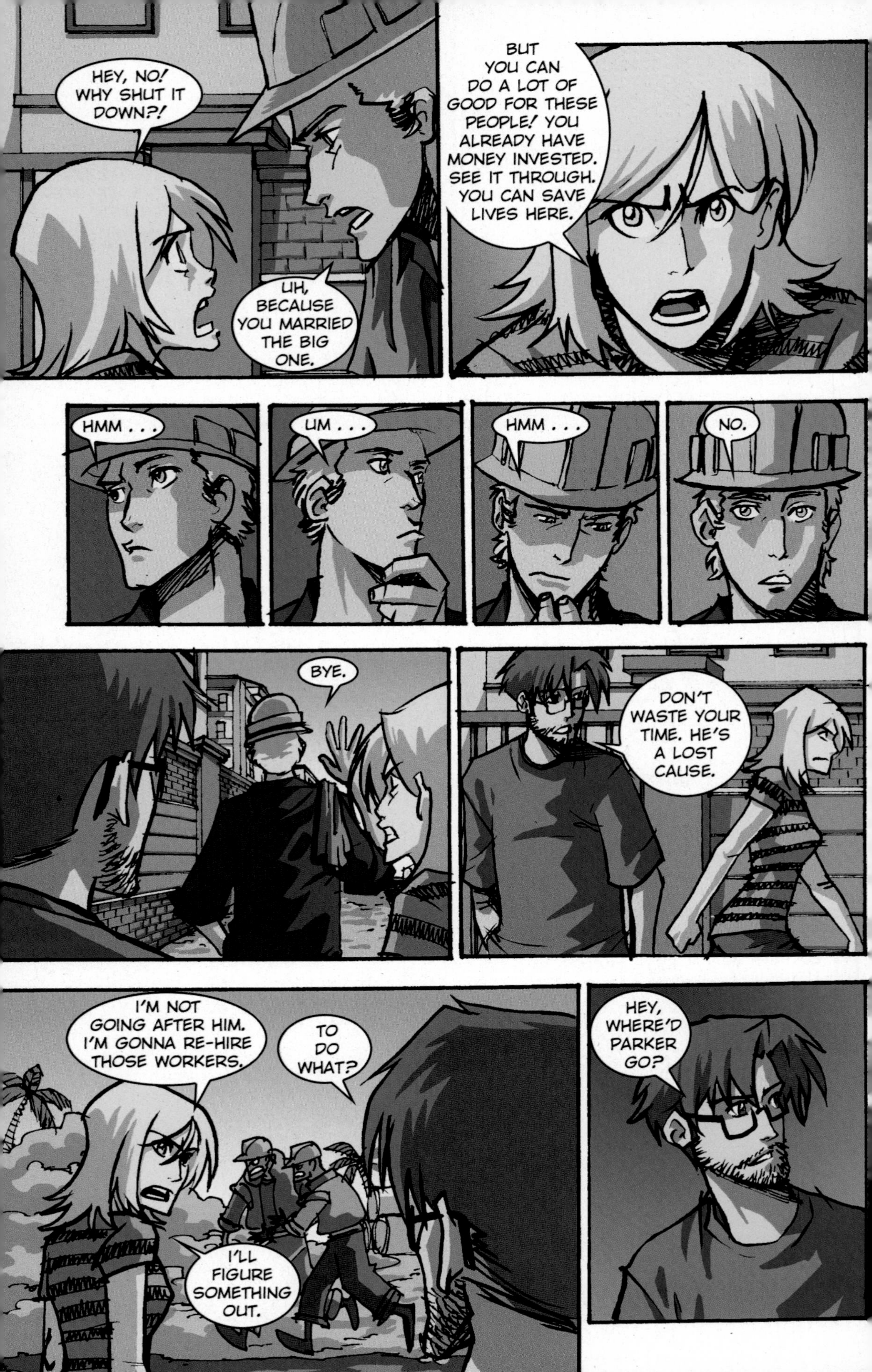
HEY, NO! WHY SHUT IT DOWN?!
UH, BECAUSE YOU MARRIED THE BIG ONE.
BUT YOU CAN DO A LOT OF GOOD FOR THESE PEOPLE! YOU ALREADY HAVE MONEY INVESTED. SEE IT THROUGH. YOU CAN SAVE LIVES HERE.
HMM . . .
UM . . .
HMM . . .
NO.
BYE.
DON'T WASTE YOUR TIME. HE'S A LOST CAUSE.
I'M NOT GOING AFTER HIM. I'M GONNA RE-HIRE THOSE WORKERS.
TO DO WHAT?
I'LL FIGURE SOMETHING OUT.
HEY, WHERE'D PARKER GO?

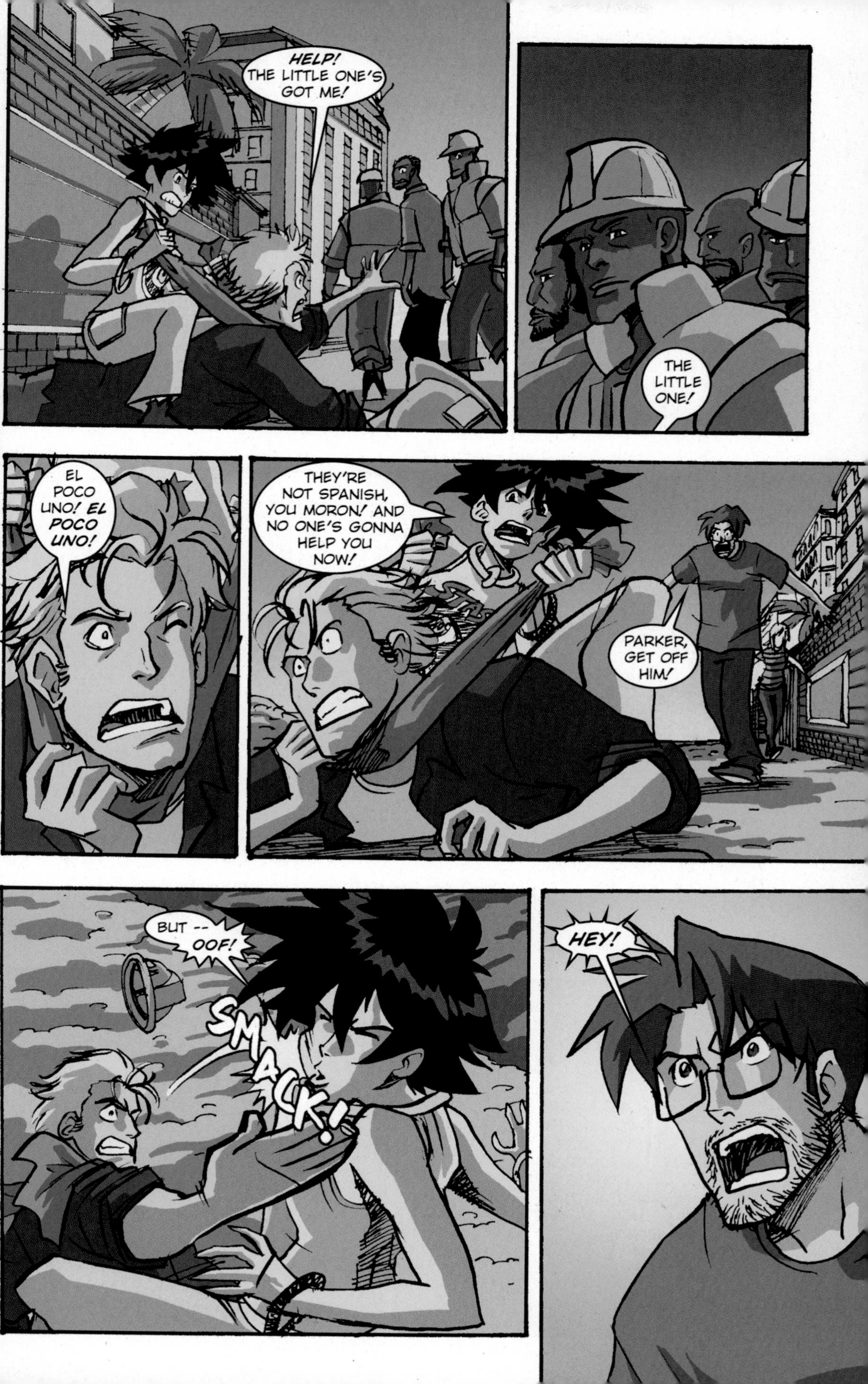
HELP! THE LITTLE ONE'S GOT ME!
THE LITTLE ONE!
EL POCO UNO! EL POCO UNO!
THEY'RE NOT SPANISH, YOU MORON! AND NO ONE'S GONNA HELP YOU NOW!
PARKER, GET OFF HIM!
BUT -- OOF!
SMACK!
HEY!

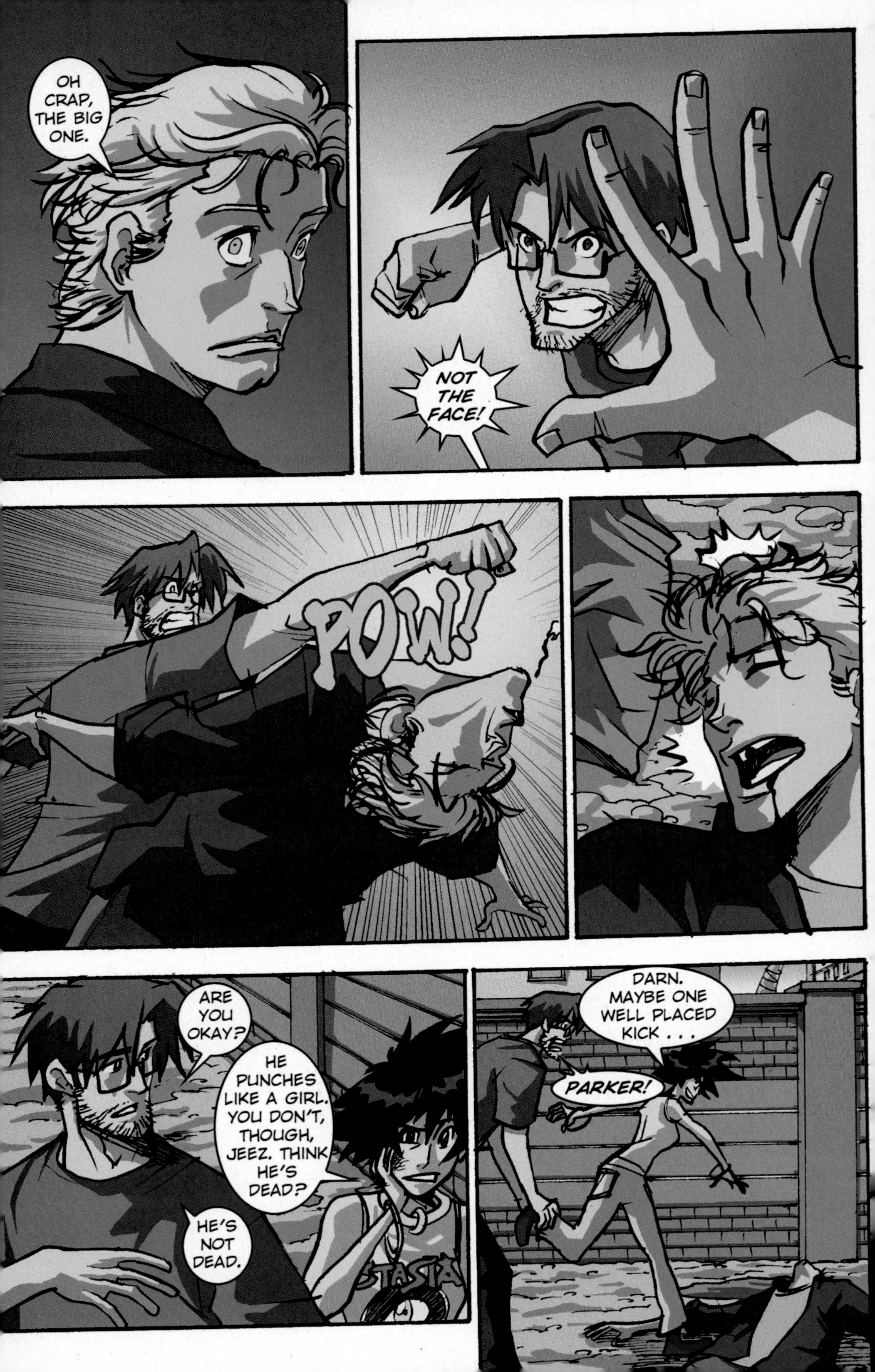
OH CRAP, THE BIG ONE.
NOT THE FACE!
POW!!
ARE YOU OKAY?
HE PUNCHES LIKE A GIRL. YOU DON'T, THOUGH, JEEZ. THINK HE'S DEAD?
HE'S NOT DEAD.
DARN. MAYBE ONE WELL PLACED KICK . . .
PARKER!
STASIA

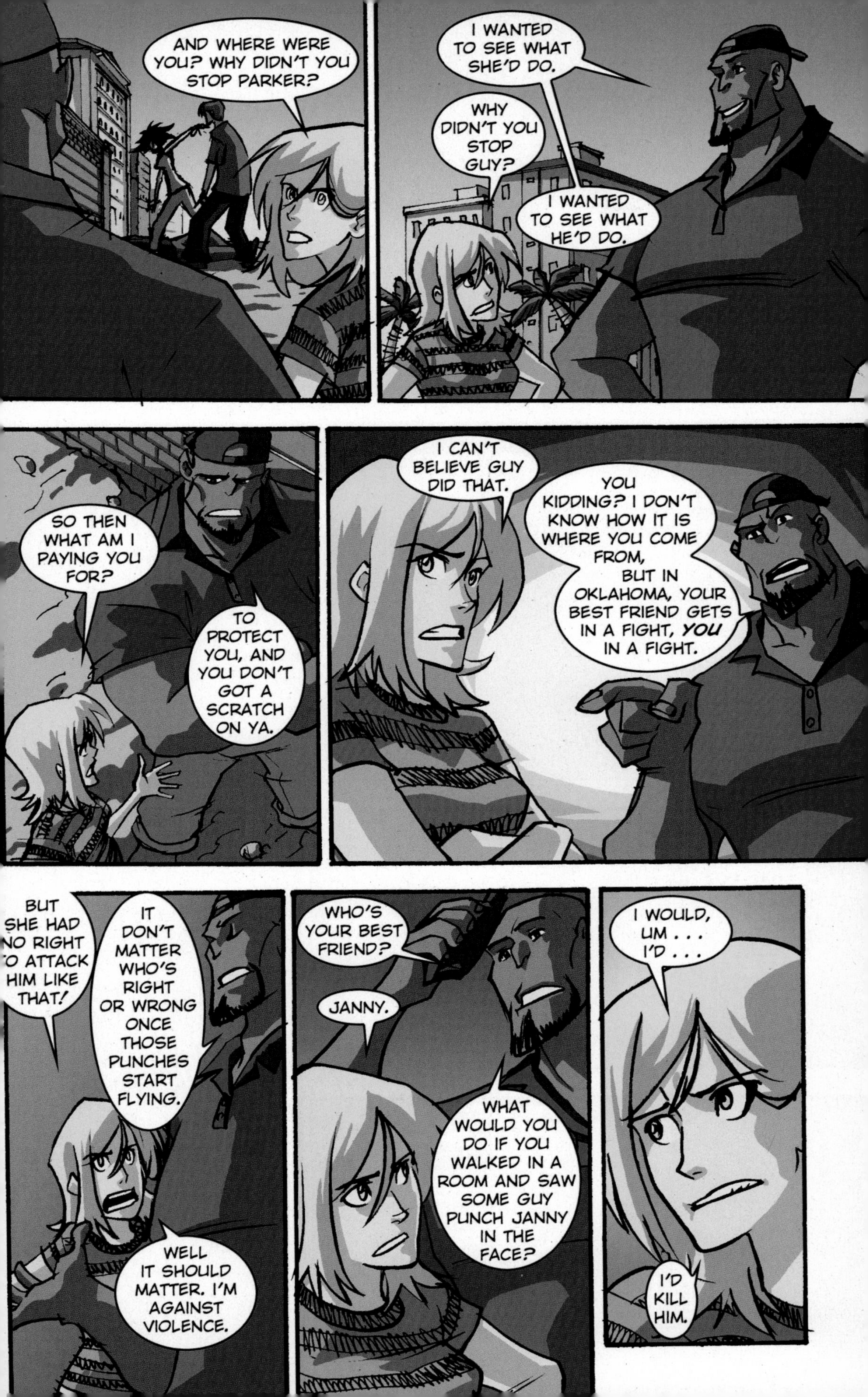
AND WHERE WERE YOU? WHY DIDN'T YOU STOP PARKER?
I WANTED TO SEE WHAT SHE'D DO.
WHY DIDN'T YOU STOP GUY?
I WANTED TO SEE WHAT HE'D DO.
SO THEN WHAT AM I PAYING YOU FOR?
TO PROTECT YOU, AND YOU DON'T GOT A SCRATCH ON YA.
I CAN'T BELIEVE GUY DID THAT.
YOU KIDDING? I DON'T KNOW HOW IT IS WHERE YOU COME FROM,
BUT IN OKLAHOMA, YOUR BEST FRIEND GETS IN A FIGHT, *YOU* IN A FIGHT.
BUT SHE HAD NO RIGHT TO ATTACK HIM LIKE THAT!
IT DON'T MATTER WHO'S RIGHT OR WRONG ONCE THOSE PUNCHES START FLYING.
WELL IT SHOULD MATTER. I'M AGAINST VIOLENCE.
WHO'S YOUR BEST FRIEND?
JANNY.
WHAT WOULD YOU DO IF YOU WALKED IN A ROOM AND SAW SOME GUY PUNCH JANNY IN THE FACE?
I WOULD, UM . . . I'D . . .
I'D KILL HIM.

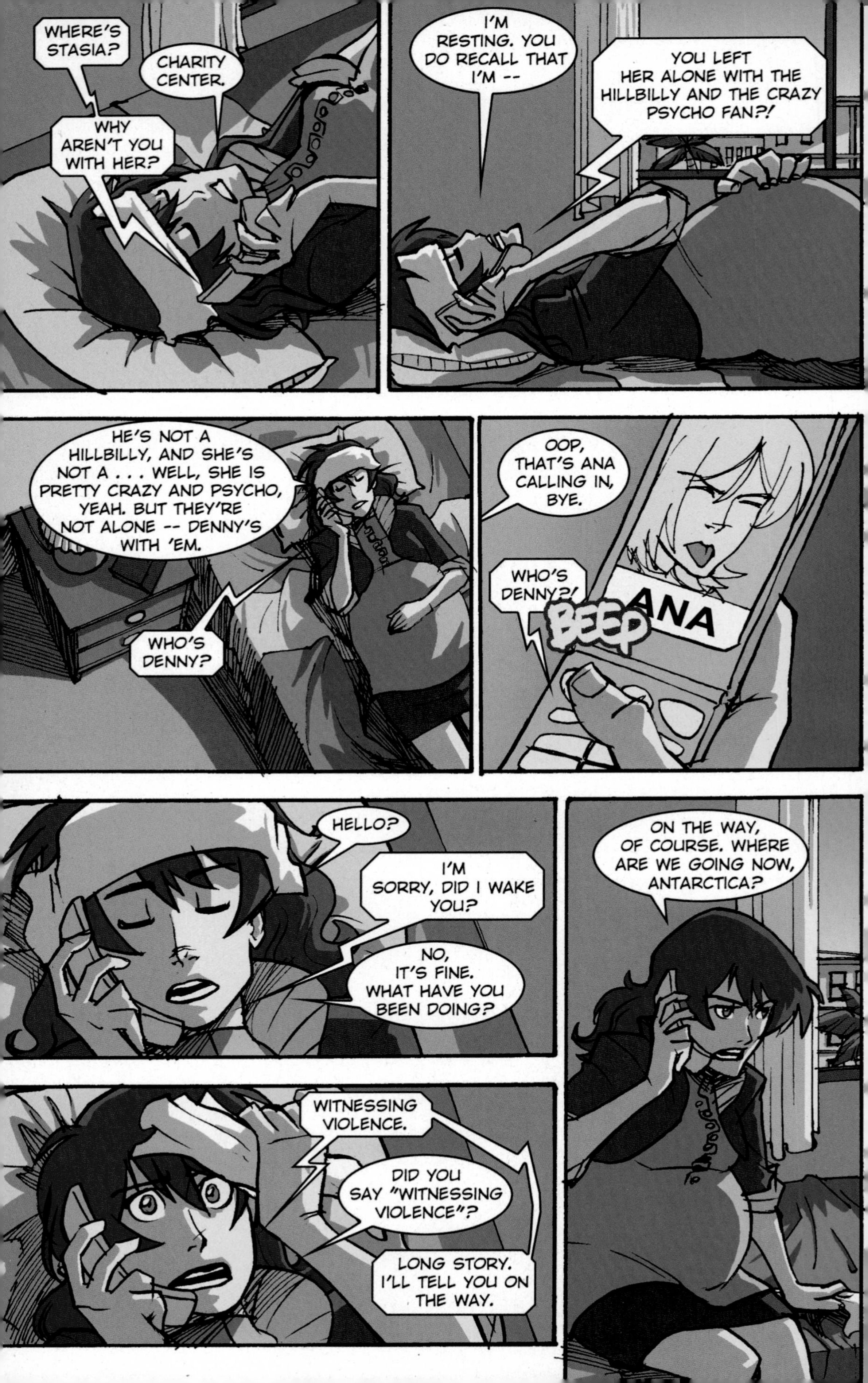
WHERE'S STASIA?
CHARITY CENTER.
WHY AREN'T YOU WITH HER?
I'M RESTING. YOU DO RECALL THAT I'M --
YOU LEFT HER ALONE WITH THE HILLBILLY AND THE CRAZY PSYCHO FAN?!
HE'S NOT A HILLBILLY, AND SHE'S NOT A . . . WELL, SHE IS PRETTY CRAZY AND PSYCHO, YEAH. BUT THEY'RE NOT ALONE -- DENNY'S WITH 'EM.
WHO'S DENNY?
OOP, THAT'S ANA CALLING IN, BYE.
WHO'S DENNY?!
BEEP
ANA
HELLO?
I'M SORRY, DID I WAKE YOU?
NO, IT'S FINE. WHAT HAVE YOU BEEN DOING?
ON THE WAY, OF COURSE. WHERE ARE WE GOING NOW, ANTARCTICA?
WITNESSING VIOLENCE.
DID YOU SAY "WITNESSING VIOLENCE"?
LONG STORY. I'LL TELL YOU ON THE WAY.

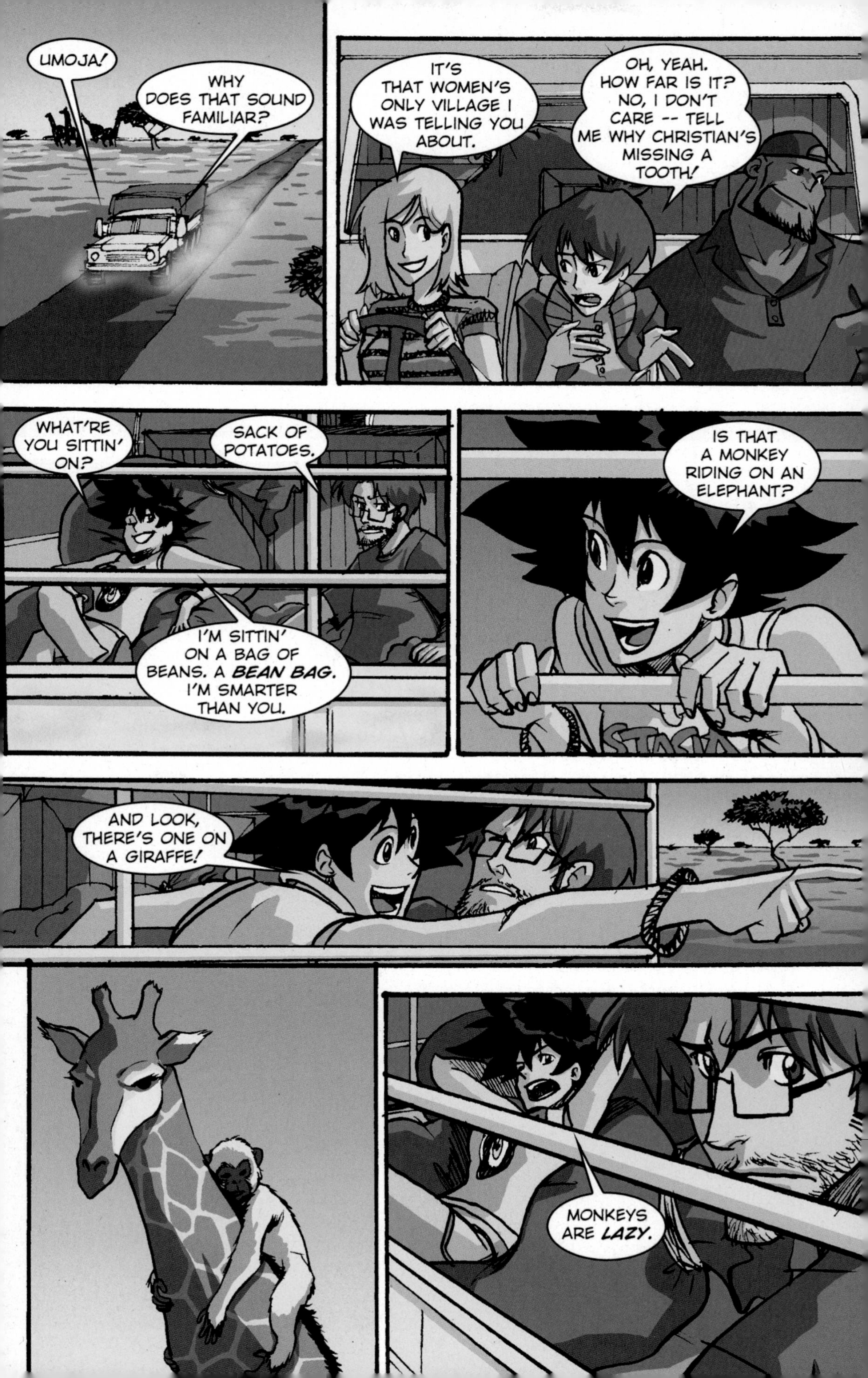
UMOJA!
WHY DOES THAT SOUND FAMILIAR?
IT'S THAT WOMEN'S ONLY VILLAGE I WAS TELLING YOU ABOUT.
OH, YEAH. HOW FAR IS IT? NO, I DON'T CARE -- TELL ME WHY CHRISTIAN'S MISSING A TOOTH!
WHAT'RE YOU SITTIN' ON?
SACK OF POTATOES.
I'M SITTIN' ON A BAG OF BEANS. A BEAN BAG. I'M SMARTER THAN YOU.
IS THAT A MONKEY RIDING ON AN ELEPHANT?
AND LOOK, THERE'S ONE ON A GIRAFFE!
MONKEYS ARE LAZY.

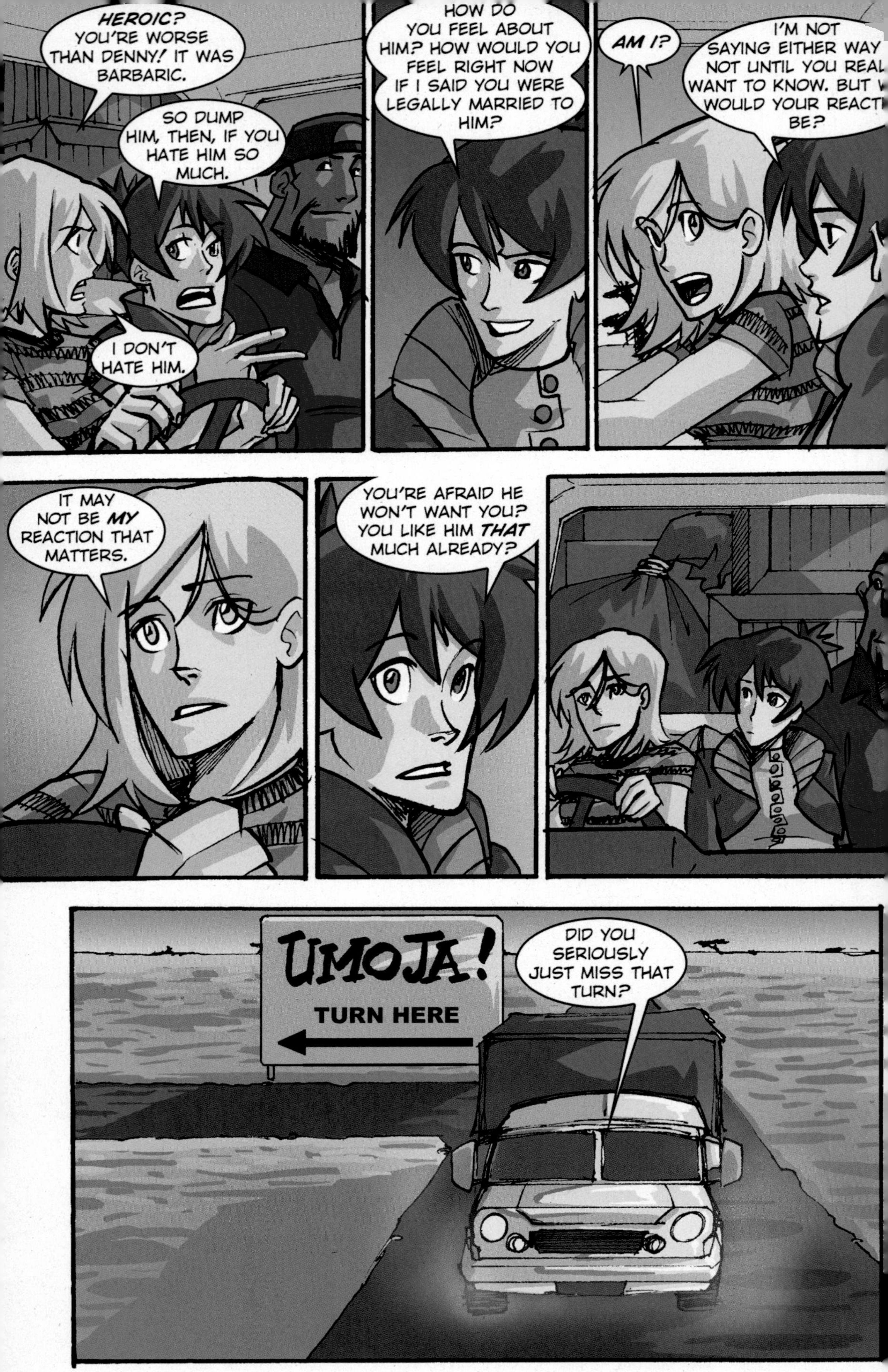
HEROIC? YOU'RE WORSE THAN DENNY! IT WAS BARBARIC.
SO DUMP HIM, THEN, IF YOU HATE HIM SO MUCH.
I DON'T HATE HIM.
HOW DO YOU FEEL ABOUT HIM? HOW WOULD YOU FEEL RIGHT NOW IF I SAID YOU WERE LEGALLY MARRIED TO HIM?
AM I?
I'M NOT SAYING EITHER WAY NOT UNTIL YOU REAL WANT TO KNOW. BUT WOULD YOUR REACT BE?
IT MAY NOT BE MY REACTION THAT MATTERS.
YOU'RE AFRAID HE WON'T WANT YOU? YOU LIKE HIM THAT MUCH ALREADY?
UMOJA!
TURN HERE
DID YOU SERIOUSLY JUST MISS THAT TURN?

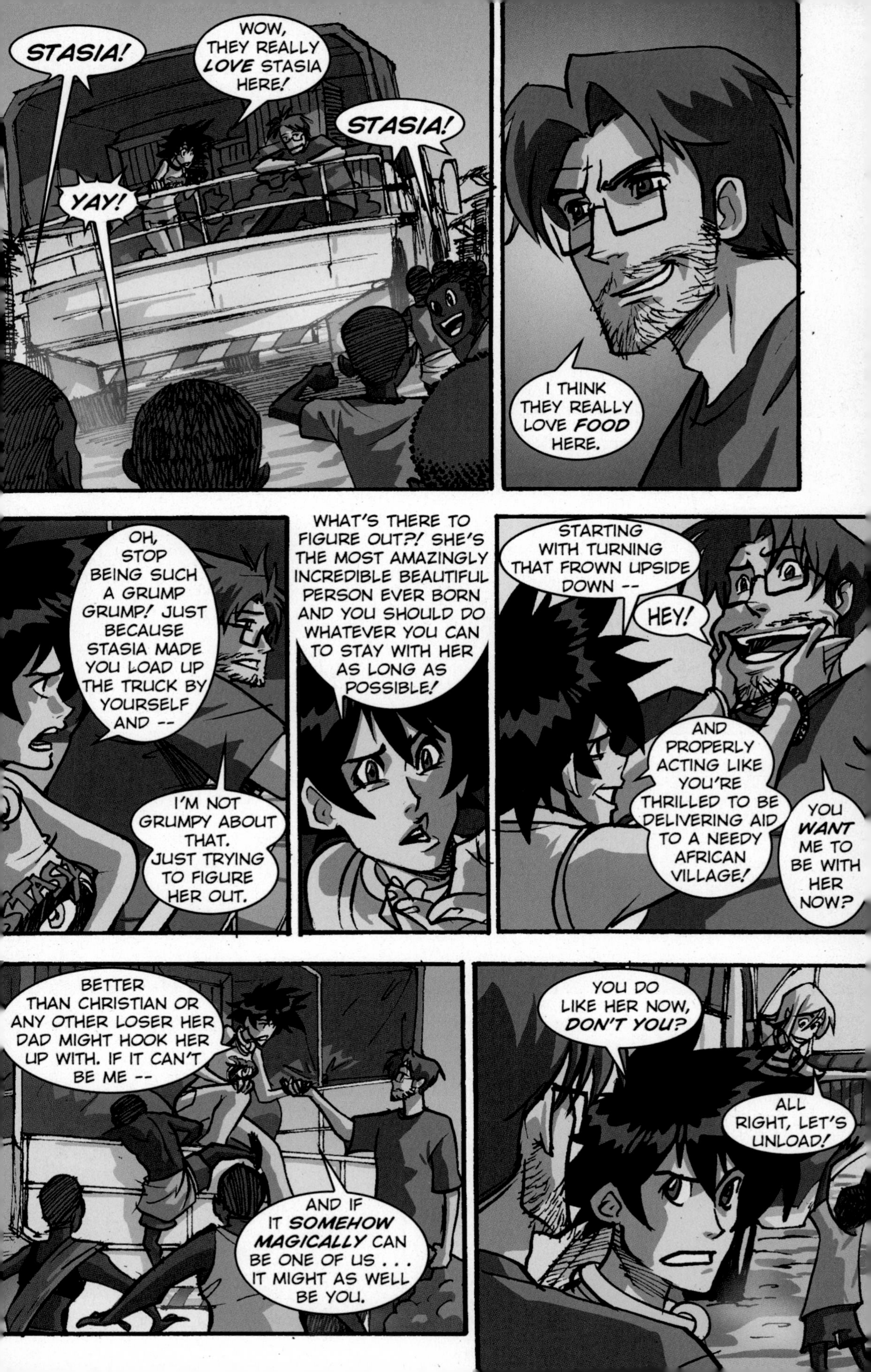
STASIA!
WOW, THEY REALLY LOVE STASIA HERE!
STASIA!
YAY!
I THINK THEY REALLY LOVE FOOD HERE.
OH, STOP BEING SUCH A GRUMP GRUMP! JUST BECAUSE STASIA MADE YOU LOAD UP THE TRUCK BY YOURSELF AND --
I'M NOT GRUMPY ABOUT THAT. JUST TRYING TO FIGURE HER OUT.
WHAT'S THERE TO FIGURE OUT?! SHE'S THE MOST AMAZINGLY INCREDIBLE BEAUTIFUL PERSON EVER BORN AND YOU SHOULD DO WHATEVER YOU CAN TO STAY WITH HER AS LONG AS POSSIBLE!
STARTING WITH TURNING THAT FROWN UPSIDE DOWN --
HEY!
AND PROPERLY ACTING LIKE YOU'RE THRILLED TO BE DELIVERING AID TO A NEEDY AFRICAN VILLAGE!
YOU WANT ME TO BE WITH HER NOW?
BETTER THAN CHRISTIAN OR ANY OTHER LOSER HER DAD MIGHT HOOK HER UP WITH. IF IT CAN'T BE ME --
AND IF IT SOMEHOW MAGICALLY CAN BE ONE OF US . . . IT MIGHT AS WELL BE YOU.
YOU DO LIKE HER NOW, DON'T YOU?
ALL RIGHT, LET'S UNLOAD!

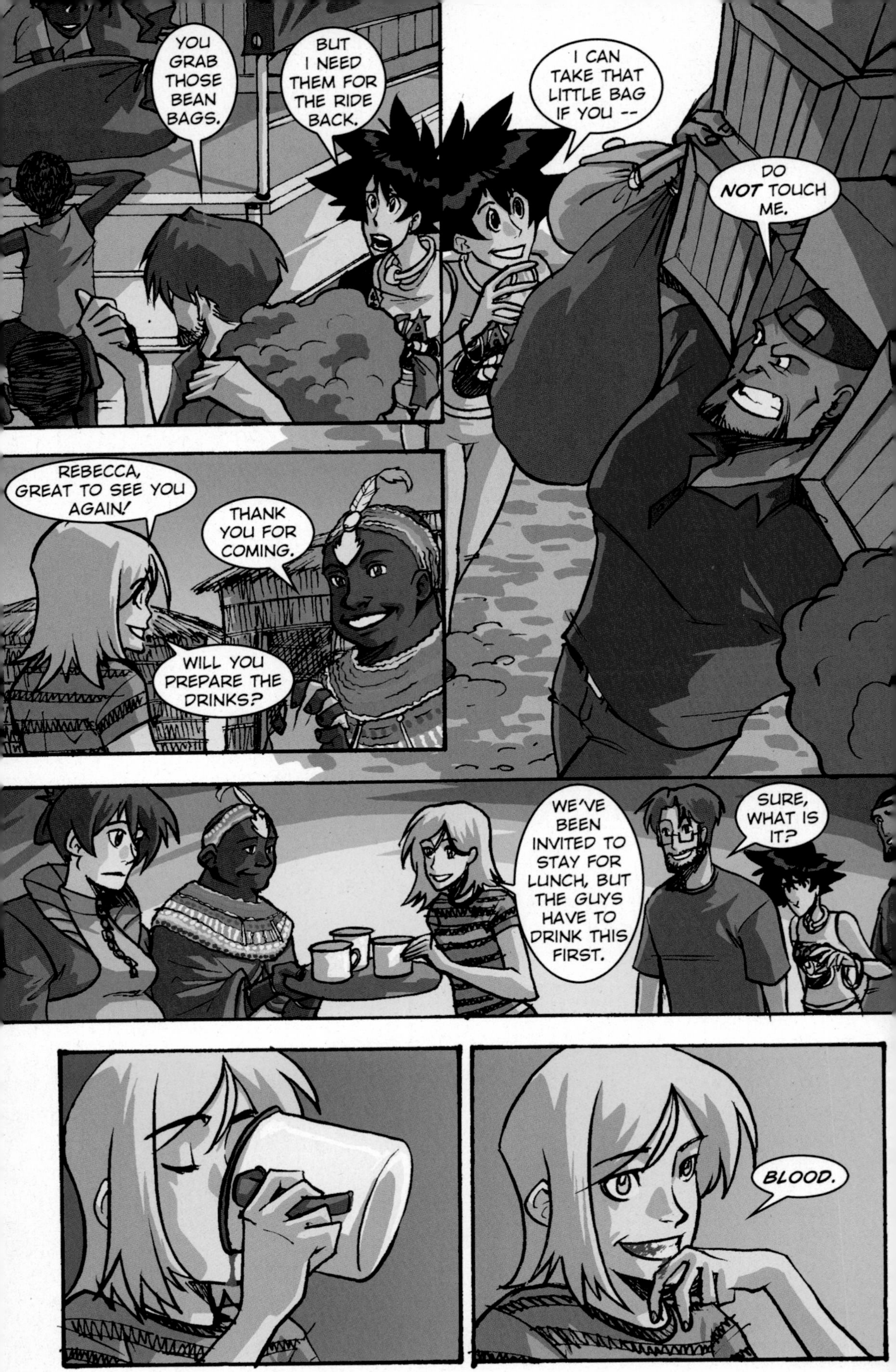
YOU GRAB THOSE BEAN BAGS.
BUT I NEED THEM FOR THE RIDE BACK.
I CAN TAKE THAT LITTLE BAG IF YOU --
DO *NOT* TOUCH ME.
REBECCA, GREAT TO SEE YOU AGAIN!
THANK YOU FOR COMING.
WILL YOU PREPARE THE DRINKS?
WE'VE BEEN INVITED TO STAY FOR LUNCH, BUT THE GUYS HAVE TO DRINK THIS FIRST.
SURE, WHAT IS IT?
BLOOD.

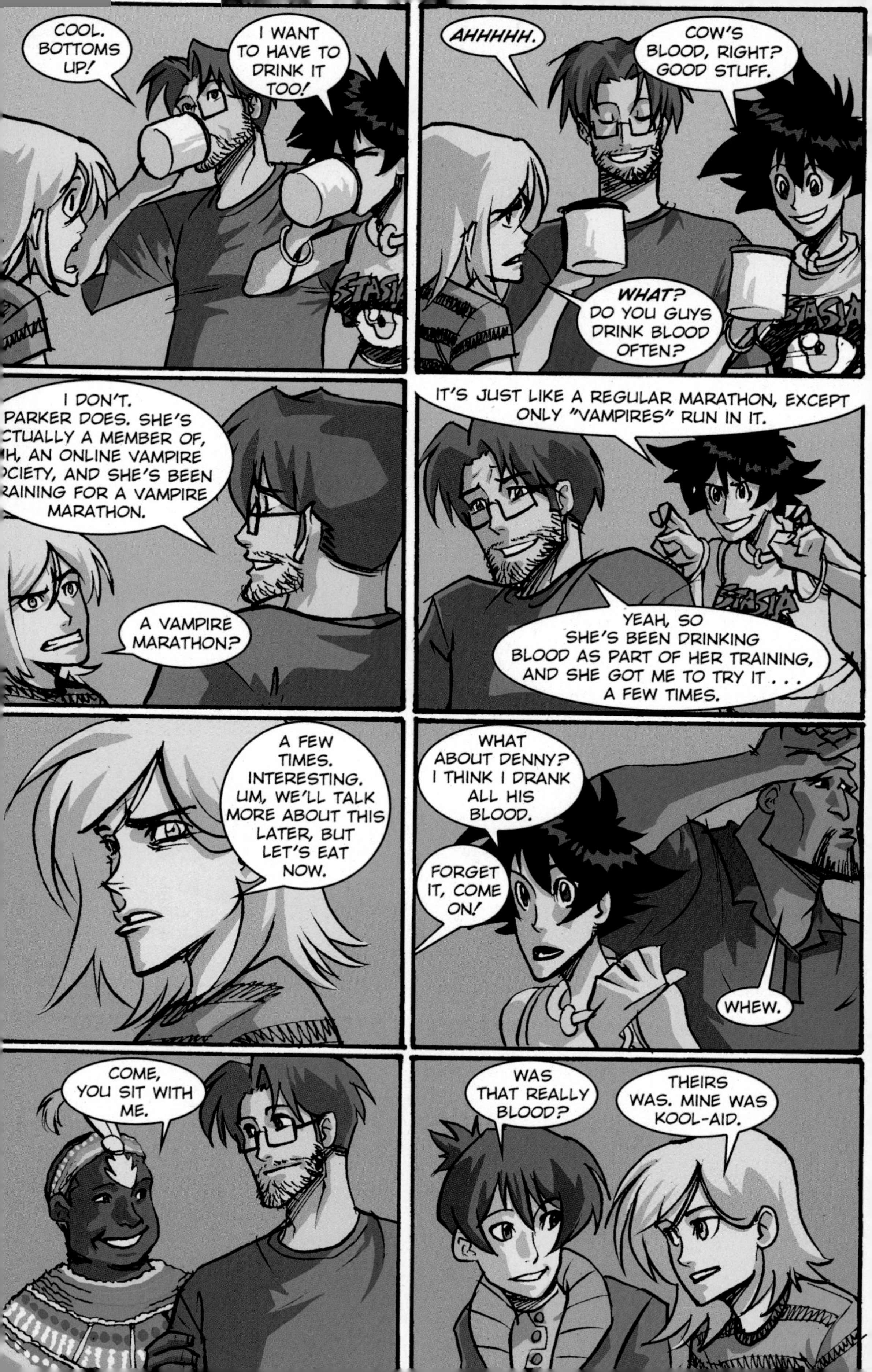
COOL. BOTTOMS UP!
I WANT TO HAVE TO DRINK IT TOO!
AHHHHH.
COW'S BLOOD, RIGHT? GOOD STUFF.
WHAT? DO YOU GUYS DRINK BLOOD OFTEN?
I DON'T. PARKER DOES. SHE'S ACTUALLY A MEMBER OF, UH, AN ONLINE VAMPIRE SOCIETY, AND SHE'S BEEN TRAINING FOR A VAMPIRE MARATHON.
A VAMPIRE MARATHON?
IT'S JUST LIKE A REGULAR MARATHON, EXCEPT ONLY "VAMPIRES" RUN IN IT.
YEAH, SO SHE'S BEEN DRINKING BLOOD AS PART OF HER TRAINING, AND SHE GOT ME TO TRY IT . . . A FEW TIMES.
A FEW TIMES. INTERESTING. UM, WE'LL TALK MORE ABOUT THIS LATER, BUT LET'S EAT NOW.
WHAT ABOUT DENNY? I THINK I DRANK ALL HIS BLOOD.
FORGET IT, COME ON!
WHEW.
COME, YOU SIT WITH ME.
WAS THAT REALLY BLOOD?
THEIRS WAS. MINE WAS KOOL-AID.

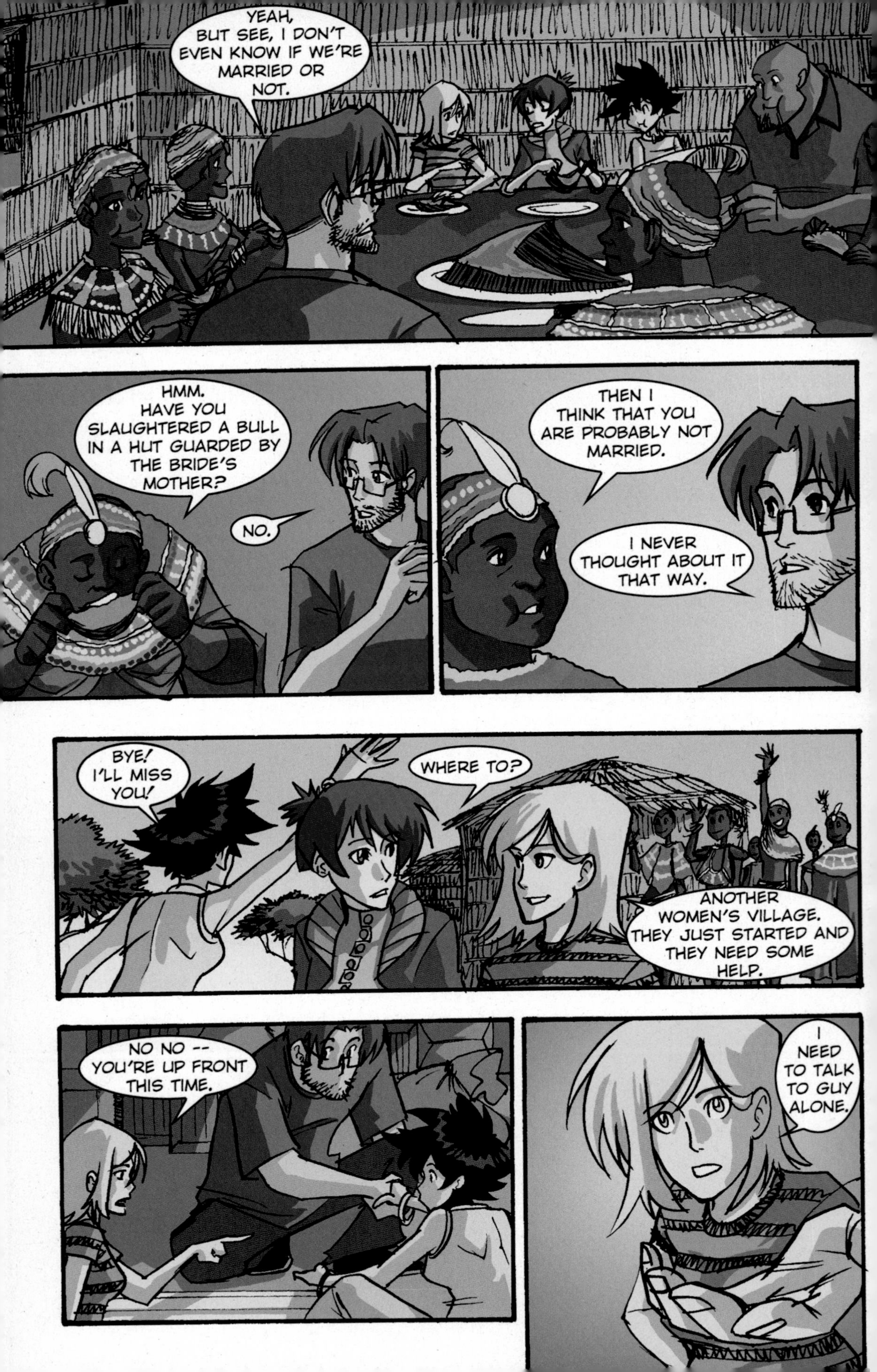
YEAH, BUT SEE, I DON'T EVEN KNOW IF WE'RE MARRIED OR NOT.
HMM. HAVE YOU SLAUGHTERED A BULL IN A HUT GUARDED BY THE BRIDE'S MOTHER?
NO.
THEN I THINK THAT YOU ARE PROBABLY NOT MARRIED.
I NEVER THOUGHT ABOUT IT THAT WAY.
BYE! I'LL MISS YOU!
WHERE TO?
ANOTHER WOMEN'S VILLAGE. THEY JUST STARTED AND THEY NEED SOME HELP.
NO NO -- YOU'RE UP FRONT THIS TIME.
I NEED TO TALK TO GUY ALONE.

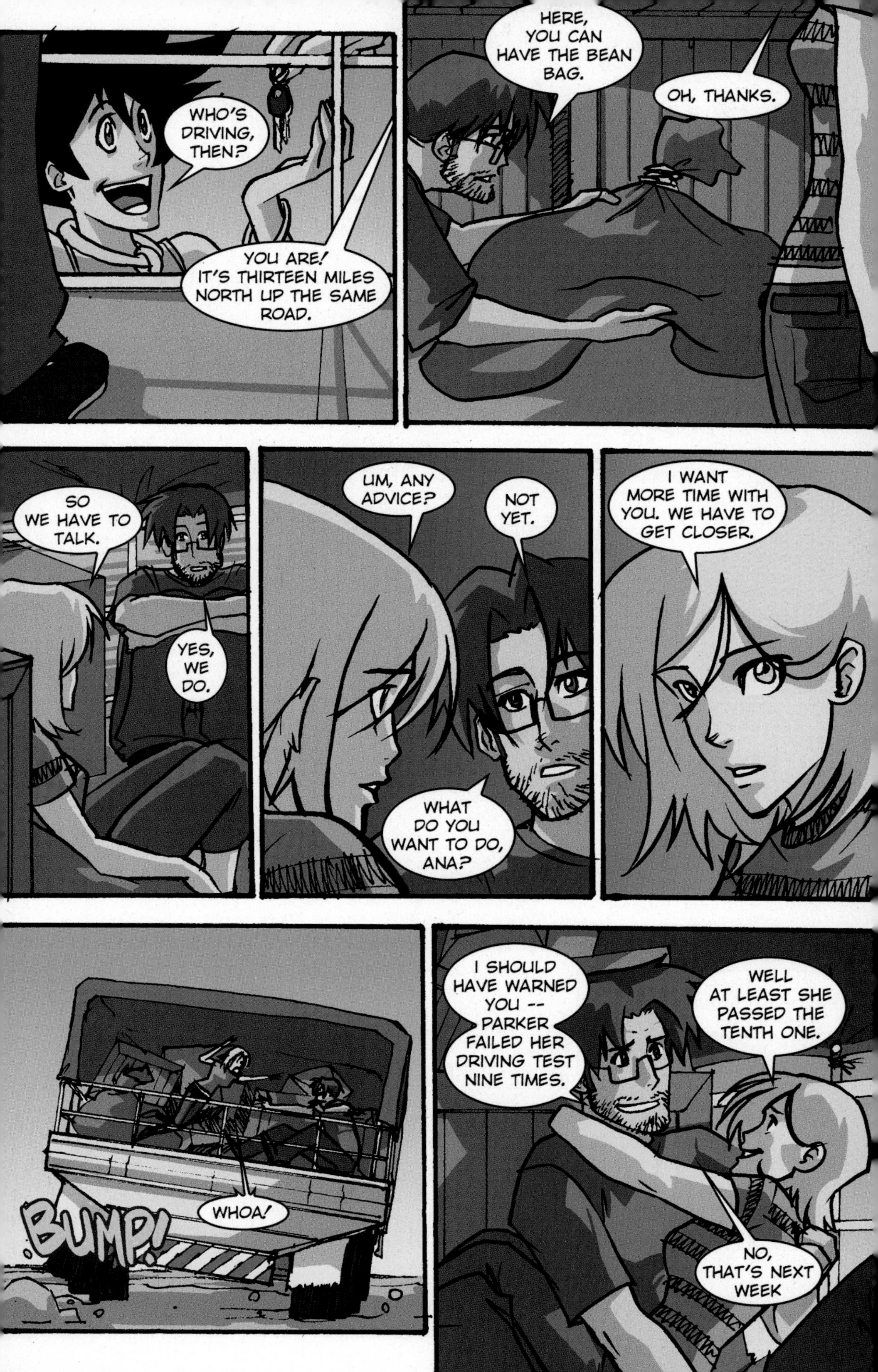
WHO'S DRIVING, THEN?
YOU ARE! IT'S THIRTEEN MILES NORTH UP THE SAME ROAD.
HERE, YOU CAN HAVE THE BEAN BAG.
OH, THANKS.
SO WE HAVE TO TALK.
YES, WE DO.
UM, ANY ADVICE?
NOT YET.
WHAT DO YOU WANT TO DO, ANA?
I WANT MORE TIME WITH YOU. WE HAVE TO GET CLOSER.
BUMP!
WHOA!
I SHOULD HAVE WARNED YOU -- PARKER FAILED HER DRIVING TEST NINE TIMES.
WELL AT LEAST SHE PASSED THE TENTH ONE.
NO, THAT'S NEXT WEEK

I THINK IT MIGHT BE SAFER IF WE STAY LIKE THIS.

I HAVE NO OBJECTION TO THAT.

UH, YOU SAID A MINUTE AGO THAT YOU NEEDED MORE TIME. IS IT RUNNING OUT?

I CAN'T AVOID HIM FOREVER. I'LL HAVE TO TALK TO HIM SOON. AND THERE'S NO WAY HE'D APPROVE OF THIS.

I KNOW YOU THINK THAT SHOULDN'T BE A BIG DEAL, BUT IT IS. HE'S MY DAD, AND MY MANAGER AND I OWE HIM A LOT.

HE'S ACTUALLY A REALLY GOOD GUY. HE'S JUST A BIT . . . CONTROLLING.

AND HE'S SCARED THAT I'M GONNA GO CRAZY AND START GIVING *ALL* MY MONEY AWAY, SO HE WANTS ME TO BE WITH A RICH GUY. AND ALL THE BETTER IF IT'S SOME IDIOT HE CAN CONTROL, LIKE CHRISTIAN.

WHY DO YOU GIVE SO MUCH AWAY?

BECAUSE I CAN. BECAUSE I MADE A HUNDRED MILLION DOLLARS LAST YEAR. I MEAN, THIS WASN'T IN MY BOOK, BECAUSE MY DAD DIDN'T WANT US TO BE SEEN AS POOR, YOU KNOW, BUT WE HAD SOME HARD TIMES. HE WAS OUT OF WORK AND . . . I KNOW WHAT IT'S LIKE TO NEED THINGS, TO NEED HELP. I JUST WISH I COULD HELP MORE.

I'M SORRY, WHAT WAS I SAYING BEFORE?

UH, YOUR DAD?

RIGHT. UM, THE THING IS I PROBABLY LET HIM CONTROL MY LIFE TOO MUCH, BUT I CAN'T GO AGAINST HIM ON SOMETHING AS HUGE AS THIS -- *MARRIAGE* -- UNLESS . . .

UNLESS YOU WERE SURE. AND YOU CAN'T BE SURE. BECAUSE YOU BARELY KNOW ME. YOU DON'T EVEN KNOW IF I LIKE YOU OR NOT.

DO YOU?

DO YOU LIKE ME?

WE'RE HERE!

SCREEEEECH!

OW.

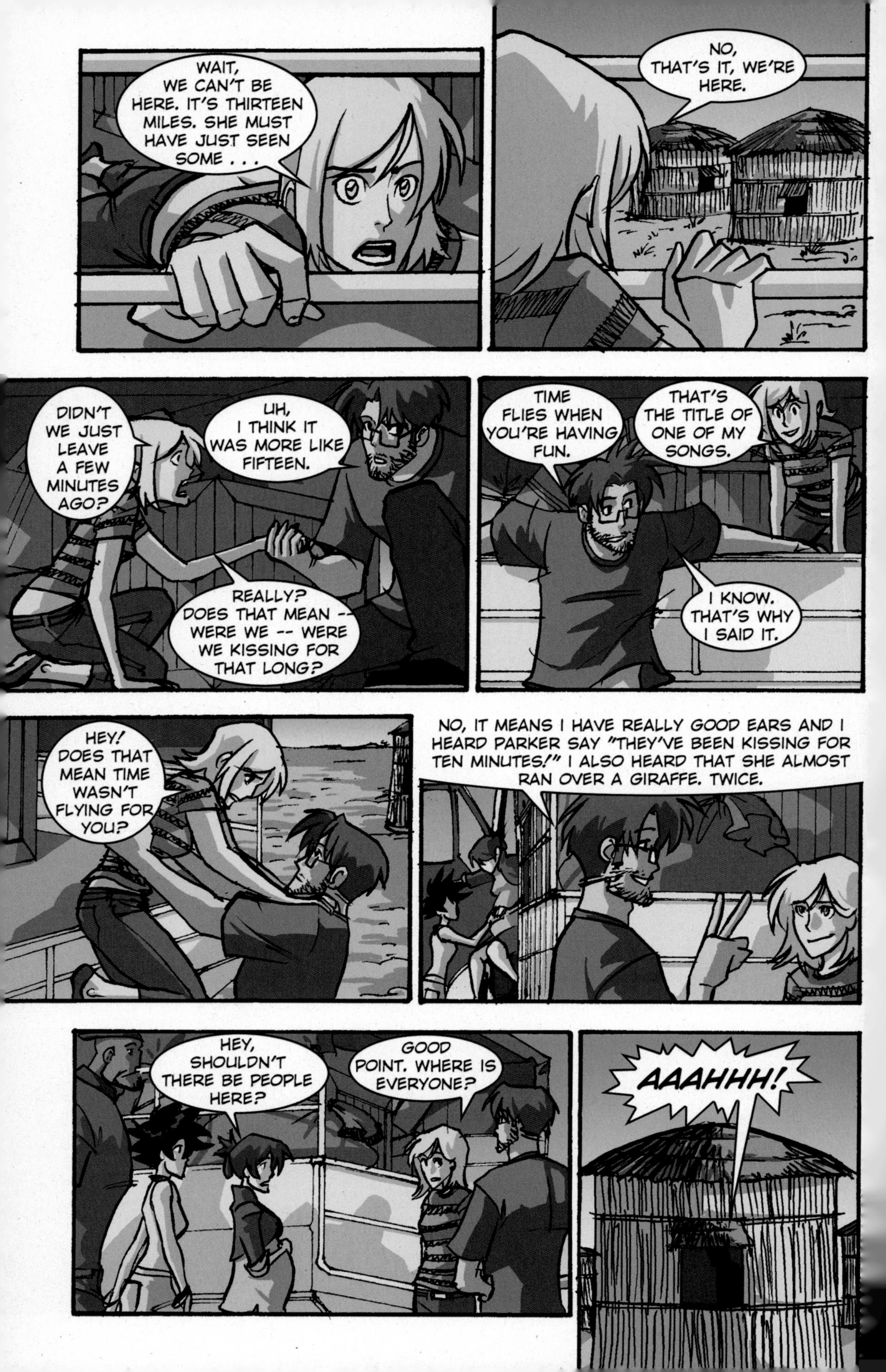
WAIT, WE CAN'T BE HERE. IT'S THIRTEEN MILES. SHE MUST HAVE JUST SEEN SOME . . .
NO, THAT'S IT, WE'RE HERE.
DIDN'T WE JUST LEAVE A FEW MINUTES AGO?
UH, I THINK IT WAS MORE LIKE FIFTEEN.
REALLY? DOES THAT MEAN -- WERE WE -- WERE WE KISSING FOR THAT LONG?
TIME FLIES WHEN YOU'RE HAVING FUN.
THAT'S THE TITLE OF ONE OF MY SONGS.
I KNOW. THAT'S WHY I SAID IT.
HEY! DOES THAT MEAN TIME WASN'T FLYING FOR YOU?
NO, IT MEANS I HAVE REALLY GOOD EARS AND I HEARD PARKER SAY "THEY'VE BEEN KISSING FOR TEN MINUTES!" I ALSO HEARD THAT SHE ALMOST RAN OVER A GIRAFFE. TWICE.
HEY, SHOULDN'T THERE BE PEOPLE HERE?
GOOD POINT. WHERE IS EVERYONE?
AAAHHH!

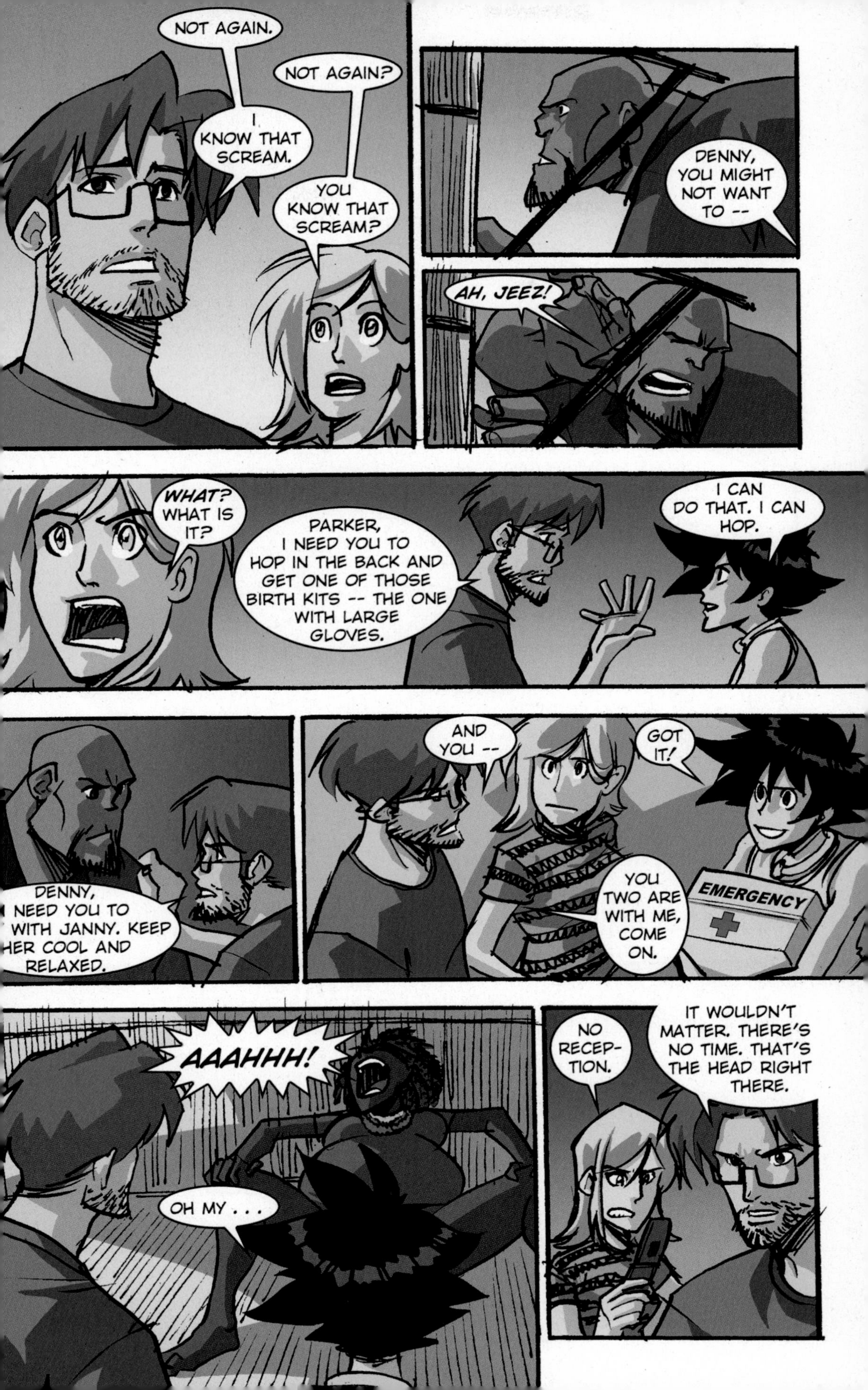
NOT AGAIN.
I KNOW THAT SCREAM.
NOT AGAIN?
YOU KNOW THAT SCREAM?
DENNY, YOU MIGHT NOT WANT TO --
AH, JEEZ!
WHAT? WHAT IS IT?
PARKER, I NEED YOU TO HOP IN THE BACK AND GET ONE OF THOSE BIRTH KITS -- THE ONE WITH LARGE GLOVES.
I CAN DO THAT. I CAN HOP.
DENNY, NEED YOU TO WITH JANNY. KEEP HER COOL AND RELAXED.
AND YOU --
GOT IT!
YOU TWO ARE WITH ME, COME ON.
EMERGENCY
AAAHHH!
OH MY . . .
NO RECEP-TION.
IT WOULDN'T MATTER. THERE'S NO TIME. THAT'S THE HEAD RIGHT THERE.

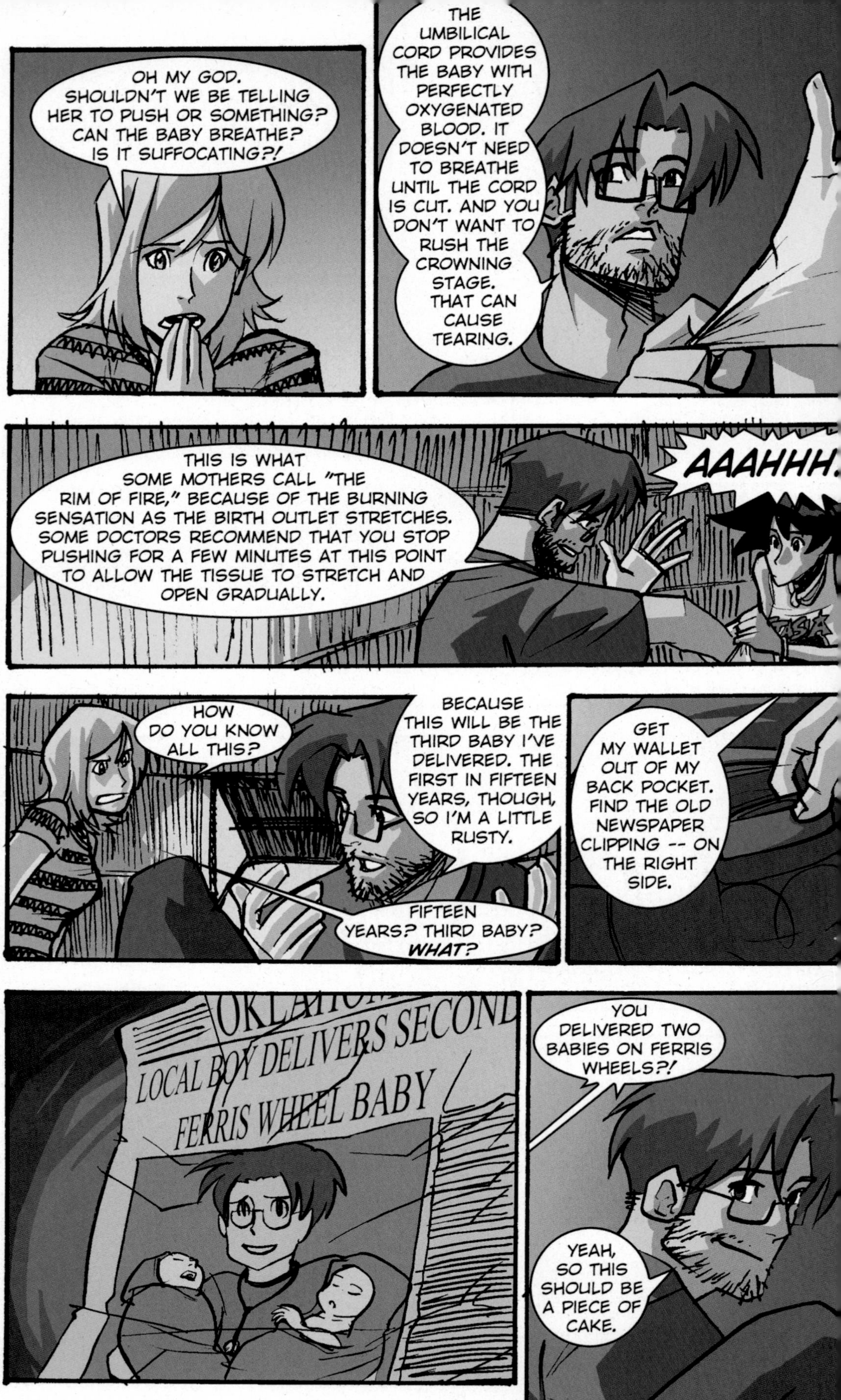
OH MY GOD. SHOULDN'T WE BE TELLING HER TO PUSH OR SOMETHING? CAN THE BABY BREATHE? IS IT SUFFOCATING?!
THE UMBILICAL CORD PROVIDES THE BABY WITH PERFECTLY OXYGENATED BLOOD. IT DOESN'T NEED TO BREATHE UNTIL THE CORD IS CUT. AND YOU DON'T WANT TO RUSH THE CROWNING STAGE. THAT CAN CAUSE TEARING.
THIS IS WHAT SOME MOTHERS CALL "THE RIM OF FIRE," BECAUSE OF THE BURNING SENSATION AS THE BIRTH OUTLET STRETCHES. SOME DOCTORS RECOMMEND THAT YOU STOP PUSHING FOR A FEW MINUTES AT THIS POINT TO ALLOW THE TISSUE TO STRETCH AND OPEN GRADUALLY.
AAAHHH
HOW DO YOU KNOW ALL THIS?
BECAUSE THIS WILL BE THE THIRD BABY I'VE DELIVERED. THE FIRST IN FIFTEEN YEARS, THOUGH, SO I'M A LITTLE RUSTY.
FIFTEEN YEARS? THIRD BABY? WHAT?
GET MY WALLET OUT OF MY BACK POCKET. FIND THE OLD NEWSPAPER CLIPPING -- ON THE RIGHT SIDE.
LOCAL BOY DELIVERS SECOND FERRIS WHEEL BABY
YOU DELIVERED TWO BABIES ON FERRIS WHEELS?!
YEAH, SO THIS SHOULD BE A PIECE OF CAKE.

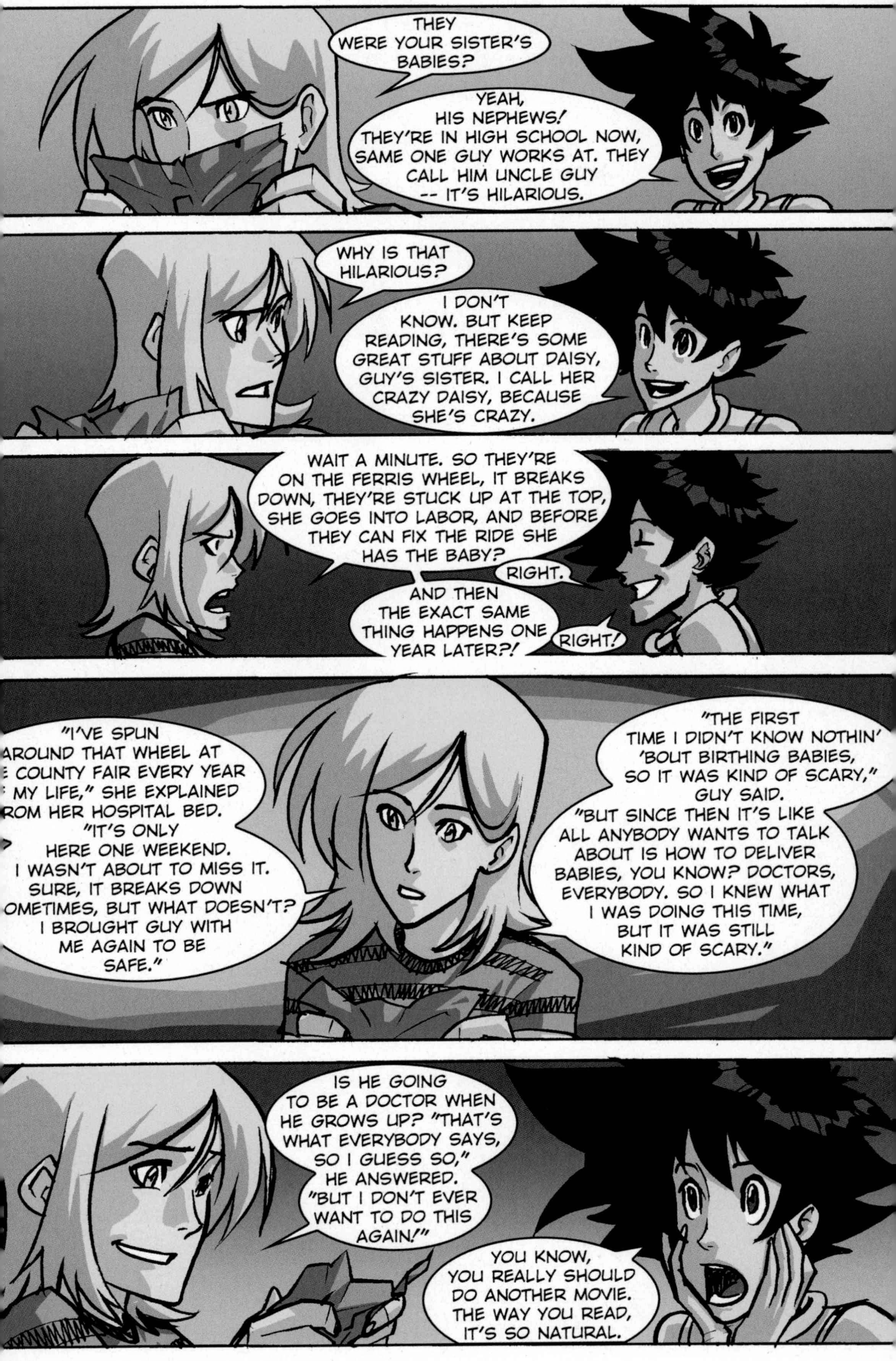
THEY WERE YOUR SISTER'S BABIES?
YEAH, HIS NEPHEWS! THEY'RE IN HIGH SCHOOL NOW, SAME ONE GUY WORKS AT. THEY CALL HIM UNCLE GUY -- IT'S HILARIOUS.
WHY IS THAT HILARIOUS?
I DON'T KNOW. BUT KEEP READING, THERE'S SOME GREAT STUFF ABOUT DAISY, GUY'S SISTER. I CALL HER CRAZY DAISY, BECAUSE SHE'S CRAZY.
WAIT A MINUTE. SO THEY'RE ON THE FERRIS WHEEL, IT BREAKS DOWN, THEY'RE STUCK UP AT THE TOP, SHE GOES INTO LABOR, AND BEFORE THEY CAN FIX THE RIDE SHE HAS THE BABY?
RIGHT.
AND THEN THE EXACT SAME THING HAPPENS ONE YEAR LATER?!
RIGHT!
"I'VE SPUN AROUND THAT WHEEL AT COUNTY FAIR EVERY YEAR MY LIFE," SHE EXPLAINED ROM HER HOSPITAL BED. "IT'S ONLY HERE ONE WEEKEND. I WASN'T ABOUT TO MISS IT. SURE, IT BREAKS DOWN OMETIMES, BUT WHAT DOESN'T? I BROUGHT GUY WITH ME AGAIN TO BE SAFE."
"THE FIRST TIME I DIDN'T KNOW NOTHIN' 'BOUT BIRTHING BABIES, SO IT WAS KIND OF SCARY," GUY SAID. "BUT SINCE THEN IT'S LIKE ALL ANYBODY WANTS TO TALK ABOUT IS HOW TO DELIVER BABIES, YOU KNOW? DOCTORS, EVERYBODY. SO I KNEW WHAT I WAS DOING THIS TIME, BUT IT WAS STILL KIND OF SCARY."
IS HE GOING TO BE A DOCTOR WHEN HE GROWS UP? "THAT'S WHAT EVERYBODY SAYS, SO I GUESS SO," HE ANSWERED. "BUT I DON'T EVER WANT TO DO THIS AGAIN!"
YOU KNOW, YOU REALLY SHOULD DO ANOTHER MOVIE. THE WAY YOU READ, IT'S SO NATURAL.

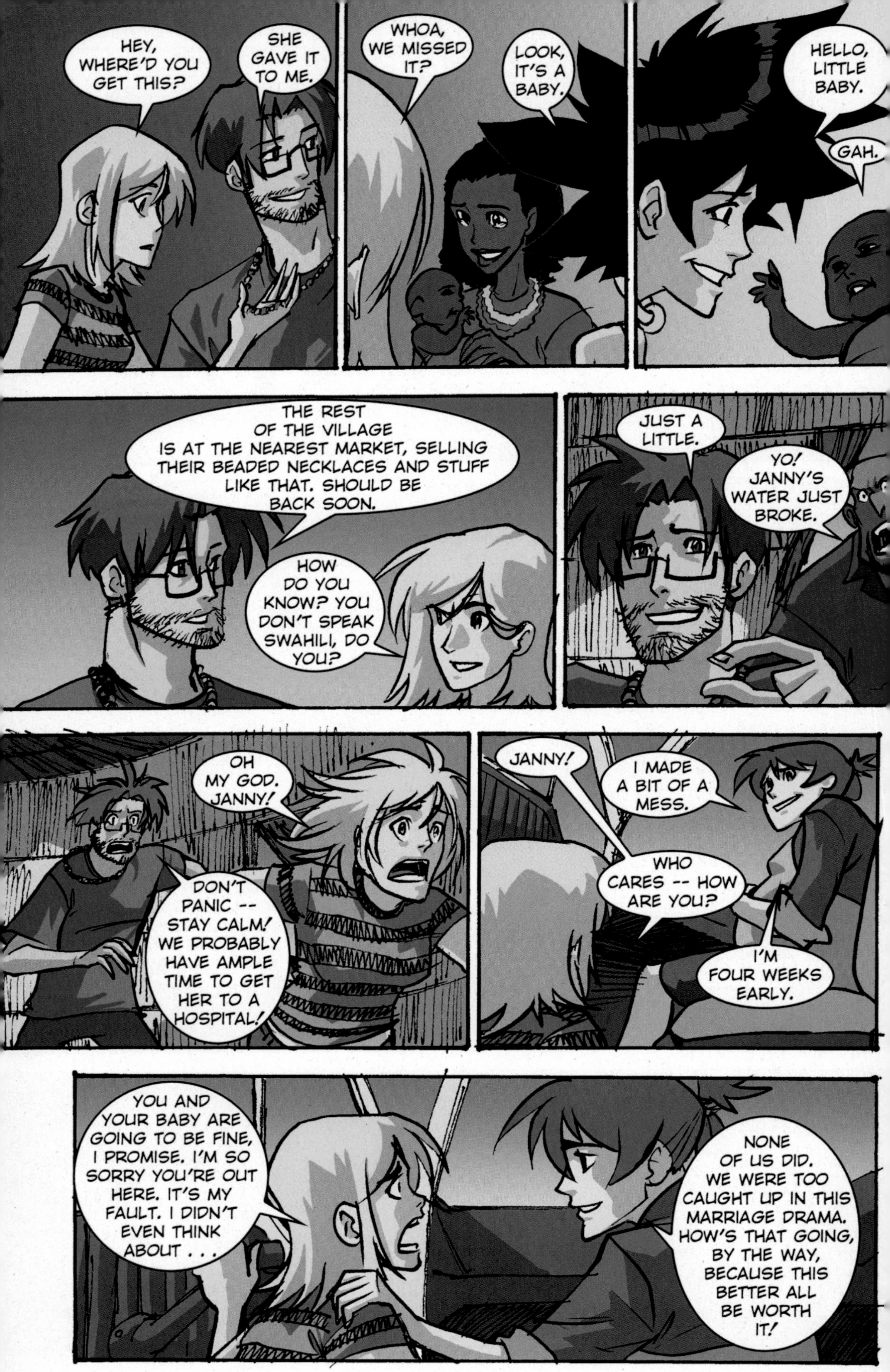
HEY, WHERE'D YOU GET THIS?
SHE GAVE IT TO ME.
WHOA, WE MISSED IT?
LOOK, IT'S A BABY.
HELLO, LITTLE BABY.
GAH.
THE REST OF THE VILLAGE IS AT THE NEAREST MARKET, SELLING THEIR BEADED NECKLACES AND STUFF LIKE THAT. SHOULD BE BACK SOON.
HOW DO YOU KNOW? YOU DON'T SPEAK SWAHILI, DO YOU?
JUST A LITTLE.
YO! JANNY'S WATER JUST BROKE.
OH MY GOD. JANNY!
DON'T PANIC -- STAY CALM! WE PROBABLY HAVE AMPLE TIME TO GET HER TO A HOSPITAL!
JANNY!
I MADE A BIT OF A MESS.
WHO CARES -- HOW ARE YOU?
I'M FOUR WEEKS EARLY.
YOU AND YOUR BABY ARE GOING TO BE FINE, I PROMISE. I'M SO SORRY YOU'RE OUT HERE. IT'S MY FAULT. I DIDN'T EVEN THINK ABOUT . . .
NONE OF US DID. WE WERE TOO CAUGHT UP IN THIS MARRIAGE DRAMA. HOW'S THAT GOING, BY THE WAY, BECAUSE THIS BETTER ALL BE WORTH IT!

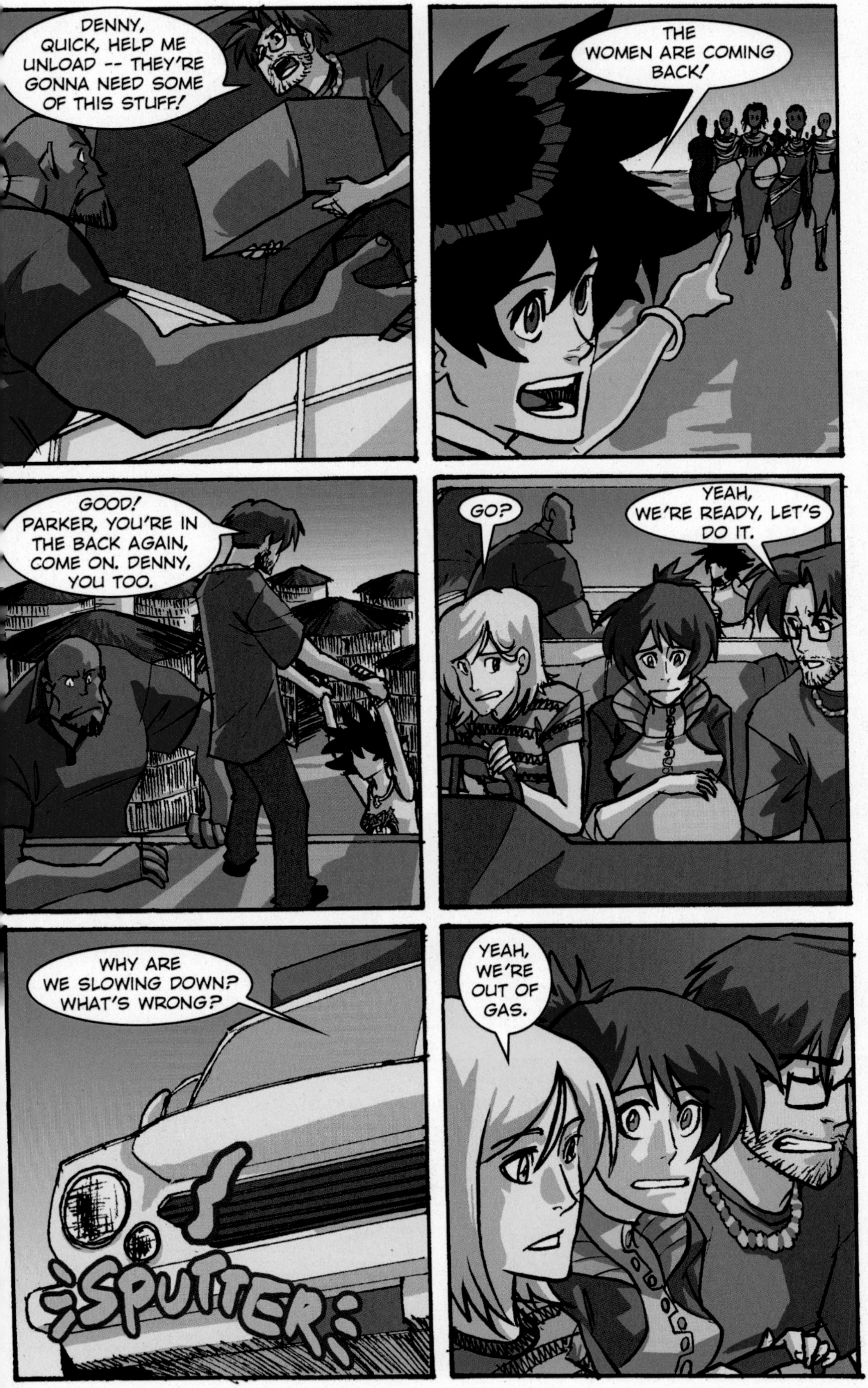
DENNY, QUICK, HELP ME UNLOAD -- THEY'RE GONNA NEED SOME OF THIS STUFF!
THE WOMEN ARE COMING BACK!
GOOD! PARKER, YOU'RE IN THE BACK AGAIN, COME ON. DENNY, YOU TOO.
GO?
YEAH, WE'RE READY, LET'S DO IT.
WHY ARE WE SLOWING DOWN? WHAT'S WRONG?
SPUTTER
YEAH, WE'RE OUT OF GAS.

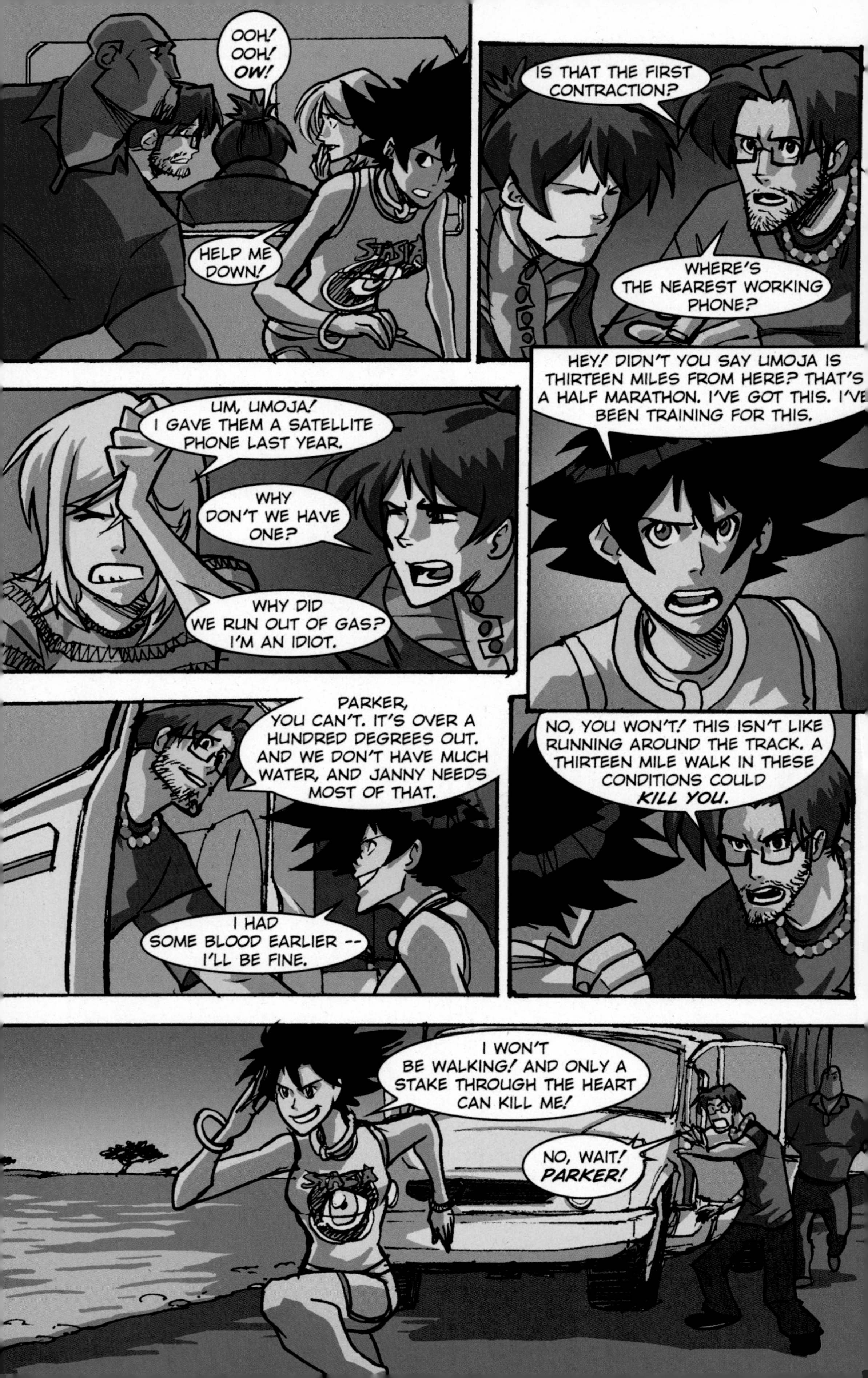
OOH! OOH! OW!
HELP ME DOWN!
IS THAT THE FIRST CONTRACTION?
WHERE'S THE NEAREST WORKING PHONE?
UM, UMOJA! I GAVE THEM A SATELLITE PHONE LAST YEAR.
WHY DON'T WE HAVE ONE?
WHY DID WE RUN OUT OF GAS? I'M AN IDIOT.
HEY! DIDN'T YOU SAY UMOJA IS THIRTEEN MILES FROM HERE? THAT'S A HALF MARATHON. I'VE GOT THIS. I'VE BEEN TRAINING FOR THIS.
PARKER, YOU CAN'T. IT'S OVER A HUNDRED DEGREES OUT. AND WE DON'T HAVE MUCH WATER, AND JANNY NEEDS MOST OF THAT.
I HAD SOME BLOOD EARLIER -- I'LL BE FINE.
NO, YOU WON'T! THIS ISN'T LIKE RUNNING AROUND THE TRACK. A THIRTEEN MILE WALK IN THESE CONDITIONS COULD KILL YOU.
I WON'T BE WALKING! AND ONLY A STAKE THROUGH THE HEART CAN KILL ME!
NO, WAIT! PARKER!

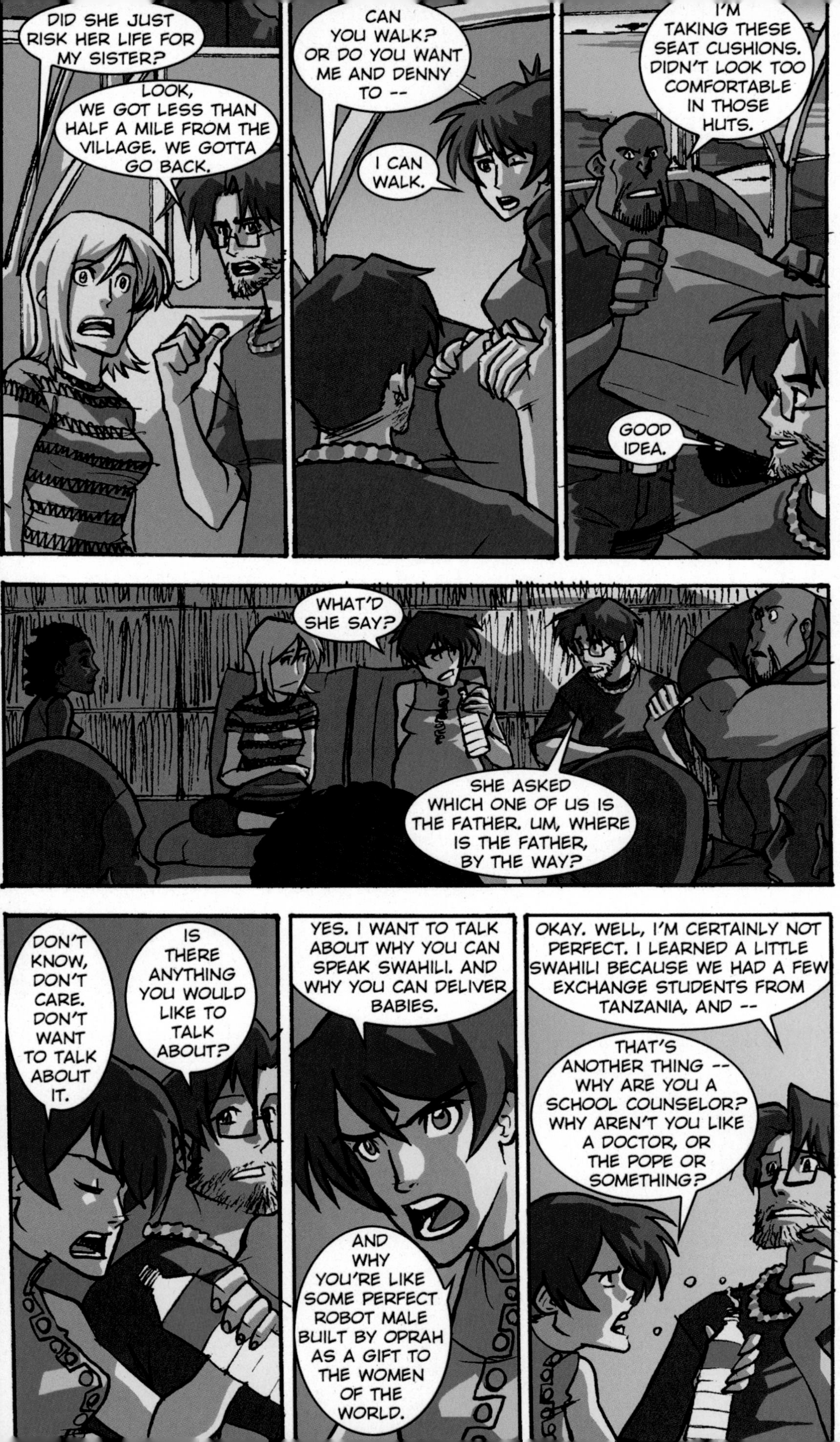
DID SHE JUST RISK HER LIFE FOR MY SISTER?
LOOK, WE GOT LESS THAN HALF A MILE FROM THE VILLAGE. WE GOTTA GO BACK.
CAN YOU WALK? OR DO YOU WANT ME AND DENNY TO --
I CAN WALK.
I'M TAKING THESE SEAT CUSHIONS. DIDN'T LOOK TOO COMFORTABLE IN THOSE HUTS.
GOOD IDEA.
WHAT'D SHE SAY?
SHE ASKED WHICH ONE OF US IS THE FATHER. UM, WHERE IS THE FATHER, BY THE WAY?
DON'T KNOW, DON'T CARE. DON'T WANT TO TALK ABOUT IT.
IS THERE ANYTHING YOU WOULD LIKE TO TALK ABOUT?
YES. I WANT TO TALK ABOUT WHY YOU CAN SPEAK SWAHILI. AND WHY YOU CAN DELIVER BABIES.
AND WHY YOU'RE LIKE SOME PERFECT ROBOT MALE BUILT BY OPRAH AS A GIFT TO THE WOMEN OF THE WORLD.
OKAY. WELL, I'M CERTAINLY NOT PERFECT. I LEARNED A LITTLE SWAHILI BECAUSE WE HAD A FEW EXCHANGE STUDENTS FROM TANZANIA, AND --
THAT'S ANOTHER THING -- WHY ARE YOU A SCHOOL COUNSELOR? WHY AREN'T YOU LIKE A DOCTOR, OR THE POPE OR SOMETHING?

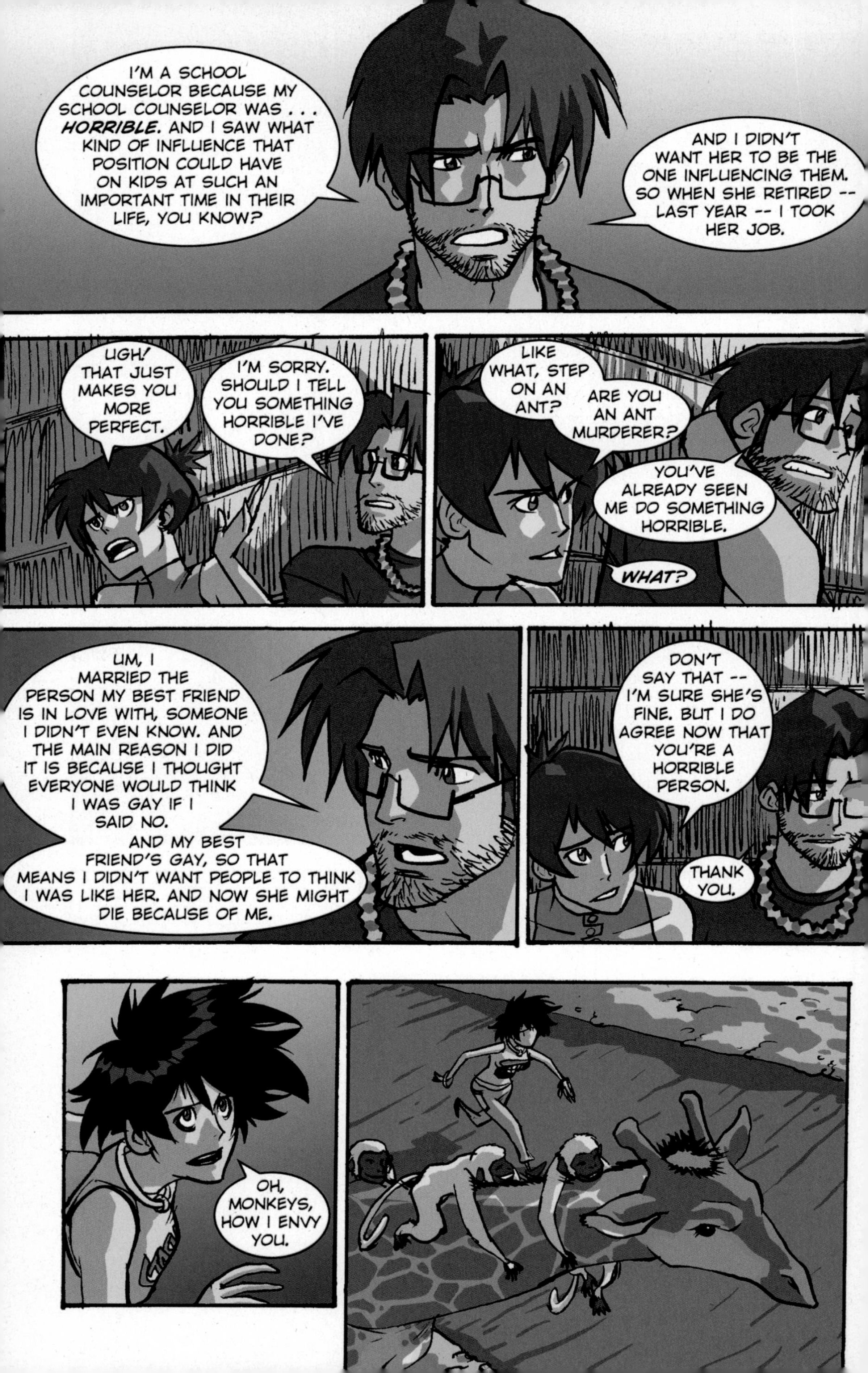
I'M A SCHOOL COUNSELOR BECAUSE MY SCHOOL COUNSELOR WAS . . . *HORRIBLE*. AND I SAW WHAT KIND OF INFLUENCE THAT POSITION COULD HAVE ON KIDS AT SUCH AN IMPORTANT TIME IN THEIR LIFE, YOU KNOW?
AND I DIDN'T WANT HER TO BE THE ONE INFLUENCING THEM. SO WHEN SHE RETIRED -- LAST YEAR -- I TOOK HER JOB.
UGH! THAT JUST MAKES YOU MORE PERFECT.
I'M SORRY. SHOULD I TELL YOU SOMETHING HORRIBLE I'VE DONE?
LIKE WHAT, STEP ON AN ANT?
ARE YOU AN ANT MURDERER?
YOU'VE ALREADY SEEN ME DO SOMETHING HORRIBLE.
WHAT?
UM, I MARRIED THE PERSON MY BEST FRIEND IS IN LOVE WITH, SOMEONE I DIDN'T EVEN KNOW. AND THE MAIN REASON I DID IT IS BECAUSE I THOUGHT EVERYONE WOULD THINK I WAS GAY IF I SAID NO.
AND MY BEST FRIEND'S GAY, SO THAT MEANS I DIDN'T WANT PEOPLE TO THINK I WAS LIKE HER. AND NOW SHE MIGHT DIE BECAUSE OF ME.
DON'T SAY THAT -- I'M SURE SHE'S FINE. BUT I DO AGREE NOW THAT YOU'RE A HORRIBLE PERSON.
THANK YOU.
OH, MONKEYS, HOW I ENVY YOU.

LET'S ALL JUST SIT IN SILENCE UNTIL MY NEXT CONTRACTION, ALL RIGHT? GUY, TRANSLATE.

SHHHHH.

HEY, WHAT'S THAT?

I SAID SIT IN SILENCE!

I HEAR SOMETHING! IT'S OUTSIDE!

YES! PARKER!

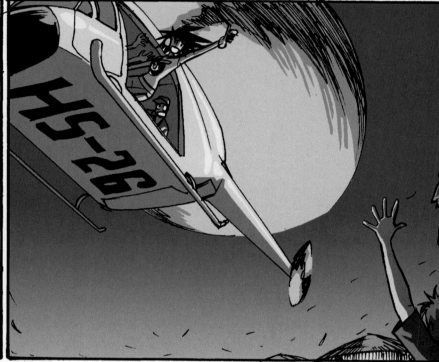

IT'S BEEN LESS THAN TWO HOURS!

THAT'S BECAUSE I'M AWESOME.

THERE'S ONLY ROOM FOR JANNY AND STASIA, BUT I BROUGHT SOME GAS FOR THE TRUCK. CAN I DRIVE?

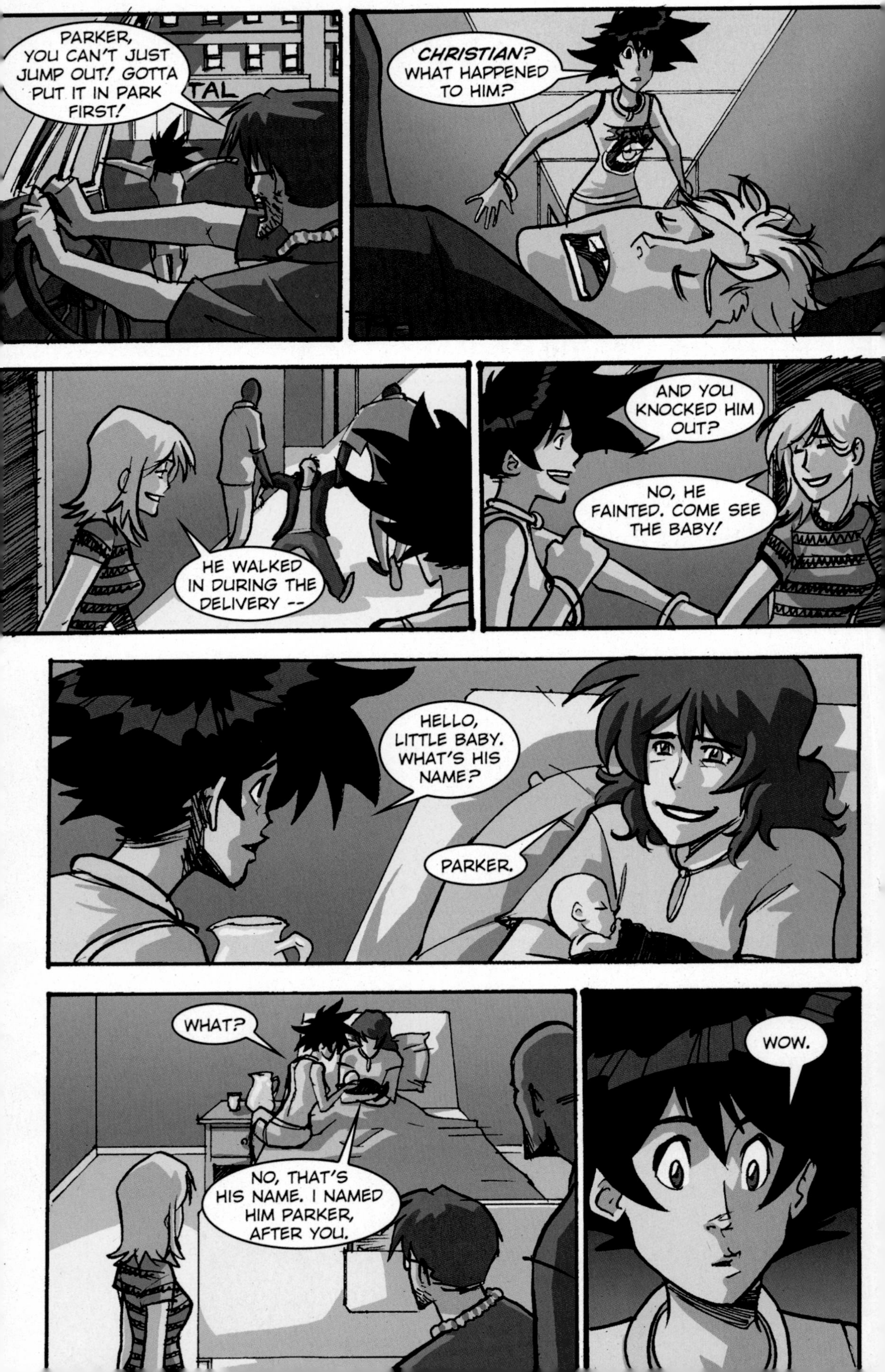
PARKER, YOU CAN'T JUST JUMP OUT! GOTTA PUT IT IN PARK FIRST!
TAL
CHRISTIAN? WHAT HAPPENED TO HIM?
HE WALKED IN DURING THE DELIVERY --
AND YOU KNOCKED HIM OUT?
NO, HE FAINTED. COME SEE THE BABY!
HELLO, LITTLE BABY. WHAT'S HIS NAME?
PARKER.
WHAT?
NO, THAT'S HIS NAME. I NAMED HIM PARKER, AFTER YOU.
WOW.

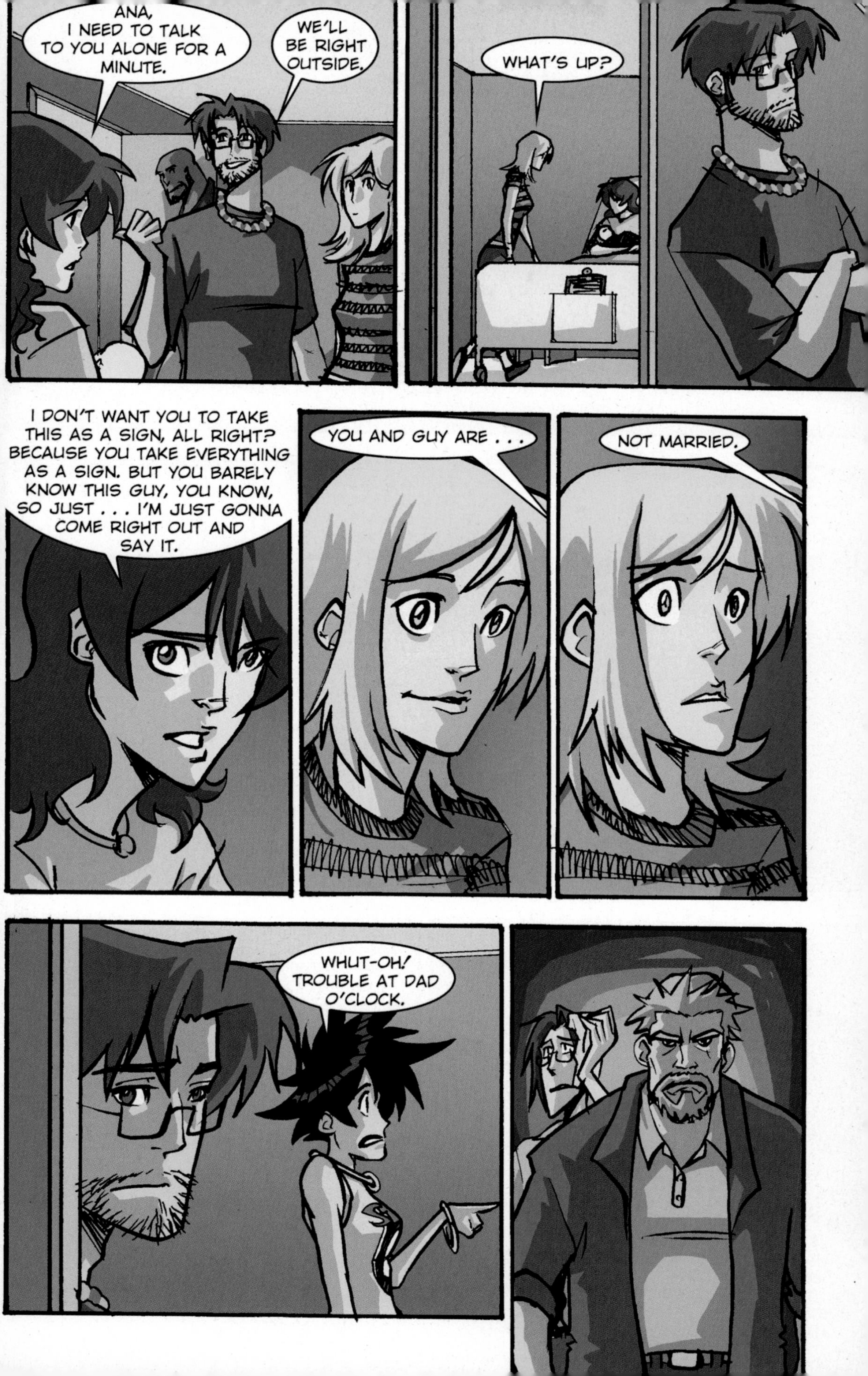
ANA, I NEED TO TALK TO YOU ALONE FOR A MINUTE.
WE'LL BE RIGHT OUTSIDE.
WHAT'S UP?
I DON'T WANT YOU TO TAKE THIS AS A SIGN, ALL RIGHT? BECAUSE YOU TAKE EVERYTHING AS A SIGN. BUT YOU BARELY KNOW THIS GUY, YOU KNOW, SO JUST . . . I'M JUST GONNA COME RIGHT OUT AND SAY IT.
YOU AND GUY ARE . . .
NOT MARRIED.
WHUT-OH! TROUBLE AT DAD O'CLOCK.

MR. TYLER, GOOD TO SEE YOU! JANNY WAS JUST MOVED TO ANOTHER ROOM DOWN THIS WAY -- LET ME TAKE YOU THERE.

I WAS TOLD --

YEAH, IT JUST HAPPENED. THE PRESS FOUND US AND THEY HAD TO FIND A MORE SECURE AREA.

RICHMOND, STAY WITH THAT ONE. DON'T LET HER NEAR MY CHILDREN!

YOUR CHILDREN ARE FINE, BY THE WAY, AND YOUR GRANDSON. CONGRATULATIONS.

NO THANKS TO YOU, I'M SURE. HE SHOULD HAVE BEEN BORN IN AMERICA, A MONTH FROM NOW!

YES, I --

GUY COOPER, THE APPARENT HUSBAND OF THE BIGGEST POP STAR IN THE WORLD -- WHO THE HECK IS HE? WE'VE GOT HIS FRIENDS AND FAMILY FOR THE HOUR, AND WE'LL BE JOINED LATER BY SOME OF HIS STUDENTS.

DON'T STAND THERE, BOY! MOVE!

OH, SORRY. UH, THIS WAY!

I WONDER IF MY SISTER'S ON THAT SHOW. SHE CAN SOMETIMES, UH -- OH, IT APPEARS TO BE ON EVERYONE'S TELEVISION. AND THERE'S DAISY, OF COURSE.

I CAN TELL YOU EVERYTHING YOU NEED TO KNOW ABOUT GUY.

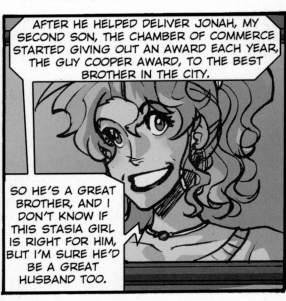

AFTER HE HELPED DELIVER JONAH, MY SECOND SON, THE CHAMBER OF COMMERCE STARTED GIVING OUT AN AWARD EACH YEAR, THE GUY COOPER AWARD, TO THE BEST BROTHER IN THE CITY.

SO HE'S A GREAT BROTHER, AND I DON'T KNOW IF THIS STASIA GIRL IS RIGHT FOR HIM, BUT I'M SURE HE'D BE A GREAT HUSBAND TOO.

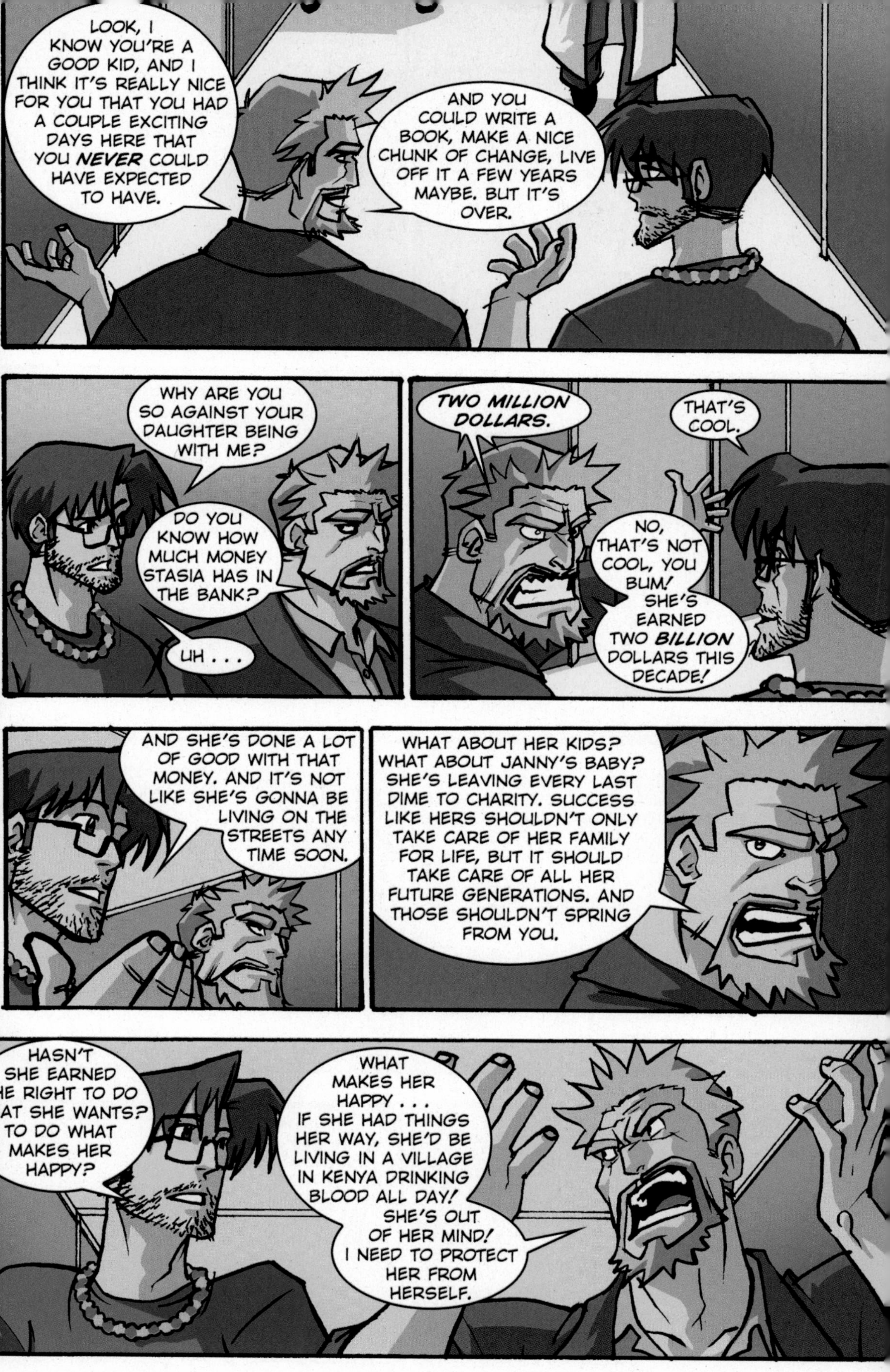
LOOK, I KNOW YOU'RE A GOOD KID, AND I THINK IT'S REALLY NICE FOR YOU THAT YOU HAD A COUPLE EXCITING DAYS HERE THAT YOU NEVER COULD HAVE EXPECTED TO HAVE.
AND YOU COULD WRITE A BOOK, MAKE A NICE CHUNK OF CHANGE, LIVE OFF IT A FEW YEARS MAYBE. BUT IT'S OVER.
WHY ARE YOU SO AGAINST YOUR DAUGHTER BEING WITH ME?
DO YOU KNOW HOW MUCH MONEY STASIA HAS IN THE BANK?
UH . . .
TWO MILLION DOLLARS.
THAT'S COOL.
NO, THAT'S NOT COOL, YOU BUM! SHE'S EARNED TWO BILLION DOLLARS THIS DECADE!
AND SHE'S DONE A LOT OF GOOD WITH THAT MONEY. AND IT'S NOT LIKE SHE'S GONNA BE LIVING ON THE STREETS ANY TIME SOON.
WHAT ABOUT HER KIDS? WHAT ABOUT JANNY'S BABY? SHE'S LEAVING EVERY LAST DIME TO CHARITY. SUCCESS LIKE HERS SHOULDN'T ONLY TAKE CARE OF HER FAMILY FOR LIFE, BUT IT SHOULD TAKE CARE OF ALL HER FUTURE GENERATIONS. AND THOSE SHOULDN'T SPRING FROM YOU.
HASN'T SHE EARNED HE RIGHT TO DO HAT SHE WANTS? TO DO WHAT MAKES HER HAPPY?
WHAT MAKES HER HAPPY . . . IF SHE HAD THINGS HER WAY, SHE'D BE LIVING IN A VILLAGE IN KENYA DRINKING BLOOD ALL DAY! SHE'S OUT OF HER MIND! I NEED TO PROTECT HER FROM HERSELF.

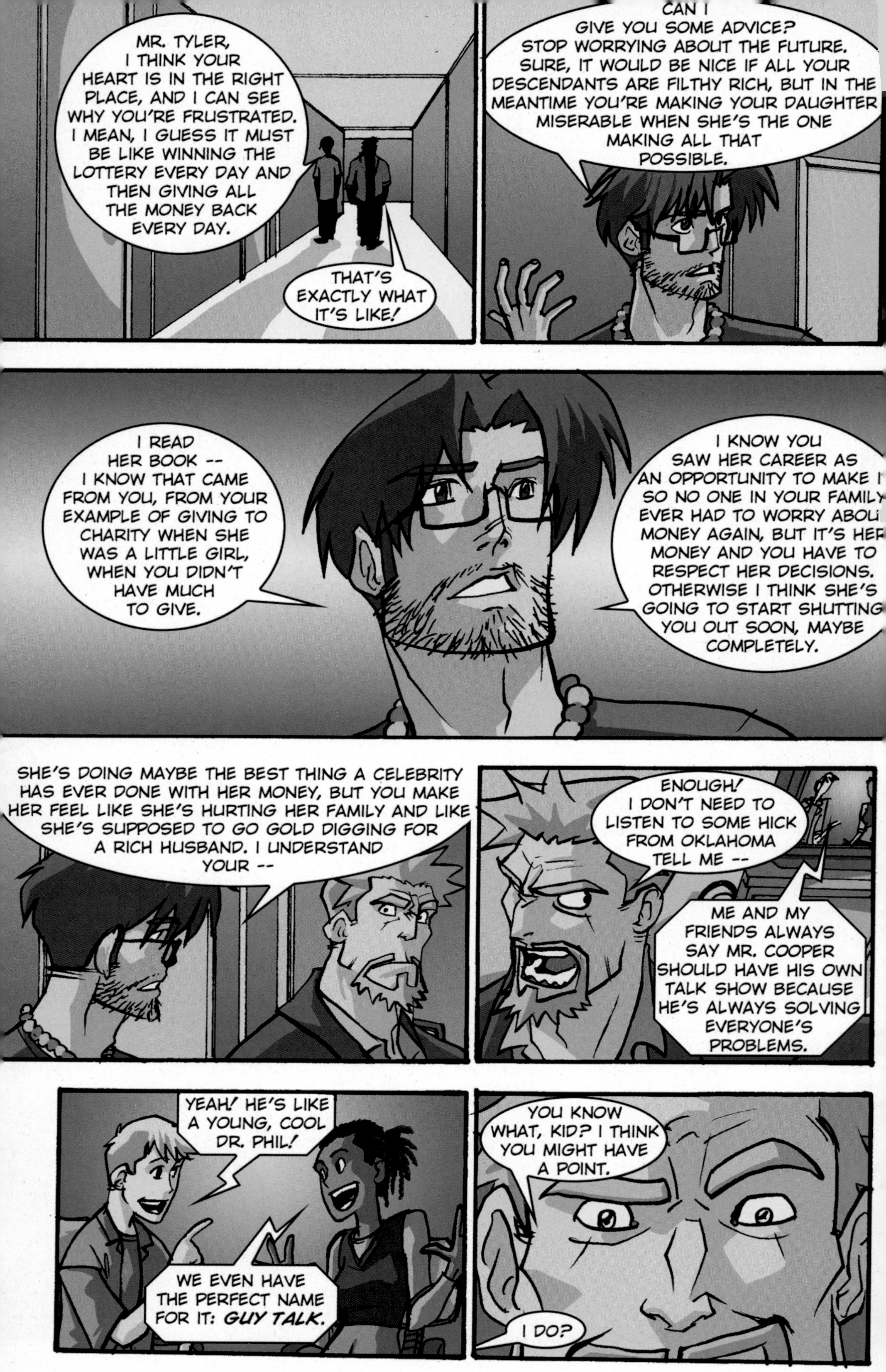
MR. TYLER, I THINK YOUR HEART IS IN THE RIGHT PLACE, AND I CAN SEE WHY YOU'RE FRUSTRATED. I MEAN, I GUESS IT MUST BE LIKE WINNING THE LOTTERY EVERY DAY AND THEN GIVING ALL THE MONEY BACK EVERY DAY.
THAT'S EXACTLY WHAT IT'S LIKE!
CAN I GIVE YOU SOME ADVICE? STOP WORRYING ABOUT THE FUTURE. SURE, IT WOULD BE NICE IF ALL YOUR DESCENDANTS ARE FILTHY RICH, BUT IN THE MEANTIME YOU'RE MAKING YOUR DAUGHTER MISERABLE WHEN SHE'S THE ONE MAKING ALL THAT POSSIBLE.
I READ HER BOOK -- I KNOW THAT CAME FROM YOU, FROM YOUR EXAMPLE OF GIVING TO CHARITY WHEN SHE WAS A LITTLE GIRL, WHEN YOU DIDN'T HAVE MUCH TO GIVE.
I KNOW YOU SAW HER CAREER AS AN OPPORTUNITY TO MAKE IT SO NO ONE IN YOUR FAMILY EVER HAD TO WORRY ABOUT MONEY AGAIN, BUT IT'S HER MONEY AND YOU HAVE TO RESPECT HER DECISIONS. OTHERWISE I THINK SHE'S GOING TO START SHUTTING YOU OUT SOON, MAYBE COMPLETELY.
SHE'S DOING MAYBE THE BEST THING A CELEBRITY HAS EVER DONE WITH HER MONEY, BUT YOU MAKE HER FEEL LIKE SHE'S HURTING HER FAMILY AND LIKE SHE'S SUPPOSED TO GO GOLD DIGGING FOR A RICH HUSBAND. I UNDERSTAND YOUR --
ENOUGH! I DON'T NEED TO LISTEN TO SOME HICK FROM OKLAHOMA TELL ME --
ME AND MY FRIENDS ALWAYS SAY MR. COOPER SHOULD HAVE HIS OWN TALK SHOW BECAUSE HE'S ALWAYS SOLVING EVERYONE'S PROBLEMS.
YEAH! HE'S LIKE A YOUNG, COOL DR. PHIL!
WE EVEN HAVE THE PERFECT NAME FOR IT: *GUY TALK*.
YOU KNOW WHAT, KID? I THINK YOU MIGHT HAVE A POINT.
I DO?

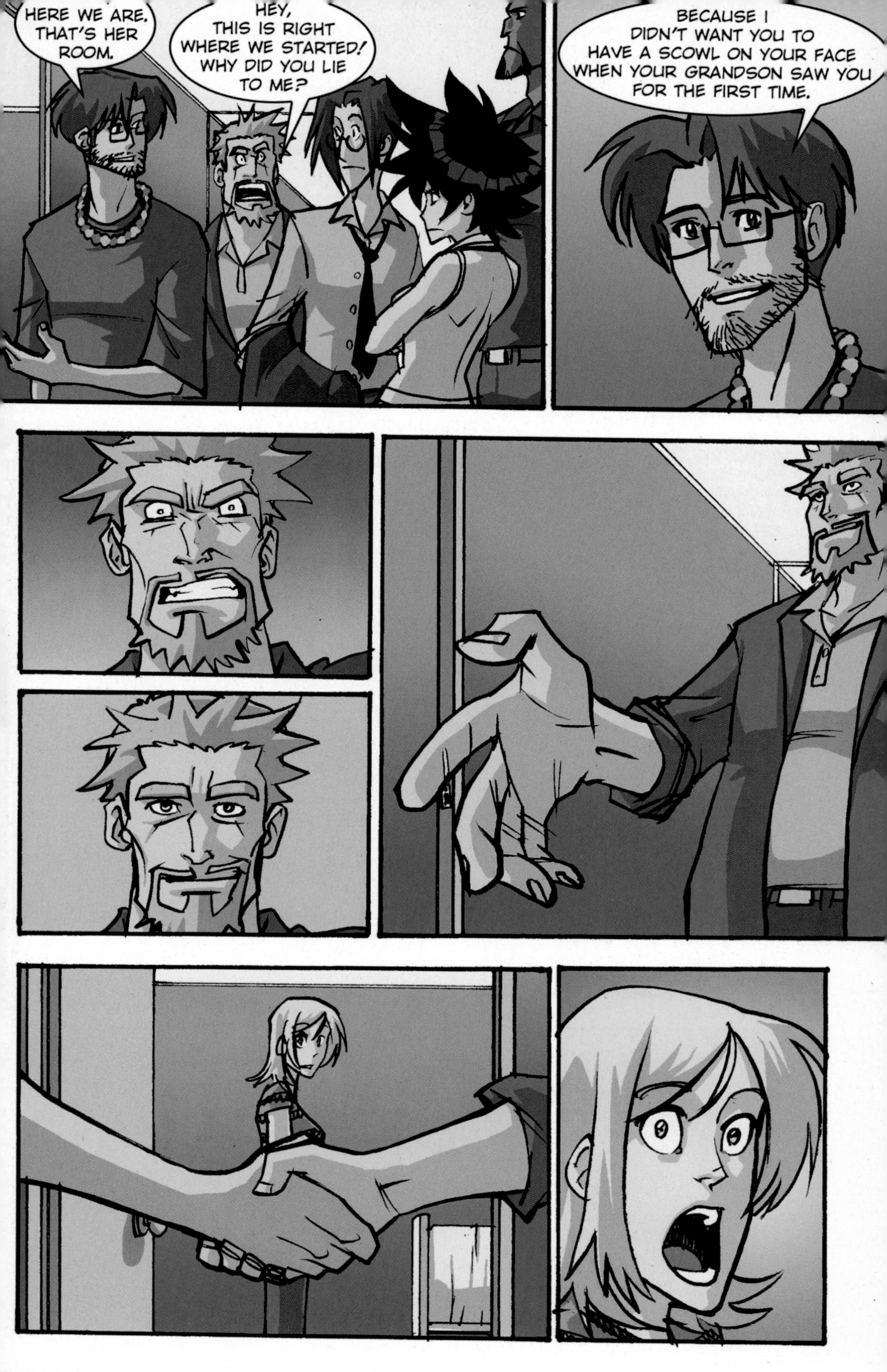
HERE WE ARE. THAT'S HER ROOM.
HEY, THIS IS RIGHT WHERE WE STARTED! WHY DID YOU LIE TO ME?
BECAUSE I DIDN'T WANT YOU TO HAVE A SCOWL ON YOUR FACE WHEN YOUR GRANDSON SAW YOU FOR THE FIRST TIME.

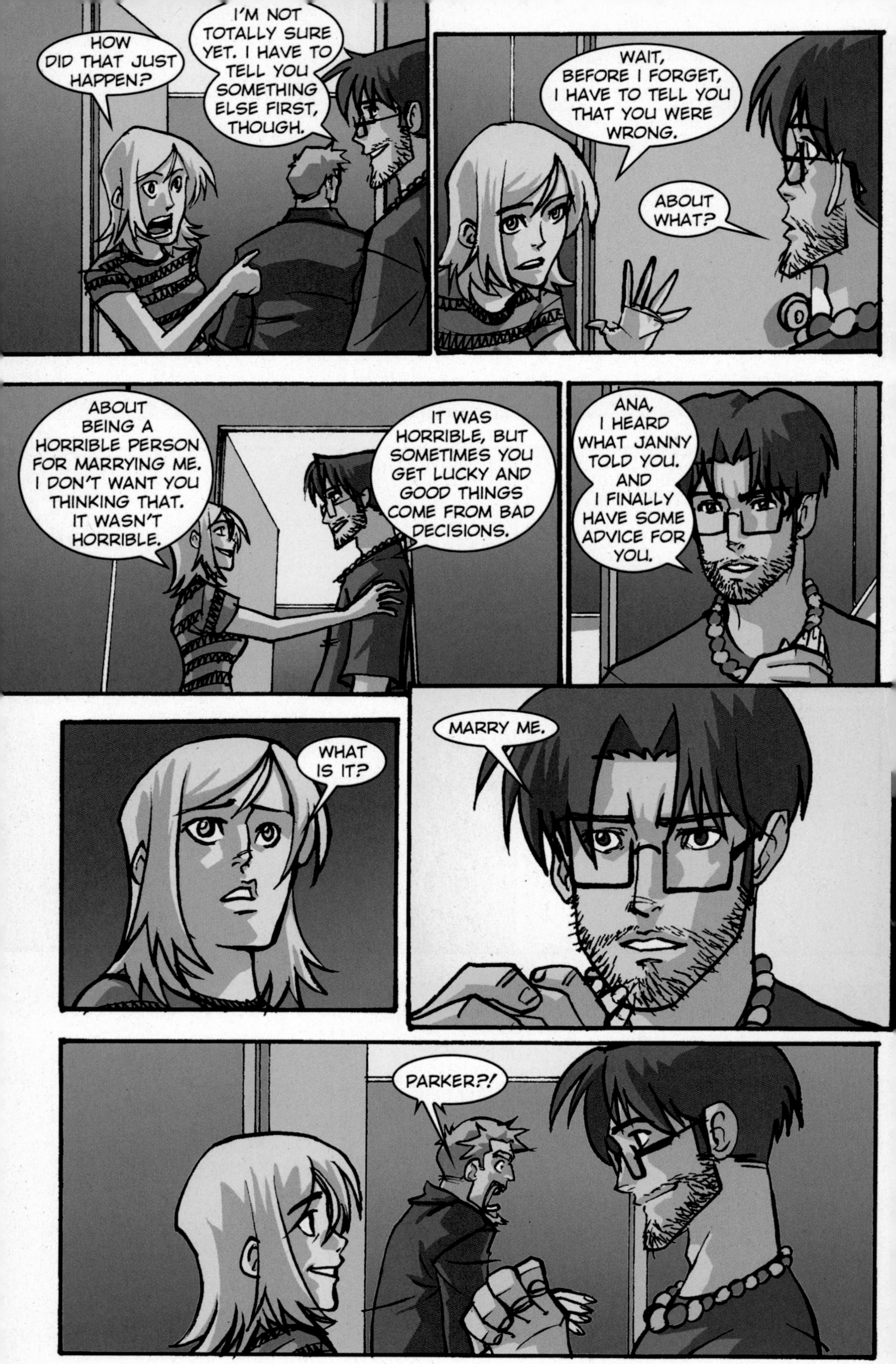
HOW DID THAT JUST HAPPEN?
I'M NOT TOTALLY SURE YET. I HAVE TO TELL YOU SOMETHING ELSE FIRST, THOUGH.
WAIT, BEFORE I FORGET, I HAVE TO TELL YOU THAT YOU WERE WRONG.
ABOUT WHAT?
ABOUT BEING A HORRIBLE PERSON FOR MARRYING ME. I DON'T WANT YOU THINKING THAT. IT WASN'T HORRIBLE.
IT WAS HORRIBLE, BUT SOMETIMES YOU GET LUCKY AND GOOD THINGS COME FROM BAD DECISIONS.
ANA, I HEARD WHAT JANNY TOLD YOU. AND I FINALLY HAVE SOME ADVICE FOR YOU.
WHAT IS IT?
MARRY ME.
PARKER?!

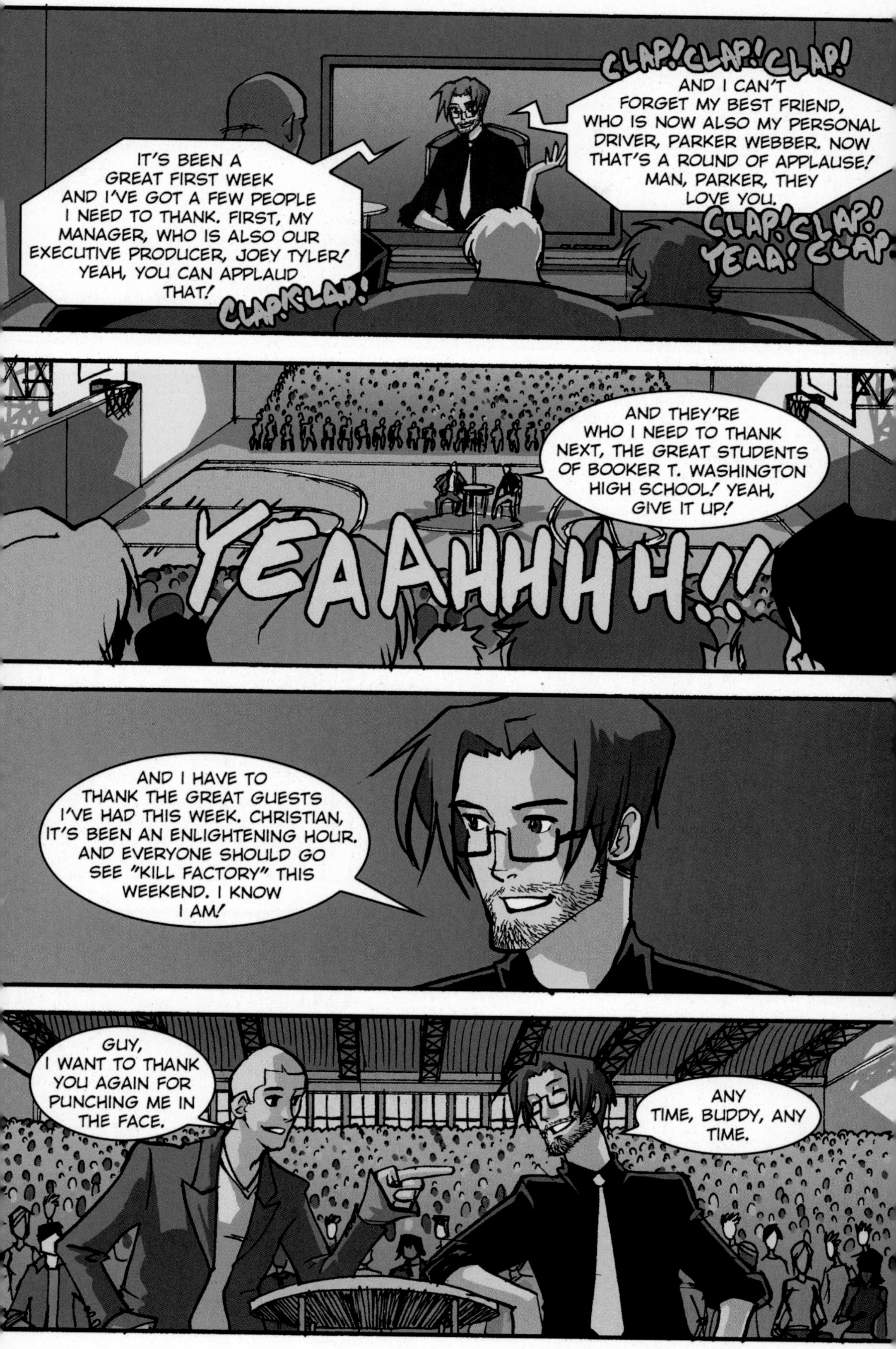
CLAP! CLAP! CLAP!
IT'S BEEN A GREAT FIRST WEEK AND I'VE GOT A FEW PEOPLE I NEED TO THANK. FIRST, MY MANAGER, WHO IS ALSO OUR EXECUTIVE PRODUCER, JOEY TYLER! YEAH, YOU CAN APPLAUD THAT!
CLAP! CLAP!
AND I CAN'T FORGET MY BEST FRIEND, WHO IS NOW ALSO MY PERSONAL DRIVER, PARKER WEBBER. NOW THAT'S A ROUND OF APPLAUSE! MAN, PARKER, THEY LOVE YOU.
CLAP! CLAP! YEAA! CLAP.
AND THEY'RE WHO I NEED TO THANK NEXT, THE GREAT STUDENTS OF BOOKER T. WASHINGTON HIGH SCHOOL! YEAH, GIVE IT UP!
YEAAHHHH!!!
AND I HAVE TO THANK THE GREAT GUESTS I'VE HAD THIS WEEK. CHRISTIAN, IT'S BEEN AN ENLIGHTENING HOUR. AND EVERYONE SHOULD GO SEE "KILL FACTORY" THIS WEEKEND. I KNOW I AM!
GUY, I WANT TO THANK YOU AGAIN FOR PUNCHING ME IN THE FACE.
ANY TIME, BUDDY, ANY TIME.

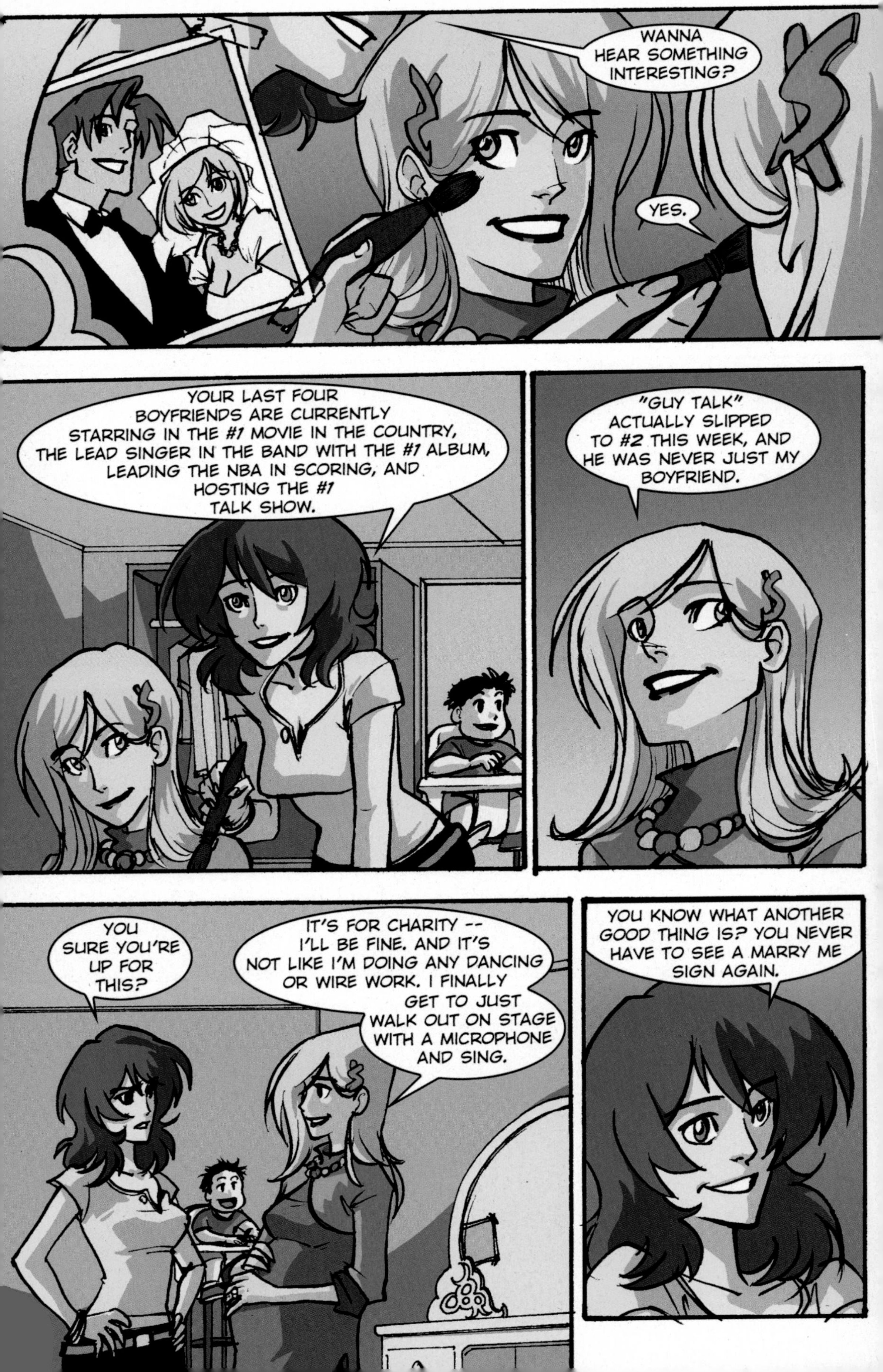
WANNA HEAR SOMETHING INTERESTING?
YES.
YOUR LAST FOUR BOYFRIENDS ARE CURRENTLY STARRING IN THE #1 MOVIE IN THE COUNTRY, THE LEAD SINGER IN THE BAND WITH THE #1 ALBUM, LEADING THE NBA IN SCORING, AND HOSTING THE #1 TALK SHOW.
"GUY TALK" ACTUALLY SLIPPED TO #2 THIS WEEK, AND HE WAS NEVER JUST MY BOYFRIEND.
YOU SURE YOU'RE UP FOR THIS?
IT'S FOR CHARITY -- I'LL BE FINE. AND IT'S NOT LIKE I'M DOING ANY DANCING OR WIRE WORK. I FINALLY GET TO JUST WALK OUT ON STAGE WITH A MICROPHONE AND SING.
YOU KNOW WHAT ANOTHER GOOD THING IS? YOU NEVER HAVE TO SEE A MARRY ME SIGN AGAIN.

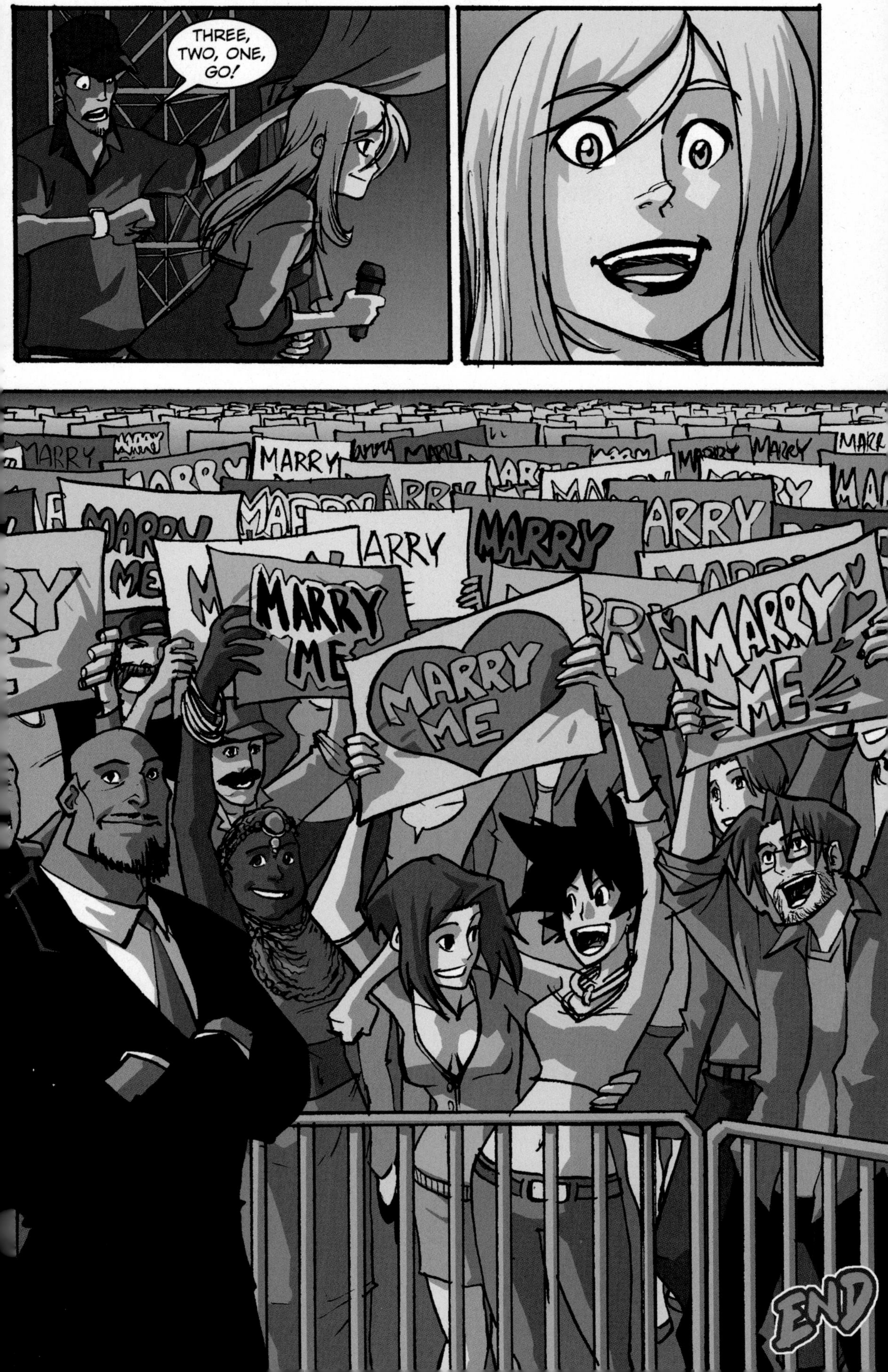
THREE, TWO, ONE, GO!
MARRY ME
MARRY ME
MARRY ME
MARRY ME
END

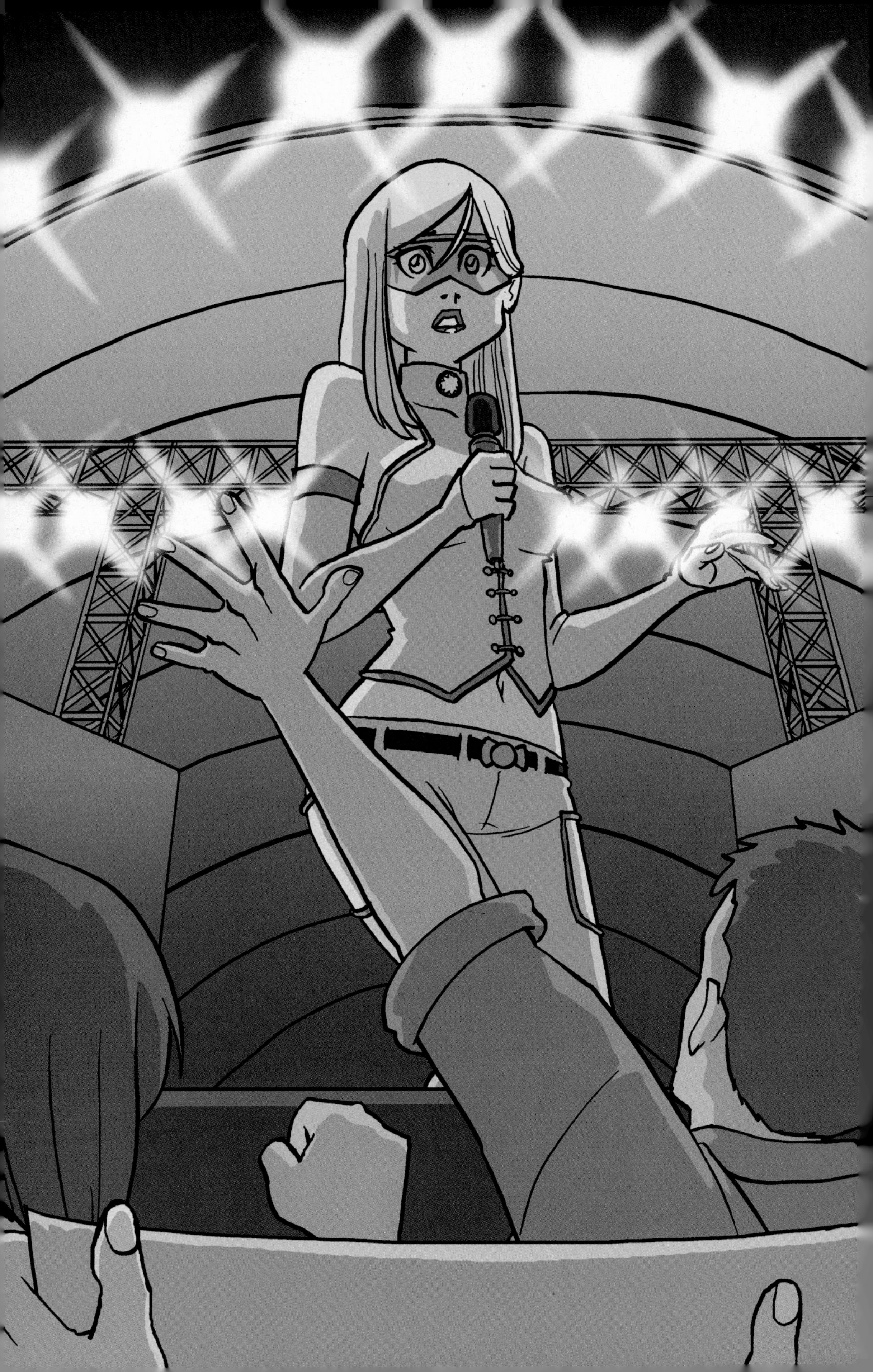

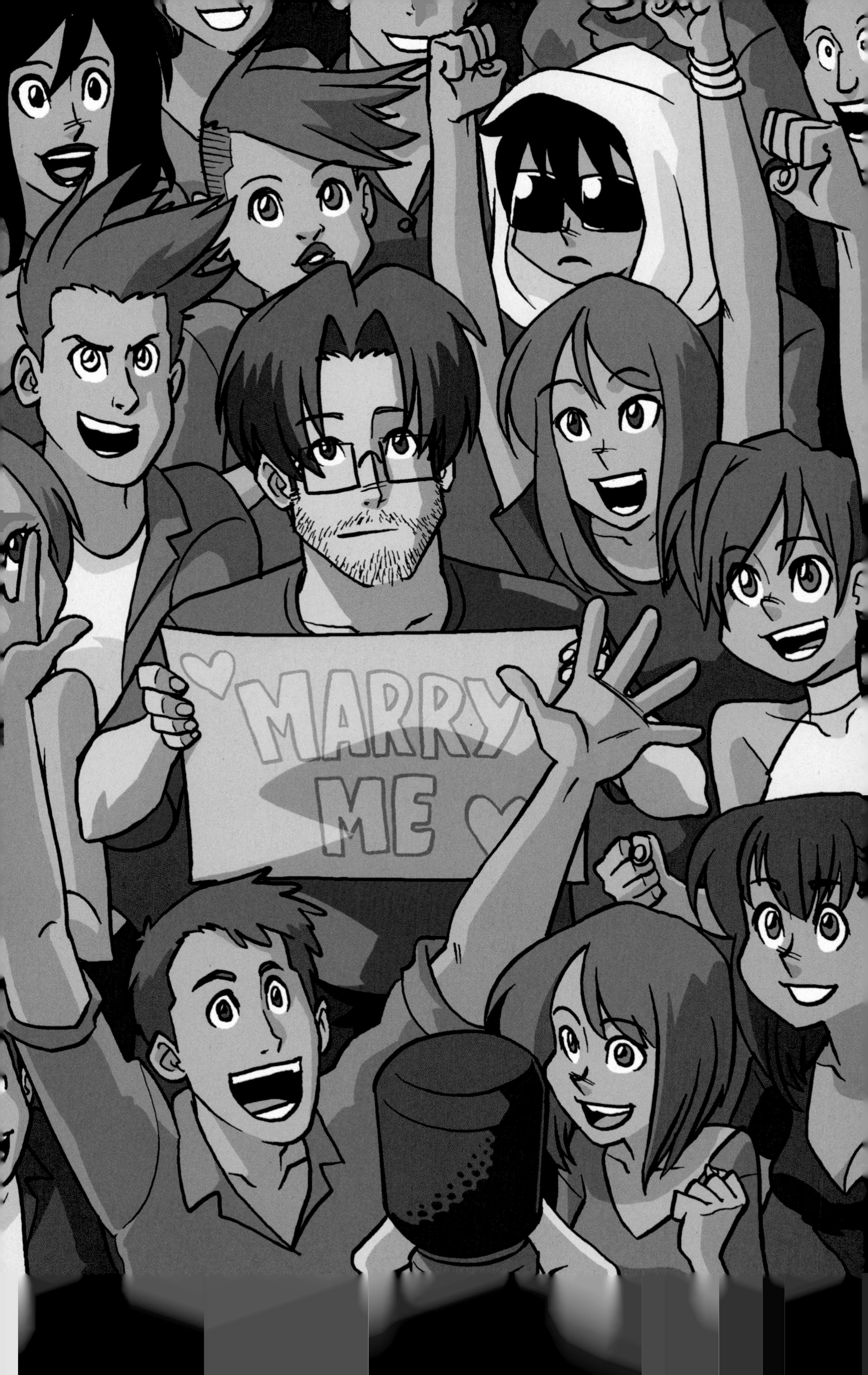
MARRY ME

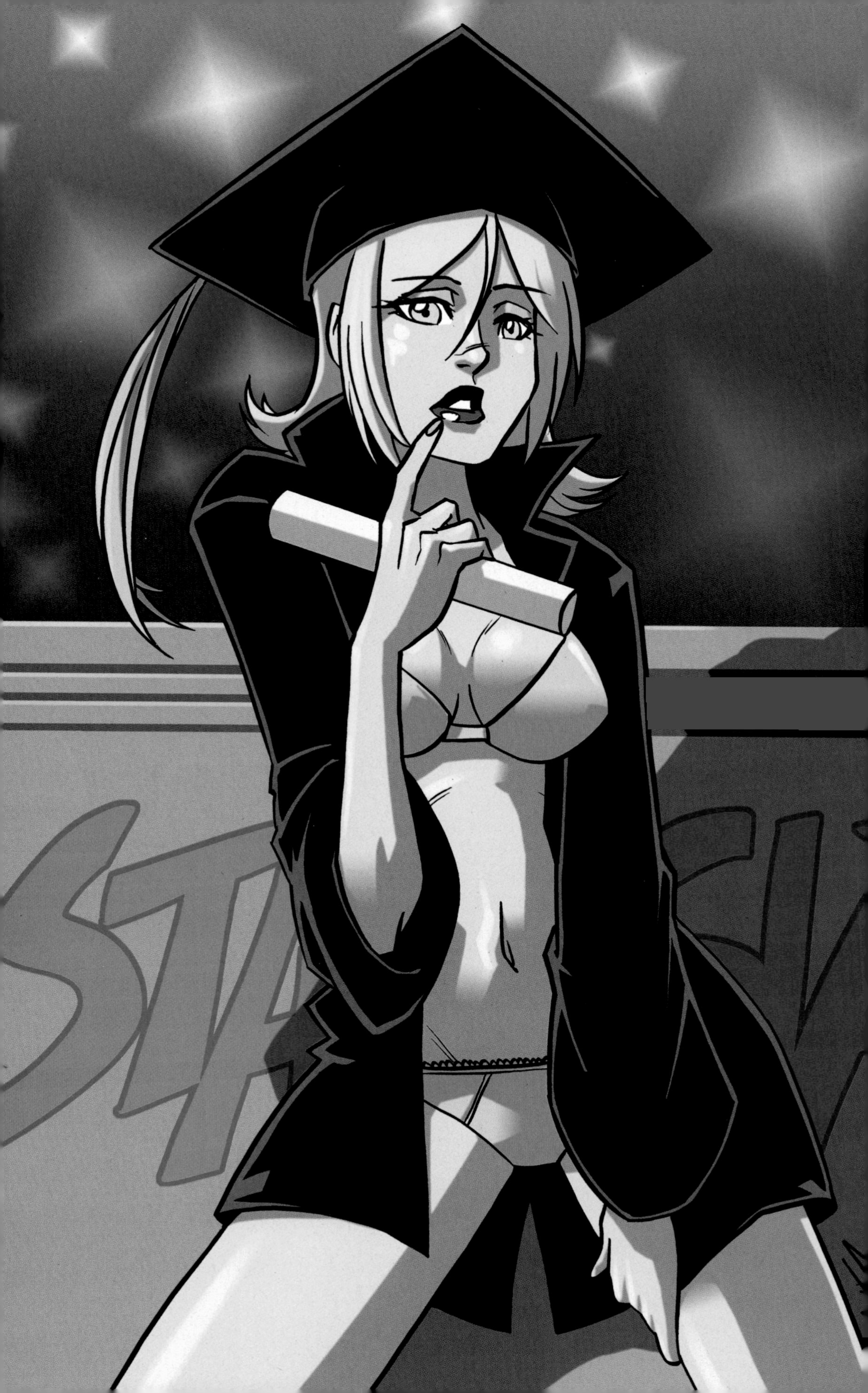

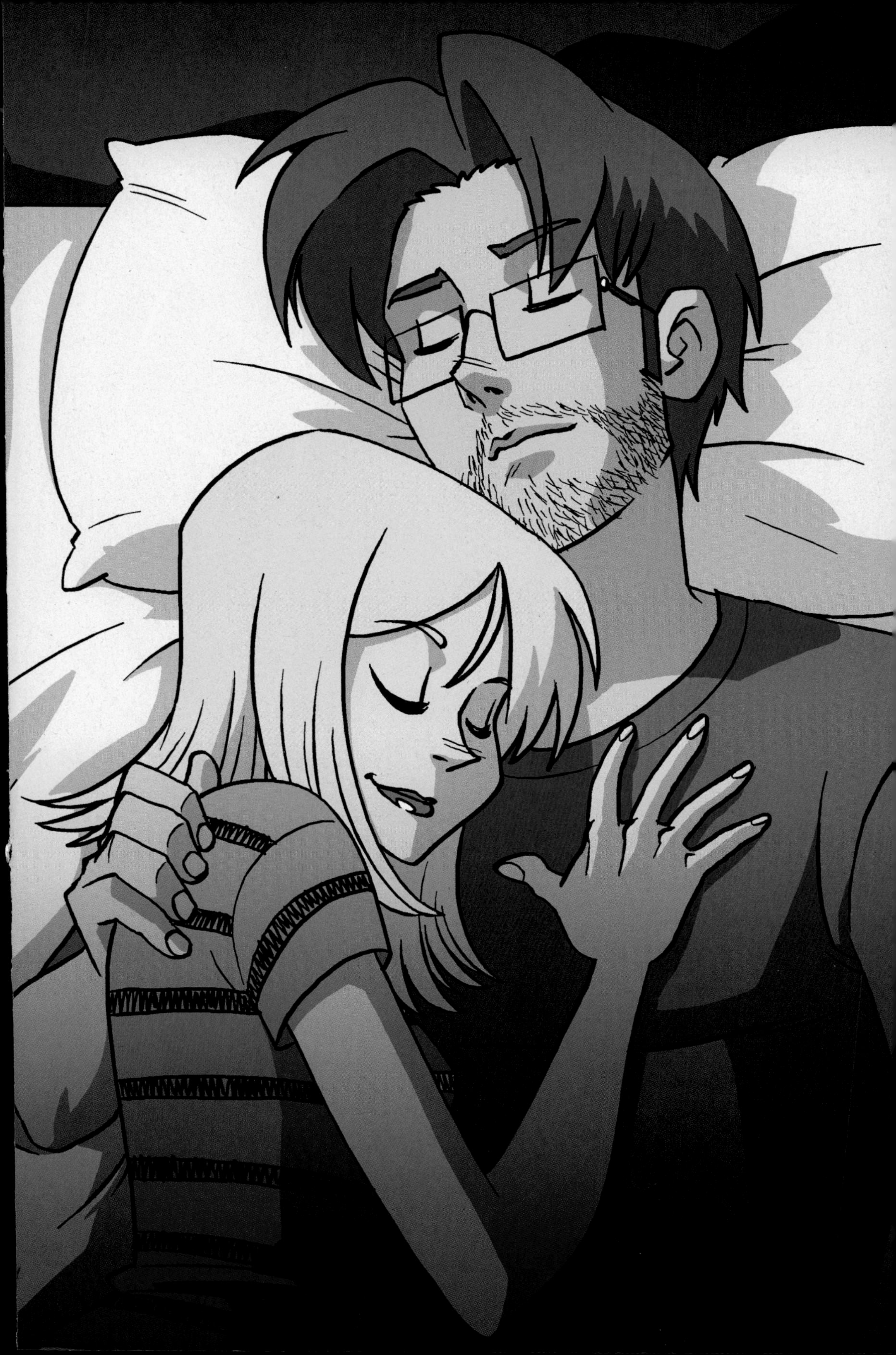

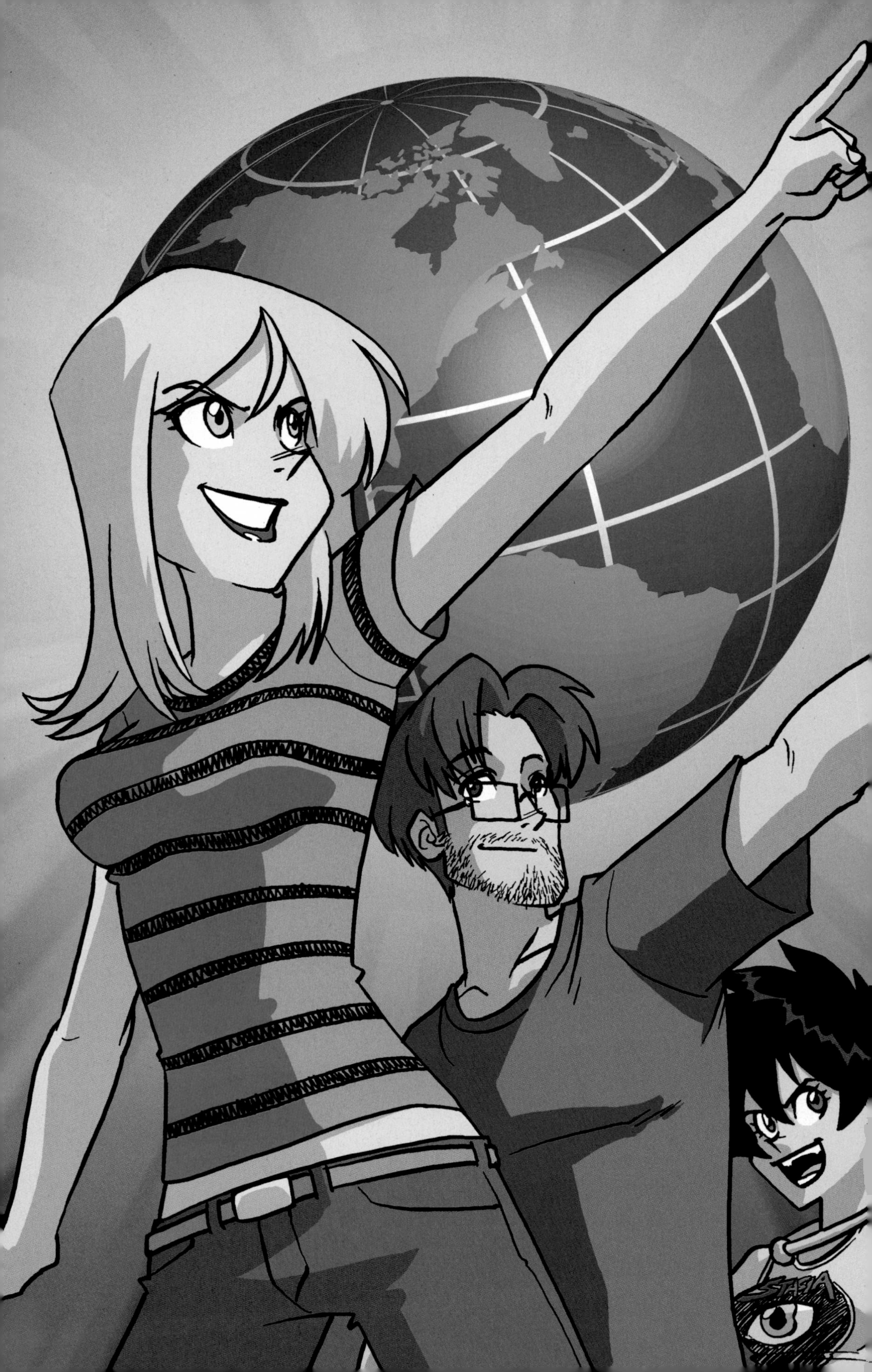
STASIA

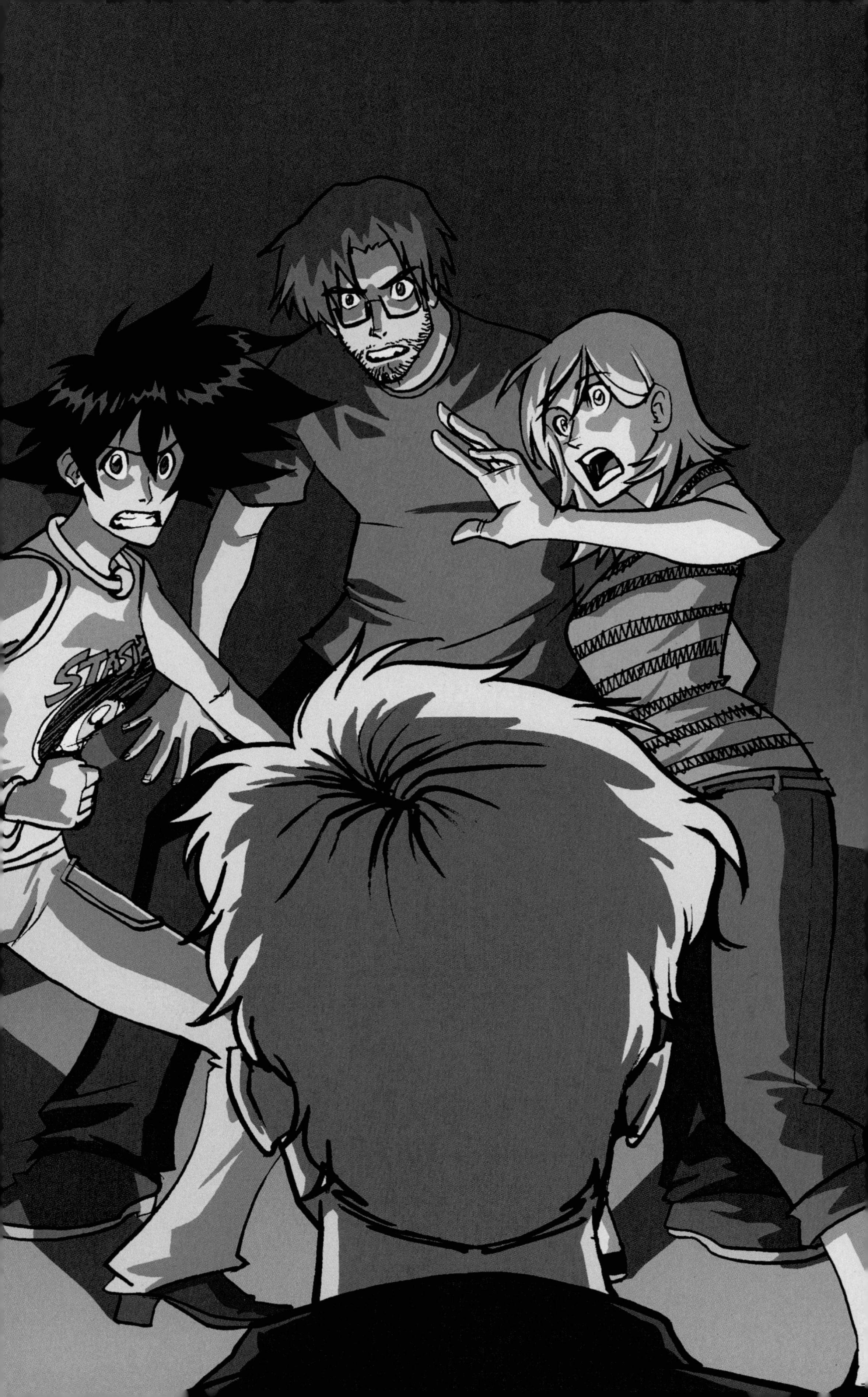

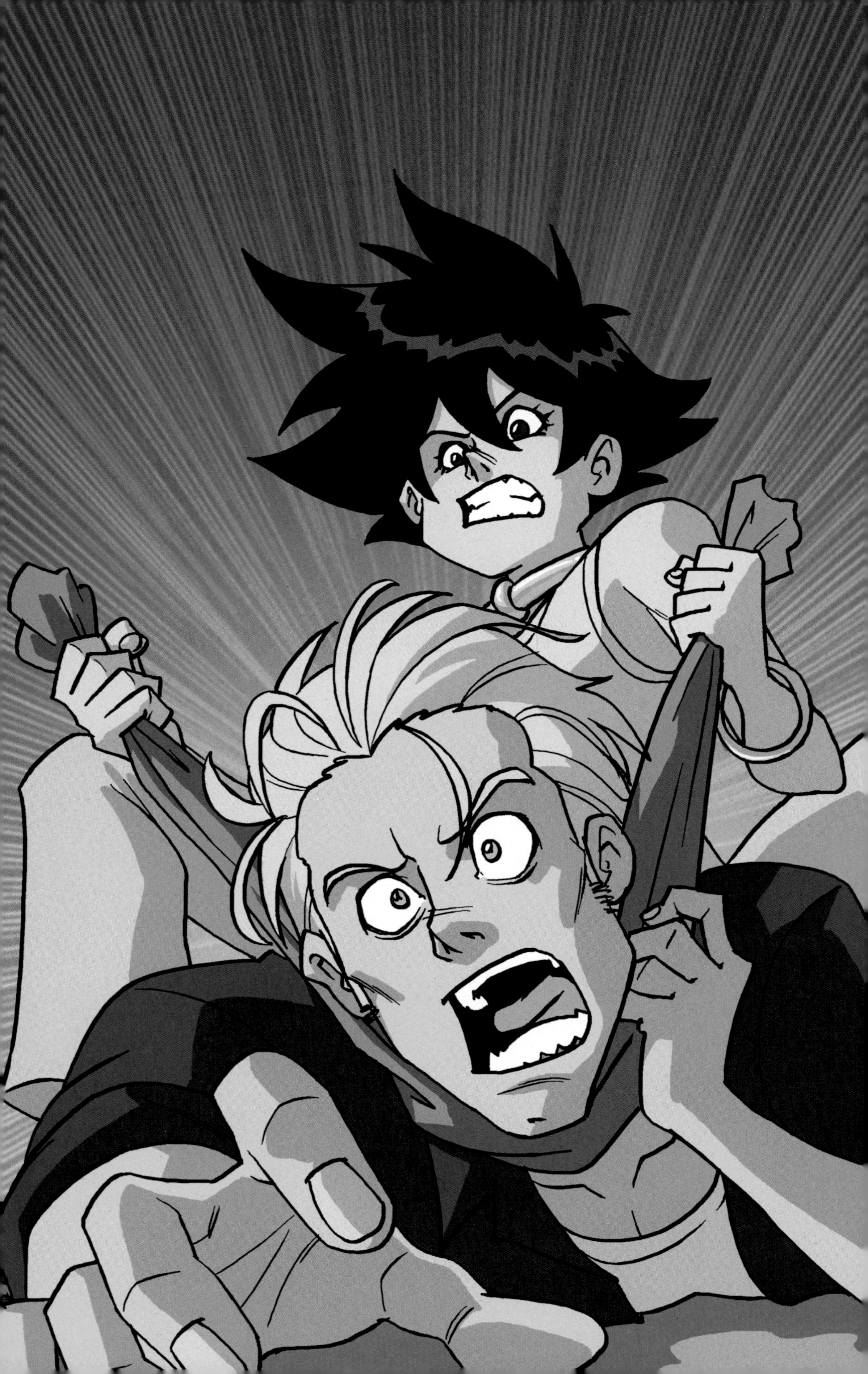

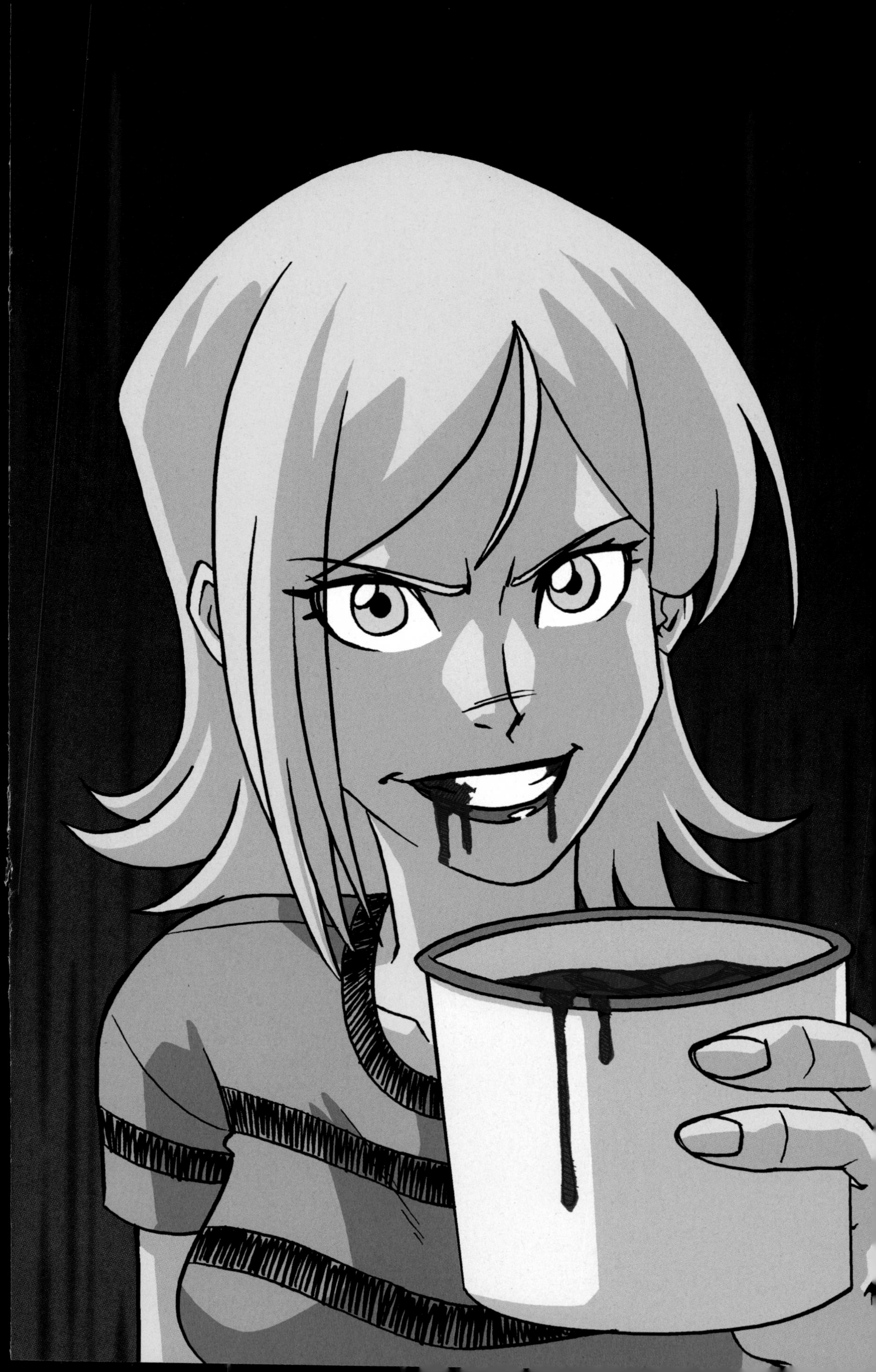

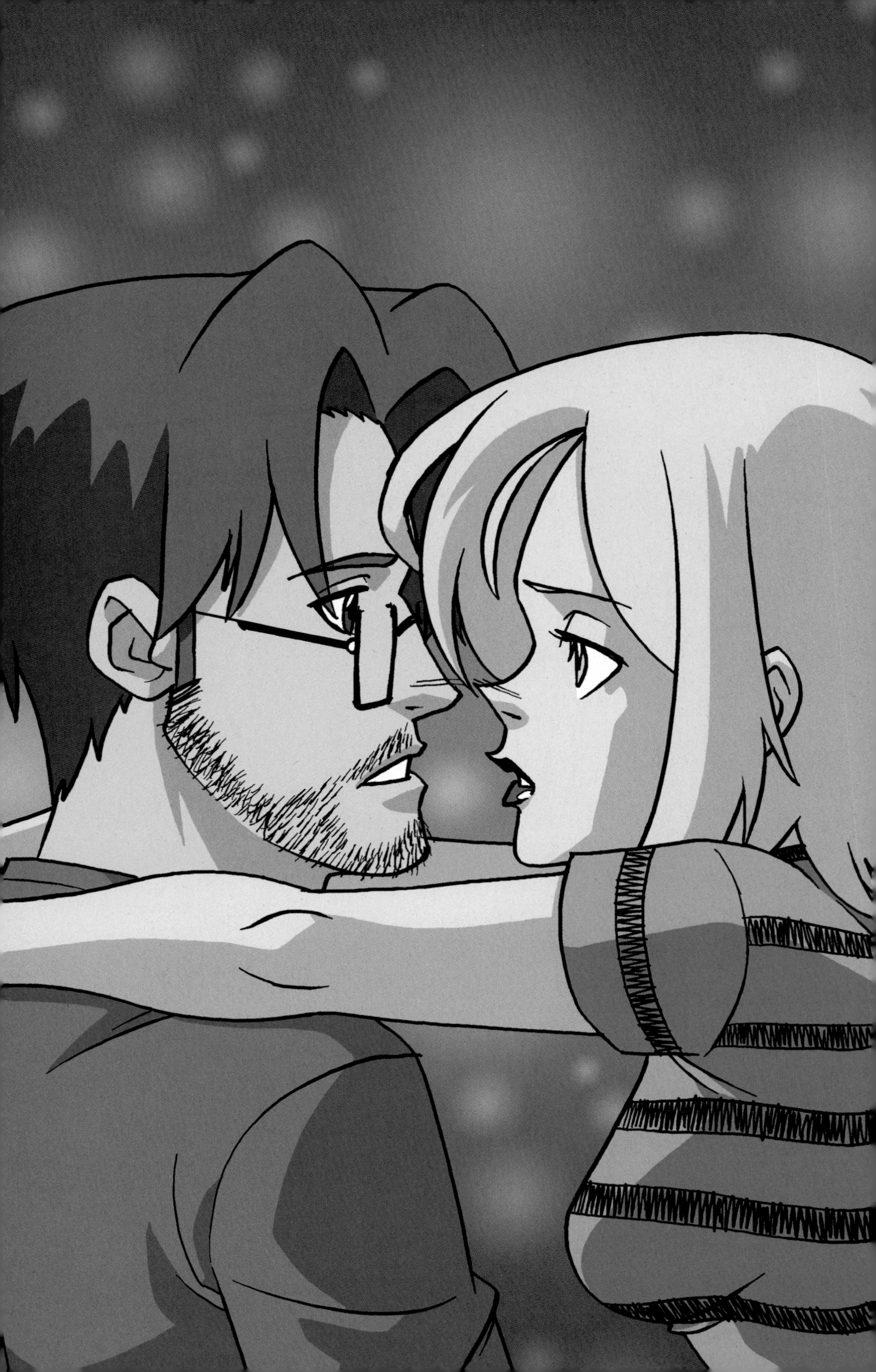

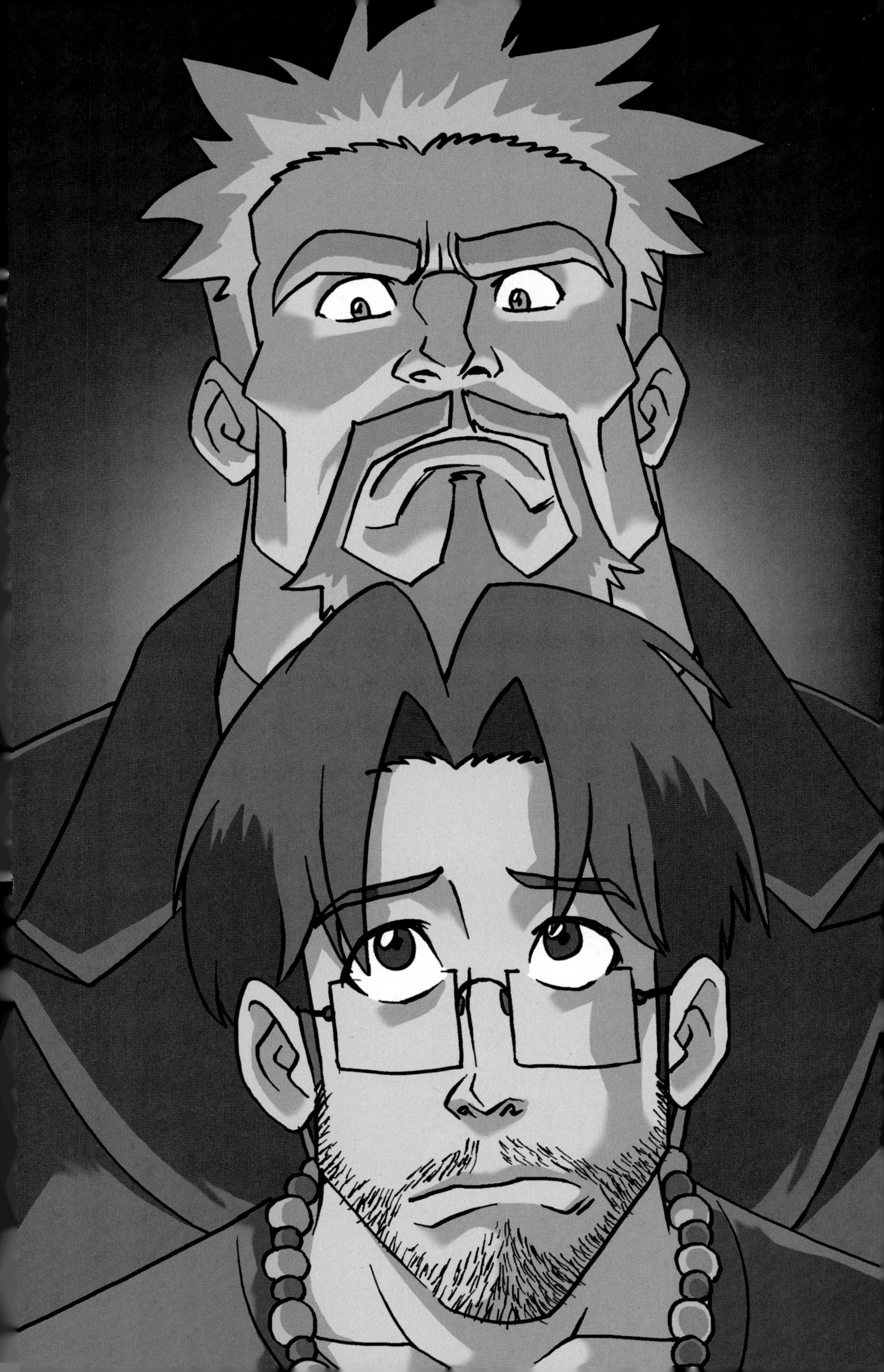

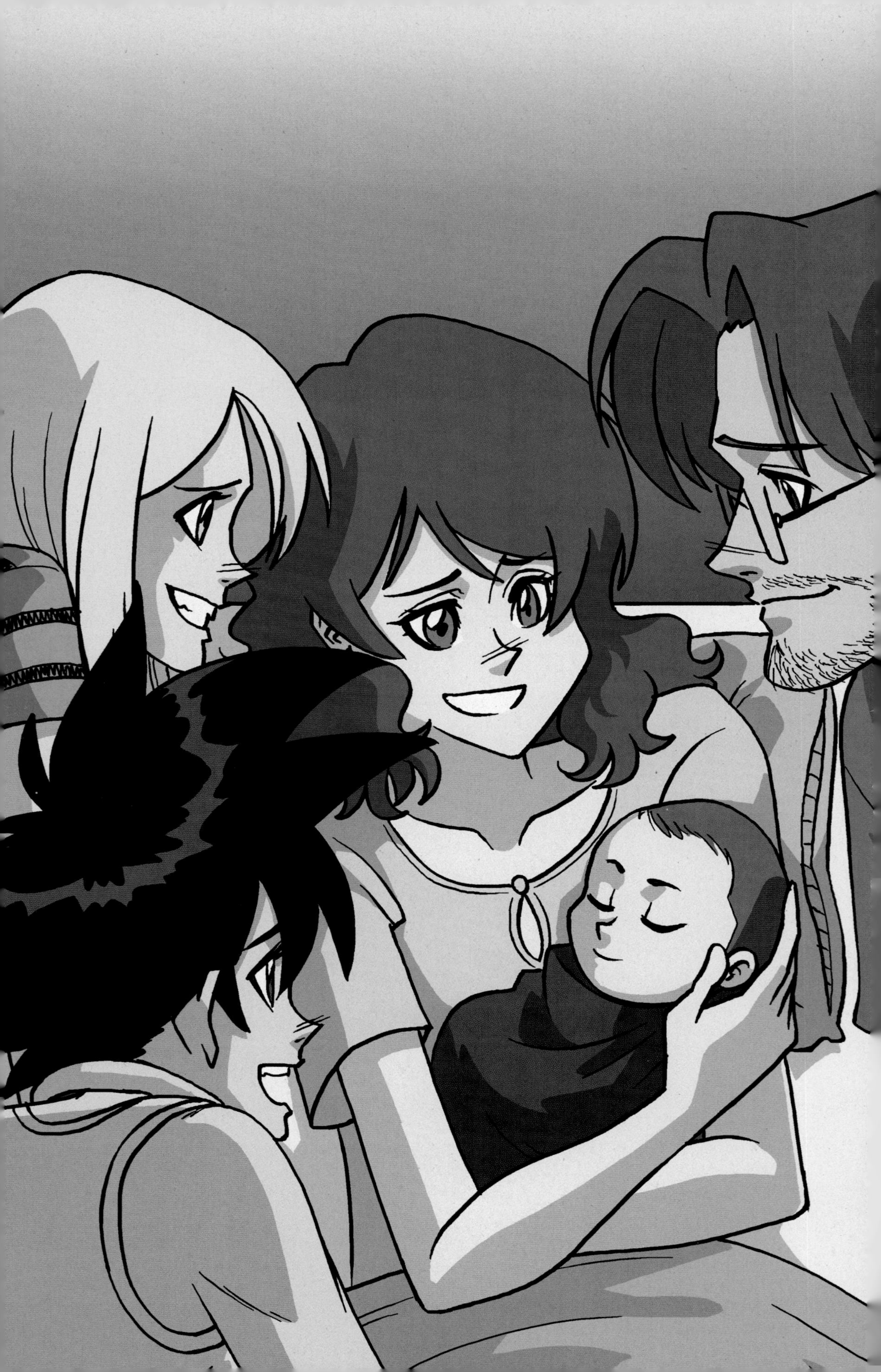